Praise for Bianca D'Arc's
Cat's Cradle

"Cat's Cradle by Bianca D'Arc kept me enthralled. I found myself immersed in the thick of the fight. I wanted to be there fighting and cheering, to be the one held by such a powerful and loyal man. ...This is a wonderful read, one I'd recommend this read to any number of readers."

~ *TwoLips Reviews*

"When it comes to shape shifter stories Bianca D'Arc is one of the masters to live up to. This is brought home again in Cat's Cradle. I am looking forward to reading more in the String of Fate Series and hope the next chapter is as well written and fun as Cat's Cradle. I love that Ms. D'Arc can add humor to her stories even in the direst of circumstances, such as Elaine's cat. It just makes me smile, even when the situations become dire. I look forward to the next in this series and Joyfully Recommend Cat's Cradle."

~ *Joyfully Reviewed*

"Bianca D'Arc has the beginning of a marvelous saga on her hands with the String of Fate series. Cat's Cradle was a wickedly blend of steadfast conflict and super erotic tension. ...I found the fast-moving plot to be thrilling, suspenseful, passionate and very satisfying. I can't wait to see what Ms. D'Arc has in store for next electrifying installment within the String of Fate series."

~ *The Romance Studio*

"...Bianca D'Arc has once again created a thoughtful, well-written story that speeds along at a fast and exciting pace. This fantastic story kept me intrigued and on the edge from start to finish... I can't wait to read the next book in this series... Ultimately, Bianca D'Arc fans will love this introduction to her newest series. If you're not already a Bianca D'Arc fan, I guarantee you will be once you've enjoyed this book."

~ *Fallen Angel Reviews*

"As with any D'Arc story, the material is wonderfully written, with attention to detail. Fans won't be disappointed and should be certain to purchase their own copy or pencil Cat's Cradle onto their TBR list. If you like heroes with bite and dig strong female protagonists, this book will definitely do you right."

~ *Whipped Cream Erotic Romance*

Look for these titles by
Bianca D'Arc

Now Available:

Wings of Change
Forever Valentine
Sweeter than Wine

Dragon Knights
Maiden Flight
Border Lair
The Ice Dragon
Prince of Spies
FireDrake
Dragon Storm

Tales of the Were
Lords of the Were
Inferno

Resonance Mates
Hara's Legacy
Davin's Quest
Jaci's Experiment
Grady's Awakening

Brotherhood of Blood
One and Only
Rare Vintage
Phantom Desires

String of Fate
Cat's Cradle

Secrets of the Ancients
Warrior's Heart

Print Anthologies
Ladies of the Lair
I Dream of Dragons Vol 1
Caught By Cupid

Cat's Cradle

Bianca D'Arc

Samhain Publishing, Ltd.
577 Mulberry Street, Suite 1520
Macon, GA 31201
www.samhainpublishing.com

Cat's Cradle
Copyright © 2011 by Bianca D'Arc
Print ISBN: 978-1-60504-909-0
Digital ISBN: 978-1-60504-870-3

Editing by Bethany Morgan
Cover by Kanaxa

First Samhain Publishing, Ltd. electronic publication: January 2010
First Samhain Publishing, Ltd. print publication: January 2011

Dedication

This book is dedicated to Mom. She's always been there for me and will always be my best and truest friend. Love you, Mom.

Many thanks to Jessica Jarman, Jambrea Jones and Valerie Tibbs for their sound advice and friendship. And a special thank you to Bethany Morgan, my fantastic editor.

Chapter One

Shihan was going to be pissed. Elaine knew she was in for it as she rounded the last corner practically on two wheels. She parked her Volkswagen bug and hopped out, only remembering to chirp the alarm over her shoulder when she reached the door of the *dojo*.

The Silent Tiger Martial Arts School was located in the basement of an office building, but at this hour, the small parking lot was relatively empty. It wasn't the safest part of town, but then, who would be foolish enough to attack a group of *jiu jitsu* students on their way to or from class? Their cars, though, were another matter. Only last week, Sergeant Riley had come out to find his SUV missing all four expensive off-road tires.

Elaine skidded down the stairs and entered the small changing room set aside for female students as quietly as possible. The lights were set low in the outer office, but that was nothing new. During class, usually only the big room was lit. She hurried into her *gi* jacket and tied the belt. *Shihan* Harris didn't take lateness well. He'd been known to send latecomers away, usually in pain.

She rushed to the curtain that separated the outer office from the *dojo* proper. There wasn't a lot of noise coming from within, but then *Shihan* might have everyone meditating. Great. She'd have to walk in on a silent room, making her tardy appearance all that much more noticeable, but it couldn't be helped. Dithering outside would only make her later. She stepped through the curtain, bowing in the ritual way.

Rising from the bow, she realized the room was nearly empty. Where were the thirty hot guys who made up the advanced class? There were only five bodies sitting or standing casually on the mats at the far end of the room. The lights were lower than normal, too. Elaine squinted as she stood in the doorway, uncertain.

She heard a muffled curse and saw a bulky form in a black *gi* heading her way. His black belt blended with the worn material of his uniform. It had to be her teacher.

"*Shihan?*"

One beefy hand waved her to silence as he drew closer. "Class is cancelled tonight. Didn't you see the sign on the door?"

Elaine felt heat rise to her cheeks. "Sorry. I was late and didn't notice. If the sign is still there, I didn't see it."

He stopped in front of her, blocking her view of the other four people in the *dojo*. Something struck her as odd about the small group at the far end of the room. She couldn't be sure from the quick glimpse she'd had, but she thought at least two were female. As far as she knew, there were only two other women enrolled in the school at present, and none were in the advanced class. Could they be students? Or merely friends of the teacher?

Speaking of whom, *Shihan* didn't look happy. Elaine gave up thinking about the visitors. She had enough to contend with at the moment.

"Go home, Elaine. Forget you came in here tonight and don't tell anyone what you've seen."

The hairs on the back of her neck stood at attention. "If there's anything I can do to help..." She had no idea where the offer came from, but the man—this normally unshakable mountain of a man—looked so different from his usual calm self, the words just popped out of her mouth before she thought twice.

"No, Elaine, but thanks. Remember, not a word."

He gave her a tight but benevolent smile and raised one hand, indicating the exit. Elaine hustled out, grabbing her knapsack from the changing room on the way. She fled up the stairs, into the dark night.

Elaine pushed open the outer door, stepped through, and ran into a wall. Well, that's what it felt like. The wall was muscular and male. Most definitely male. He smelled tangy and wild in the most delicious sort of way. Warning bells sounded through her brain. Elaine sprang back as the door slammed shut behind her.

Eyes the color of midnight snow narrowed and pinned her in place.

"You shouldn't be here."

Elaine stared at the man, noting her own odd reaction to his nearness. He made her body tingle. But his accusatory tone got her back up, and his size gave rise to a shiver of fear she didn't like at all.

He also stood entirely too close. Elaine backed away to put some space between them. Enough to defend herself, should that prove necessary, though his size alone gave her pause. She was only a green belt. She knew a lot compared to the newer students, but she was on the lowest rung of the advanced ranks. She had a lot to learn before she would blithely take on a guy this size.

"I was just leaving." She hefted her knapsack, putting even more space between herself and the stranger.

"Are you a student here?"

Fear rose in her throat. What kind of weirdo played twenty questions with a strange woman he met on the street after dark? The answer couldn't be anything good. Still, she had to approach from a position of power. She couldn't let him see her misgivings.

"What gave me away?" Trying for a disdainful air she raised

11

one eyebrow and glanced down at the uniform she wore.

The man didn't rise to her mocking tone, but tilted his head in a puzzled sort of way. "There usually aren't females in Harris's advanced class."

That told her he was either familiar with the school or some kind of stalker who watched the *dojo* at night. The first idea offered some comfort, but the latter was downright frightening.

She shrugged, edging away. "I was promoted recently." She had to get out of here.

The mysterious man nodded, silky locks the color of darkness swaying gently with his movements. His hair was long for a guy, but it fit him. Gave him a somewhat cavalier look that few men could pull off. The guy was hot with a capital H, but he was also kind of creepy, and he was standing between her and the parking lot.

"Class was cancelled this evening. Didn't you see the note?"

She followed his gaze over her shoulder to the scrap of paper on the door flapping in the slight breeze. The same scrap of paper she'd completely missed on her way in.

"Must've missed it when I chirped my car." Again, she tried to work her way around him to the relative safety of the parking lot, but he sidestepped, countering her move and striking fear into her heart she fought to hide.

"What kind of car?"

She heard the suspicion in his tone, and it didn't bode well. She tried to see around his broad shoulders, but he was just too big.

"A VW."

"Color?"

"Lime."

He shook his head and finally stood aside. The parking lot beyond was empty.

"Shit!" She started forward, uncertain what to do, but needing to look around to verify that her beloved bug was gone.

Things had just gone from bad to worse, and the stranger behind her seemed even more sinister. She really had to get out of here.

He came up beside her—not too close this time, thankfully. "I saw two guys driving away in a green bug when I walked up."

"Dammit!" She moved farther away from him, and this time he stayed put. Swinging her knapsack around, she dug inside for her cell phone. The man just stood there, watching from a few feet away. She found the little phone and flipped it open only to curse again. The damned battery was dead.

And the stranger now knew it. Her gaze shot up to meet his in the darkness. All she saw from the shadows were two pinpoints of light—sinister-looking reflections from his eyes. A shiver swept down her spine. This man could be dangerous, and she was in a very weak position.

"Don't look at me like that. I won't eat you for dinner, kitten." As if sensing her fear, he stepped back and raised his hands, palms outward. His voice dropped low, sending another kind of shiver through her.

She didn't know why, but his gestures and words calmed her a little, though she was pointedly aware of her predicament. As a last resort, she supposed she could go back into the *dojo*, but it was the very last thing she'd consider. Her teacher had made it abundantly clear she wasn't welcome there tonight.

She weighed her options, finally deciding on a course of action.

"Do you have a phone?" She asked the stranger.

"Sorry." He held his position, a comfortable distance away, his pose completely unthreatening now, though his size made her hyper-aware of how male he was and how small she was in comparison.

Elaine stuffed the useless phone back into her pack and swung it over her shoulders again. She was still dressed in her black *gi*, but that couldn't be helped. Sure, she looked a little weird running around the streets in a martial arts uniform, but it was night and the black fabric might just help her blend into the background. The less attention she drew walking alone at this time of night in this neighborhood, the better.

She started walking.

"Where are you going?"

"Home." She needed to get away from this disturbing man as soon as possible.

"I'll walk with you." He was right behind her when she turned, much too close. She gasped, stumbling backwards as he watched, making her feel even clumsier, but his eyes were calm, measuring and all too cunning.

"I'll be fine on my own." She backed away, watching him to see if he followed, but he remained motionless, much to her relief.

"It's not safe down here at night."

She couldn't help the ironic laugh that escaped. "No kidding."

He sighed, shaking his head as one corner of his mouth quirked up. "I know I frightened you, and I'm sorry. I'm a friend of your teacher's. My name is Cade. I help out with the advanced class now and then, but I haven't been here in a while."

"Well, it's nice to meet you, Mr. Cade—"

"Just Cade."

She nodded warily. "Cade, then. But like I said, I'll be fine."

"As you wish." He inclined his head, those fascinating eyes holding her gaze. It was as if he could see right through her, but she knew she was imagining things. The guy was super hot, but cool as ice. If they'd met under other circumstances, she would've been very attracted to him, but at this point, there was just no way of knowing if he was on the level—or some kind of pervert serial killer.

Elaine suppressed a shiver, hefted her pack and began walking once more. She kept an eye on Cade, but he didn't move to follow. She waved at him once before turning the corner and applying her feet to the pavement, making tracks away as fast as possible without drawing undue attention.

The key was to walk swiftly and silently and without drawing the eye of the more undesirable elements that came out around here when the sun went down. She'd keep an eye out behind her as well, just in case this Cade guy really was a perverted serial killer stalking her backtrail. With that frightening thought, she put on extra speed.

Cade eyed his companion across the dimly lit parking lot. Mitch made a short movement, a code signal he read easily.

Follow? Mitch asked with just the slightest movement of one hand. Cade shook his head and replied with another gesture.

Guard.

Mitch nodded and prowled out of sight. Cade knew his comrade would keep an eye on the group in the *dojo* while he checked out the uninvited guest. Following in her tracks, Cade headed away through the darkened streets of the unquiet city.

The woman moved gracefully for one not of the blood. She had an athletic build beneath the shapeless *gi* top, but the supple cotton of the pants revealed glimpses of a very shapely ass Cade would love to sink his teeth into. Strange, that reaction. Few women stirred his inner beast on such short acquaintance, but this one had intrigued him from the moment he'd caught her scent, just seconds before she'd slammed into him outside the *dojo*. She'd had that deer-in-the-headlights look on her face for a moment, and her innocence shone through like a beacon before she shielded her light behind a façade of wary vigilance. In Cade's experience, that sort of thing couldn't be faked.

But questions remained. What was she doing there, tonight of all nights? Was her presence really as guiltless as she wanted him to believe? Or was there something more sinister in play?

Cade was determined to find out. To that end, he followed the woman, stalking her through the city streets as she made good time. She'd walked about a mile and a half when her path took her into a small park. The shadows lengthened under the trees, and the hair on the back of Cade's neck stood up straight. Didn't she realize the chance she was taking? A woman alone, in the dark of night, on foot, with no cell phone and no means of protection. She was an assault waiting to happen. Cade picked up his pace, cutting the cautious distance he'd kept from his prey.

He entered the shadows of the park and caught sight of her ahead. She was remarkably silent for a human, though she'd never match his kind for stealth. Still, he had to admire the smooth way she moved. Off to her right, on an intercept course with her path, Cade caught sight of trouble.

A man, armed with something that glinted in the pale light. A blade of some kind perhaps. Cade could see well in the dark—better than any human, at least. He sniffed and caught the scent of magic. Things grew more complicated, but he had to follow the woman and find out more about her. He didn't want Others getting involved. This was his mission. His alone.

He stepped out into the weak light. It was enough for the Other to see him. Gazes met across the distance of the dark park, testing, probing. Cade allowed his eyes to glow for a moment, knowing the Other would see the challenge and understand what he was up against. A moment later the Other withdrew.

Cade moved swiftly after his prey.

A short distance from the small park, the woman stopped in front of an old apartment building. The big central library was around the corner and this apartment building was dwarfed by the monolithic library structure. It only had a few stories and probably a dozen small apartments on each floor. He did a quick circuit of the place and noticed which lights were already on. Once the woman went in, he'd do another circuit and look for any new lights. That would give him a place to start his investigation.

A few moments later, he'd noted only one light going on during the reasonable timeframe for her to get inside and up to her apartment. He would check it out, but chances were he would find her place on his first try. Unless she was playing some much deeper game, the woman was as innocent as she appeared. Cade would find out for sure though. More than his own life depended on it.

It was an easy jump from the ground to the sturdy fire escape for one of his kind, but he was careful to keep to the shadows. He ascended to the target window, bypassing the one with the light in favor of the one above. He'd keep watch from above the apartment where he thought the woman had gone and learn what he could through her open window.

She had safety locks that only allowed the window to go up a few inches. In case of emergency the locks could be easily removed from the inside to allow the tenants to make use of the fire escape. It was a good system that allowed fresh air in while keeping cat burglars out.

For the most part. Cade had to stifle a snicker at his own thoughts. It might work against burglars, but definitely not against cats.

In fact, there was an orange tabby eyeing him from the other side of the screen. The house cat had staked out the niche between the screen and the sill as his own personal resting place. Cade wasn't too worried the short meow of respectful greeting would give away his presence. Most cats liked him, sensing the dominant male in the pride right off, even when he was in human form.

His mark entered the room from what must have been the bathroom, her black *gi* top hanging open. The rank belt was neatly folded and sitting on the couch next to her knapsack. She shrugged out of the cotton jacket and folded it, placing it on top of the bag. She had a black sports bra on underneath, and it showcased a lithe, powerful body with all the right curves. Cade's mouth watered, but he squelched the response. He had work to do. More importantly, he needed to discover if this woman really was the innocent she seemed.

She reached into her bag and snagged the dead cell phone, plugging it into a charger on a small end table next to the couch. Sighing, she flopped onto the couch and picked up the hard-wired phone that sat on the same small table.

From the conversation, it was clear she was reporting her car stolen to the police. Cade could easily hear both ends of the conversation with his acute senses, and felt certain the call was legitimate and aboveboard. He also learned all kinds of personal information about Elaine Spencer as she recited it for the police. Cade was tempted to take notes, but knew he would remember every last detail about this puzzling woman. For some odd reason, she fascinated him.

She hung up the phone and stared at nothing for a few minutes before finally rising off the couch. She came to the window and Cade dropped back, farther out of sight. The well-fed tabby greeted her with a purr as she stroked his fur.

"Well, Chuck, they stole my car." She sighed heavily as the cat turned to offer his tummy to rub. She stroked the small feline with delicate, loving hands. Cade wasn't unaffected, and the response made him angry. She was human, dammit. She shouldn't have this kind of effect on him, yet when her eyes filled with tears, he wanted to kiss them away and hold her tight.

But she didn't know she was being observed. She wiped away a tear and kept talking to the tabby cat, her gaze fixed on something in the distance only she could see.

"That on top of the fiasco with *Shihan*. I'll be lucky if he doesn't make me do knuckle push-ups on telephone books at our next class. He was not a happy camper when I walked in." The cat meowed as she stepped away.

Cade followed her progress to the small kitchenette, where

she poured herself a glass of ice water.

"There was something weird about the people in the *dojo*, though I can't quite figure what it was." She continued chatting with the cat as she moved about the apartment. "And that guy outside. Hubba hubba, Chuckie. I mean that guy was downright scary, but totally hot, too."

She giggled at her own words and drank the rest of the water, placing the glass in the sink. "I bet he's got a girlfriend. Or two. Hell, he's probably married. All the hot ones are." She collapsed onto the couch, and the cat jumped down from the windowsill and made his way over to his mistress. The tabby was obviously very loyal to the woman and that bode well for her. "But I don't need anyone else if I have you, Chuck."

She hugged the big tabby cat and rubbed her face in his orangey fur. Cade spent a brief, senseless moment imagining her doing the same to him. Damn, he really had to get his mind out of his pants. Or rather, out of *her* pants.

The woman let the cat curl up on her lap and reached for the remote control. She flipped through channels for a while until she settled on a local news channel. Cade settled in to watch her, wondering when she'd get around to taking the rest of her clothes off. He wasn't usually a peeping tomcat, but he'd give just about anything for a peek at the rest of her sultry skin. And hey, it was his job, after all.

The news channel broke into their own coverage of a human-interest story with an alert, and Cade snapped to his senses. He could hear every sound from inside the room, so hearing the newscaster wasn't difficult at all. But what he was saying, sent ice into Cade's veins.

"—police and the fire department are on scene now. The fire appears to have started in the basement of the building at 121 Water Street, in a space used by a martial arts school. The headquarters of Brown Investments occupies the upper floors of the office building, and we'll have a spokesman from Brown with us momentarily. Right now, all we can tell you is that the building is fully engulfed in flames, and there are unconfirmed reports of casualties. Arson is suspected due to the rapid spread of this fire, and investigators are already on scene."

Cade didn't wait to hear any more. Bounding down the fire escape, he used all his speed to get back to the *dojo*, cursing himself for a fool. He should never have left his post. He flipped open his cell as he ran, speed dialing Mitch.

Not only did he not get an answer, the line didn't even connect. Something was wrong with Mitch's phone. This was not good. Anything that could take Mitch out had to be serious. The tiger wouldn't have gone down quietly.

Chapter Two

"Oh no!" Elaine leaned forward to watch the building she'd just left not an hour before going up in flames on the news. She had to get over there, but her car was gone. Dammit!

Throwing on a black sweat jacket over her sports bra, she looked up a cab company's phone number in the phone book and gave them a call. They promised to send someone right over. Grabbing her purse, she headed for the door, stopping only to unplug the lightly charged cell phone. It didn't have much juice, but it would have to do. She'd ask the cabbie to wait for her, but if he wouldn't, she'd probably have enough power to at least make one call to get another cab. She scribbled down the number of the cab company on a scrap of paper and stuck it in her pocket.

When she finally got to the scene, the fire was almost out. There were lots of fire trucks blocking the road, but the cabbie got her as close as possible. He stopped at the head of the block and let her out on the corner, refusing to wait. She shrugged and started toward the flashing lights further up the block. Elaine had no idea what she could do to help, but she needed to tell someone that there there'd been at least five people in the basement when she'd left.

The building was reduced to charred rubble. It was amazing how much damage could be done in such a short time. Elaine's pace slowed as the enormity of the horror started to set in. She'd just come upon the row of trees and bushes separating the property lines when a hand shot out and dragged her into the darkness. She didn't even have time to scream.

Cade cursed when her scent wafted to him on the evening breeze. It wasn't an echo from before. It was fresh. As if merely thinking about the beautiful, perplexing, annoying woman had conjured her.

He poked his head out of the shrubbery and sure enough, there she was, walking down the street toward him. Her gaze was glued to the pile of smoldering ash that had once been an office building and home of the Silent Tiger *dojo*.

Cade couldn't let her talk to the cops or firemen. She'd undoubtedly tell them what she'd seen in the *dojo* before Harris sent her packing. Cade didn't know exactly what she had seen, but he couldn't take any chances.

The fire had been a hit. No natural fire moved that fast or burned that hot. And he smelled the scent of burnt flesh. Someone—or several someones—had died in the fire. Cade wished to hell he'd been there to stop it.

But he'd found Mitch. The tiger was down. Hurt bad and bleeding from more places than Cade could count, but alive, for the moment. Cade had to get him out of here and get him patched up or even the stubborn tiger might yet bleed to death. Saving Mitch—the only witness who might be able to help him figure out what had happened here—had to be the first priority.

A plan formed in his mind. It wasn't a great plan, but it would kill two birds with one swipe.

He waited impatiently while the woman drew closer. A few more steps and he would pounce. Shock etched her features as she drew even with his hiding place.

He didn't give her a chance to scream. He pulled her back into the shadows, one hand covering her mouth, the other quelling her movements. She was so shocked, she didn't even fight back, though he knew she was highly trained. He had precious seconds before her training would kick in. He had to stop her from giving away their position.

"Don't struggle. I won't hurt you. I need your help. My friend is seriously hurt."

She stilled when her foot brushed up against Mitch's prone body. Cade pushed her head down so she could see him.

"I found him like this. He needs help, but I can't bring him to the cops. The people who torched the building are too close. They'll finish the job on Mitch if we go out in the open. Will you help us? I know you're a nurse."

He felt her calmness, her questioning, and he judged it safe enough to loosen his hold on her. A show of good faith on his part might go a long way toward securing her cooperation. He needed it, as he hadn't needed anyone's help in a long time. It wasn't a comfortable feeling, but he would deal. Mitch had to be the priority now.

Cade gingerly let go of her mouth. "Please don't give us away. I won't hurt you."

"How did you know I was a nurse?" She whirled on him, putting about a foot of space between them as she moved into a ready stance. It was a subtle move, but he noted it with something like satisfaction. She was calm enough to ask questions, but on guard enough to be wary. It was a good combination.

"I saw the I.D. tag on your pack before, when you left the *dojo*. Remember me?"

"Yeah, I remember you." Her tone was leery. "Did *Shihan* make it out?" She didn't take her gaze from him, but nudged her head back toward the ruined building.

"I don't know. I, uh..." he paused to try to look sheepish. Manipulating someone as quick as this woman would be difficult, but he was a master. "I followed you home to make sure you made it safely."

"You what?"

"Look, I didn't feel right about letting you go off into the night like that. So I followed you. Made sure you made it home okay then came back here to find the place in flames. I don't know if anyone made it out. All I know is, whoever did this will probably come back once the officials clear out. We can't be found here."

"Dammit!" She looked torn, her gaze moving between him and the injured man on the ground.

"Look, Harris asked Mitch and I to guard the perimeter tonight. I'll be the first to admit, we did a shitty job. I let you distract me, and my friend paid the price. Maybe even Harris. I don't know yet who made it out and who didn't, but we won't find out from the cops."

"How do I know you're telling the truth?"

Cade thought for a second. "Harris had a series of passwords shared among his top students. You claimed to be in the advanced class, so you should know them, right?"

She nodded. "He told me last month when I joined the class. At the time I thought it was just a foolish game."

Cade's expression hardened. "Harris had reasons for everything he did. If I say chrysalis to you, what does that convey?"

"Emergency," she answered automatically, her eyes widening. "So if I ask you what day it is?" One of her eyebrows rose in challenge.

He didn't hesitate. "The farthest yet from the beginning."

"Damn." She shook her head. "He told me anyone who knew his code was one of his select group."

"At your service." Cade made a mocking little bow. "But we don't have time for this. I need to know if you'll help us. Mitch needs medical care, and I need to figure out what happened here and what I can do about it."

Elaine bit her lip in indecision. On the one hand, something fishy was definitely going on, but she couldn't just let a man bleed to death. She dropped to one knee, checking over his extensive injuries. Nothing looked too deep from what she could see in the gloom under the trees, but the slashing wounds were in odd, parallel patterns all over his body, and he was still bleeding. A lot.

"All right. How do we get him out of here?"

"I have a car around the corner. I was going to carry him through the trees when I saw you walk up. For Harris's sake, you can't tell the cops what you saw earlier tonight."

"But I didn't see anything. Just four people in the distance, sitting in a darkened *dojo*."

"Damn, you saw more than I thought. You can't tell anyone. I bet Harris said the same when he sent you out of there."

She recalled *Shihan's* words and nodded. This strange man seemed to know things, and try as she might to be reasonable, she felt a sort of weird trust in him. She knew his friend needed her help though at first look, none of his injuries seemed beyond her abilities to patch up. Of course, common sense told her to run as far and as fast from these two as possible.

The emotional side of her personality told her to help them. It was instinctual, not reasonable, but Harris had been working on her to trust her instincts more. In this situation, it just might get her killed if this guy turned out to be an ax murderer, but she had to go with her gut.

"All right. Let's get him to the car, then we'll head for my apartment. I have a guest room and big first aid kit. It's not fancy, but it'll do."

"Thank you." Cade touched her hand, drawing her attention. The look in his icy eyes made her shiver, but not with cold. No, he was looking at her with heat and respect, and genuine gratitude. She'd never seen quite that combination and couldn't believe she'd ever thought his eyes lifeless and frozen. No, the ice in his gaze was, in truth, the hottest of fires, flashing and sparkling with life.

She moved away from his disturbing touch and went to her patient.

"Let me just tie a tourniquet on his leg before you lift him." She took a strip off Mitch's tattered shirt and bound it around a muscular thigh, but had a hard time pulling it tight enough. Cade stepped in and did the honors, seeming to know just the right amount of pressure to put on the wounded leg. He'd most likely done this before. Elaine nodded at him as she moved back and was astounded by the easy way Cade lifted his huge friend, without any outward sign of strain. He loped off into the trees separating one office complex from the next, and she followed closely behind, cursing herself for a fool with every other step.

The car was dark and nondescript. Cade draped his friend across the backseat and motioned for her to take the passenger side, but she demurred.

"I should ride in back with him."

But Cade shook his head. "It's not safe. He might change."

"Change what?" She was baffled by the terse words.

Cade held up one hand for silence as he rounded the car and opened the driver's side door. "Not now. Get in the front." She still hesitated. "Just do it. Someone's coming."

She heard the faint sound of a vehicle heading their way and didn't argue further. Cade had the car in gear and moving almost before she'd shut the door.

"Duck down. I don't want anyone to see you with me if it can be helped."

She saw the merit in that idea and crouched a bit below the dashboard.

"Corner of Lincoln and Bayberry."

"What?"

"That's where my apartment is."

"Yeah," Cade managed a tight grin, "I know. I followed you home before, remember?"

A cold feeling shivered up her spine. "Oh. Yeah."

"Look, I'm sorry. At the time, I wasn't sure of you, but if you were on the level, I wanted to be sure you made it home safe. If not, I wanted to know where you went."

"So you expected trouble tonight?"

Cade turned a corner, making her clutch the armrest as the force pushed her into the door.

"I always expect trouble." He sighed heavily. "But yeah, I knew they were taking a risk going to the *dojo*."

"They? The people I saw inside?"

His features clouded as he stopped at a red light. Sparkling chips of ice glittered down at her when he turned his head and pinned her with his gaze.

"You'd do better to forget them. There are forces at work here you don't understand, and you don't want to. Believe me." The light turned, and he shifted his attention back to the road and the mirrors, keeping a careful watch on their backtrail.

Elaine had had about enough. "Why should I? I don't even know you."

"It's safer that way." He pulled into the underground parking garage below her building and found a dark corner to park the car. "We'll only impose on you long enough to get Mitch patched up and make a few calls. After that, if all goes well, you'll never see us again."

"Why? What are you running from?"

"It's better you don't know any more than you do already."

Cade got out of the car, sniffing the air cautiously before opening the back door and hoisting his friend out. He jerked his chin to indicate she should precede them.

She dug out her key and opened the private elevator that would take them to her floor. At this time of night, few people were awake, so they didn't run into any of her neighbors, thank goodness. She had no idea how she would've explained such odd company in the middle of the night and was glad she didn't have to.

Elaine unlocked her apartment door and led the way to the guest room, stripping off the comforter. Cade deposited his friend on the clean white sheet with surprising gentleness. Elaine went into the kitchenette and grabbed her first aid supplies while Cade stripped off the tattered rags that had once been a dress shirt and trousers from the injured man.

She went back into the room and got her first real look at the extent of Mitch's injuries. The sheer brutality made her gasp. It looked like he'd been savaged by a bear. Or some other wild animal with huge, sharp claws. He had long, bloody, parallel furrows etched all over his body.

"What the hell did that?"

"Nothing you want to meet on a dark night," Cade said with grim humor. "Come on, I'll help you. Tell me what to do."

They spent the next half-hour bathing the gouges and dabbing on disinfectant, during which time, Mitch remained mercifully unconscious. Elaine located a huge bump on the man's head, but what worried her more was the fresh needle mark she found near his left kidney. He'd been drugged, which was probably why he was still out. The head injury alone wasn't serious enough to keep him unconscious this long.

"Bastards!" Cade cursed when she found the needle mark.

"Why would they hurt him like this, only to drug him unconscious? It doesn't make much sense."

"They wanted him to suffer. To know he'd failed to defend the ones we were sworn to protect. They fought him to get close enough with the needle. That's what caused this damage. But their real objective was to incapacitate him. It's the highest form of insult among our people."

"What are you? Some kind of black ops guys or something? I mean, I knew *Shihan* Harris was ex-military, but I never heard he was into that clandestine stuff."

"Black ops? Now that's an interesting idea. But even if I were, you know I couldn't tell you anything. The less you know—-"

"Yeah, yeah. I heard that before." She sighed and got to her feet. "I think all we can do now is wait until he comes out from under whatever they gave him. His vitals are strong— surprisingly so, considering how much blood he must've lost. His wounds are deep, but nothing deadly, and his pupils are reacting normally, so I don't think the bump on the head is too serious. Still..." she thought hard about whether or not to offer her next suggestion.

"What?" Cade had a way of seeing way too much.

"I have a friend in the building who's a doctor. If he doesn't come around soon, I think we might want to ask her to have a look. I'm a nurse, Cade. I don't feel comfortable making these kinds of judgments if his life hangs in the balance."

"Do you trust this woman?"

"With my life. Gina and I grew up together. She's the one who convinced me to go into nursing and even helped me get this apartment. She's on the next floor."

Cade seemed to weigh the options. "Let's watch him for an hour or two. If you still think it's necessary, we can ask your friend to take a look at him, but the fewer people who see us here, the better."

"Okay." She yawned, the adrenaline rush wearing off. "You might as well stay here tonight. Your friend won't be much good until whatever they gave him wears off and even then, his wounds are pretty extensive."

Cade cursed inwardly even as his frozen heart thawed, looking at their petite rescuer. She was dead on her feet.

"You should get some rest. I'm going to make some calls on my cell so they can't trace them back to you."

"I thought you said you didn't have a cell phone?" Anger showed in her eyes.

"To be accurate, I never said I didn't. I only said I was

sorry."

She shook her head. "Semantics. You lied by omission. You could've saved me a lot of trouble if you'd just let me use your damned phone."

"At the time, I needed you out of there as quickly as possible. If you'd called a cab, I would've had to wait with you."

"But you followed me all the way here. It would've been quicker to call a cab."

"Yes, but then you might've been there when the attack went down." He saw understanding dawn in her eyes. He expected fear to follow soon after, but was surprised by the steadfast light that shone instead. She looked like she might've wanted a piece of the fight. Cade had never known a human woman to look forward to battle—not like a shifter female—but this small woman came damned close.

He looked down at his friend, still unconscious on the bed. "But it's all beside the point now. I'll stay here and watch over Mitch. If we're gone when you wake, don't worry."

"I seriously doubt your friend will be able to move for a few days at least." She yawned as she headed for the door, pausing with her hand on the knob. "I don't know why, but I trust you. Don't make me regret it."

She left before he could answer, but what could he say, really? She'd gone farther than he could have expected any human to go in helping them. She'd shown either a remarkable amount of trust or a foolhardy level of disrespect for her own safety. The latter worried him while the idea that she trusted him warmed something in his soul he hadn't known existed.

The woman was dangerous. In more than just the obvious ways.

Cade flipped open his small phone and started making discreet calls. He had to know who'd made it out of the *dojo* and where they'd gone. If not for Mitch, he would be tearing up the town already, searching, but he owed Mitch his life and had to be certain the tiger would recover before he went hunting.

He heard the shower go on in the other room. Images of their hostess wet and naked flashed through his mind, killing his concentration and heating his blood. The little human was getting to him and if he wasn't careful, she could provoke him into acting on the desire that flared every time she was near.

But she wasn't Other. She couldn't handle what might be unleashed. For her protection, he had to keep a lid on the reaction that shook him every time he caught her scent. It didn't make any sense. No human woman had ever had this kind of effect on him before. In fact, no female of any species had ever provoked his cat in such a way.

Cade took a deep breath and tried to ignore the scent of the woman that permeated her home. It wasn't as bad in the guest room, so he made his calls from there, keeping a close eye on Mitch. There was no way to know what the bastards had injected him with, and Cade didn't like the fact the tiger had been out so long. His body chemistry and natural healing ability should have counteracted whatever they'd given him by now.

Unless they knew what he was and had come armed for bear...or cat shifter, as the case may be.

The odds were that whoever had fought and managed to subdue Mitch had known just how to take him down. The claw marks meant there was a blood traitor working with them. Only another shifter with superior fighting skills, or a major amount of luck on his side could have hoped to distract Mitch enough for a shot to be delivered. Cade could almost see it. They'd probably sicced the shifter on him first and when he was in prime position, another had come up behind—or maybe several others—and jabbed him in the back with the needle. Mitch wouldn't have gone down quietly.

Cade made his first call to Maggie, the coordinator of tonight's activities. If anyone would know the outcome of the fire, it would be her.

"Where are you?" Her worried voice came over the line immediately.

"Safe for now. Mitch was drugged and hurt. I'm sticking with him 'til he comes out of it. What have you got for me?"

"Harris got out with the others. They're in transit. Molly and Steve were injured pretty badly, but they got to the healer in time, and he says they should be okay."

"So everybody got out on our side?"

"Yes, thank heavens. It was close though, from what little I've heard. We're keeping everybody at the gamma safe house for now."

"You got enough crew to man the perimeter?"

"It'll be tough with you and Mitch down, but we'll manage. We need to find a way to get them to safety. Harris was our best hope, but tonight proves he's been made."

"Undoubtedly. We can't use him again."

"He knows that, but he still wants to help. Remember his wife…"

"How could I forget?" Cade sighed, remembering the young cub named Willa who'd married the human, Harris. She'd been headstrong and full of life. She'd loved the human, though her parents and pack had disapproved loudly. Harris had proven himself over the years though. He was skilled and could hold his own, even among Others. It had been pure bad luck when his wife was caught out alone, hunted and killed.

Harris had his revenge, stalking and taking out the men who'd killed his wife—with Clan approval and assistance. He'd been a steadfast ally ever since, and a good friend to the shifter community.

Cade finished the call and dialed the next number. He had to talk to Harris. Someone had died in that building and if it wasn't one of theirs, Harris probably had something to do with it.

"How is everyone?" Cade asked as soon as Harris picked up on the other end.

"We're good. Molly and Steve got a knocked around some,

but they'll be okay."

"So I heard from Maggie. Damn, Harris, I'm sorry I wasn't there."

Condemning silence greeted his statement. After a long pause, Harris spoke again. "I figured you were taken down."

"Mitch was. An Other distracted him while someone jabbed him with a needle. He's still out."

"Where were you?"

"Off following your student home. Her car was stolen from the lot, and she walked."

A muffled curse on the other end of the line followed Cade's words. "Didn't she have a phone?"

"Dead battery."

"Sounds convenient." Speculative silence stretched for a moment. "If it was anyone other than Elaine, I'd be suspicious, but she's as straight as an arrow. And though she doesn't know it, her best friend is one of you. That's how she came to me. Her friend, Gina, asked me to let her in, and I've never regretted my decision. Until now."

"Is this Gina a doctor by any chance?"

"As a matter of fact, she is. My Willa used to go to her."

Cade hated the note of devastation in the man's voice. It was a brutal world they lived in and Harris was one of many Cade had known through the years, whose life had been ripped apart by prejudice and hate.

"Someone was in the building. Your doing?"

"I got one, Molly and Steve got one apiece, but they didn't go quietly."

"Ever see them before?"

Harris sighed. "Cleaning crew and the night watchman. They were armed for bear."

"So that's how they found out?"

"Must've been watching me for weeks. I recall we had some staff turnover in the building a few weeks back. That's when they must've come in."

"Look, Harris, I'm sorry—"

"Save it. Given the circumstances, I probably would've done the same, but I am suspicious that her car was stolen at just the right time. Could've been to lure you away—or more likely—to keep you occupied with her, distracted, so that when they made their move, you'd be taken by surprise."

"And have an innocent civilian to protect," Cade added, not liking the way the scenario unfolded. "Damn, you're right."

"But she's an independent type and decided to hoof it. Saved some trouble. It got her and you out of the way before they made their move."

"Disgustingly neat." Cade recalled the dark park. "There was an Other in the park on her way. I showed myself to him, and he backed off. He had a knife."

"Also a little too convenient. Maybe, seeing you leave, they wanted to make sure you went all the way home with her."

Cade shook his head. "These bastards are getting way too crafty."

"Such is the challenge we face," Harris said wisely. "Learning from our mistakes means we won't repeat them. Tonight we got lucky. Everyone's okay, and we took out three of them."

"Good point. But we have three hurt and a civilian who's seen way more than she should have. We're at her place."

"You're kidding." A bare hint of incredulous laughter found its way into the *Shihan's* tone.

"'Fraid not. When she saw the fire on the news, she called a cab and headed back over there. I saw her coming down the street and pulled her aside to help Mitch. She gave us a place to hole up and treated Mitch's wounds."

"Good girl." Harris said in approval. "I've been working on her to trust her instincts. Sounds like tonight was the ultimate test."

Cade heard the shower shut off and moved to stand in the open doorway. A moment later, Elaine emerged from a doorway on the other side of the room with a towel wrapped like a turban around her head and a long, terrycloth bathrobe swathing her body. She jumped when she saw him standing across from her, in the doorway to the guest room, her eyes going wary.

"You want to talk to her? It might help put her at ease." Cade spoke into the small phone, but knew she heard every last syllable.

Harris agreed and Cade moved into the room, handing her the phone. She looked uncertain, but took the slim device and said hello. Harris spent a few minutes on the line with his student, and Cade could sense the easing of her fears and the elevation of her curiosity. It was written all over her pretty face, but Cade wouldn't satisfy any of that curiosity. He couldn't. She was already in enough danger just for taking them in.

He approached the windows in the darkened apartment from the side, tugging the shades closed and pulling the curtains. No sense offering a target for anyone who might be watching. Cade didn't sense any danger in the immediate area, but he knew damn well that could change awfully fast.

He paused a moment to greet the cat, receiving a deferential tail curl and rub of the tabby's soft fur against his hand. Like most housecats, this one liked him.

The soft scent of woman drew nearer and his phone was held out in a feminine hand. "He wants to talk to you again." Damn, she smelled good.

Cade took the phone, careful to avoid touching her soft skin any longer than absolutely necessary. This woman was temptation itself, even in a somewhat frumpy bathrobe. Her delicate scent simply stole his breath.

He finished up with Harris in short order and closed the phone. The cat rubbed up against him affectionately. Too bad his owner was watching Cade with such a puzzled expression.

He couldn't afford to satisfy any of the questions he could almost see buzzing around her, but felt the alien desire to do just that. It was a strange sensation. Never before had he been tempted to reveal anything about the nature of his challenges to a human who didn't already know about the Others.

This girl was as naive about the real world as most of the rest of humanity. Cade wouldn't be the one to enlighten her, but damn, he was tempted. He wanted to let his cat out to play with the alluring female. Worse, his inner beast wanted to rub up against this female much the way the tabby cat was rubbing all over him. It was a base level instinct that he had to fight to control.

That was new. A human female had never attracted him this strongly. It was new... and dangerous.

"That call went a long way toward easing my remaining fears, but—"

A crash from the other room interrupted, setting them both into motion.

Cade leapt through the guest room doorway first, to find Mitch in the grip of convulsions. His body seized on the bed and Cade held him down, reaching inside his mouth to be certain his friend wouldn't choke on his own tongue.

"I'm calling Gina." Elaine moved swiftly to the phone and called her upstairs neighbor, the doctor—who, according to Harris, was also a shifter. The Lady was truly smiling on him this night.

Mitch's body eased and a moment later there was a discrete knock on the apartment door. Elaine let her friend in and Cade immediately recognized the scent of shifter—another tiger, if he wasn't much mistaken. What were the odds? He stood from Mitch's side to greet the doctor, who eyed him warily.

"We're friends of Harris," Cade said softly.

Mitch made a growling sound deep in his throat, and the pretty doctor immediately went to him. Elaine moved to the other side of the bed, ready to assist her friend if necessary.

"What happened to him?"

"The scratches are nothing," Cade said. "The real problem is whatever they injected him with."

Gina's gaze rose to meet his. "How long ago?"

"About three hours."

"And he hasn't awakened once?"

"No. He's been out since I found him."

"Not good." The doctor turned to look at her human friend, regret clear on her face. "There's only one thing I can think to do without access to a laboratory. Besides, it would take too long to figure out what they gave him."

"What are you going to do?" Elaine asked, clearly ready to help in whatever way she could.

"Ellie, we need to draw blood." Elaine immediately rooted through the doctor's small bag and took out the necessary supplies, but when she would've used the big needle on Mitch, the doctor stopped her. "Not his. Mine."

"You're a Universal then?" Cade asked, satisfied when the doctor nodded.

"What the hell are you two talking about?"

Gina turned to her friend with a look of resignation. "How long have we known each other?"

"Forever." Elaine answered immediately.

"And you trust me, right?"

"With my life."

Cade liked how immediate and unequivocal her answer was.

"Then trust me now, Ellie. It's the only chance he's got."

Mitch began thrashing on the bed, slow at first, but Cade feared the tiger was building up to another seizure. Cade moved in and held him while the women worked out what would be done. He watched with satisfaction as Elaine—or Ellie, as her friend called her—drew blood from Gina.

Gina took the needle and quick as a rabbit, stuck it into

Mitch's vein. She was fast and accurate. Both good traits in a doctor. But then, this doctor was no ordinary woman.

"I don't get it," Elaine muttered, her gaze both puzzled and fascinated as she watched the procedure.

Gina sighed deeply as she finished and turned back to her friend. "Ellie, I went into medicine because of my blood. Remember that time in sixth grade when half the class was quarantined because we'd been exposed to meningitis?" Elaine nodded. "Ellie, I actually got the disease. I almost died, but then something inside me killed the bug. My mother recognized what happened, and she quietly inoculated the rest of the kids. A few of them would have died if she hadn't."

Gina's mom was a nurse. Elaine had sought her advice on more than one occasion as she went through nursing school and began working in the field. But this kind of thing was beyond anything Elaine had ever even heard of before. It was almost too fantastic to believe.

"So you think injecting this guy with your blood will heal him? Gina, you don't even know what blood type he is!"

Gina shook her head, that soft, knowing smile on her face. "It doesn't matter. I'm a Universal."

"Universal what? Blood type? That's good, but it won't heal him."

"Yes it will. Being a Universal means more than just blood type. My blood has Universal antibodies, among other things. It's a rare phenomenon and not something I want known, but it's real. I promise. You'll see. Look, he's already quieting down." Gina turned back to her patient, but Elaine gasped as she looked once more at the man. He was... changing.

"Look at his hands!"

In place of the scratched, calloused human hands she saw something that resembled paws, covered in tawny fur. And where he'd had short, clipped nails before, he now sported two-inch claws. Elaine tugged at Gina's shoulder to get her away from the guy, but she didn't move. In fact, Gina's expression seemed sort of sadly resigned when she turned to look at her.

Gina did something strange then. She turned her gaze to Cade as if seeking permission.

"You have to tell her," Cade said enigmatically, shrugging as he returned his attention to Mitch.

"It's all right, Ellie." Gina turned back to her. "He's a shifter."

"A what?"

"A shapeshifter. Darn it, Ellie, I didn't want you to find out like this—or at all, to be honest. Shapeshifters live in secret. I'm sure you've heard the rumors. You know they would hunt us if we came out in the open."

"Us?" Elaine staggered back just the tiniest bit, in shock. "You're saying you're one of them too?"

Gina nodded sadly. "I'm like this man." She gestured toward her patient. "Tiger Clan."

"Holy shit." The expletive was a whisper of shock as Elaine collapsed into the chair at the side of the bed and just stared at her friend. Gina was claiming to be a tiger? And the guy in the bed was too?

Well, she could see the claws and—holy shit—paws at the ends of his arms. There was definitely something hinky about that guy.

Her gaze shifted to Cade, watching her with those mysterious eyes. She'd bet money he was one of them, too. Which meant...

"Is *Shihan* Harris a shifter too? Is what happened tonight connected with all this?"

Cade whistled between his teeth, a strange sort of smile touching just the tips of his sensuous lips. "You're quick. Harris isn't one of us, but his wife was. She was hunted and killed. He's been our ally ever since."

"Ally? Is this some kind of war?"

Gina stepped in. "Most shifters just want to live in peace, but there are certain factions that want to kill us and all Others."

"Others?"

"Other magical races. Supernaturals. There are a few different kinds and not all of them are peaceful. In fact, some of the Others fight against us, trying to get rid of the competition, so to speak. Which is probably what happened to this man." Gina turned to check her patient. He was calmer, but his hands remained shifted. "I'm sure you noticed the claw marks. Too big for any normal kind of animal you'd find on a nice suburban street. This was done by an Other."

"Why did they attack him? And what the hell were you doing at the *dojo* tonight?" She turned her questions toward Cade, who watched her with those creepy eyes of his.

"Harris helps protect people who needed to find a new place to live. He helps us get them in and out of the city, and get settled. But he's been made. The new cleaning crew at the building was in on the attack tonight, as was the night watchman."

"Damn," Gina muttered.

"Yeah," Cade agreed. "It's a tough break for our side."

Elaine watched, amazed, as Mitch's hands began to shift back to normal. "His hands," she whispered, drawing the attention of both Gina and Cade, who immediately looked at Mitch.

"That's a good sign." Gina's smile was relieved. She checked her patient's pupils and vital signs. "I don't know what they gave him, but it had to be fierce to put down a tiger of his size."

"He's an Alpha." Cade said quietly.

Gina looked impressed while Elaine was just puzzled by the cryptic words.

"That's probably what saved him. I'd guess the stuff would've killed a lesser man outright. It was probably a poison, not just a tranq."

"Yeah," Cade agreed, "when he went into convulsions, I guessed it was something more powerful. Up 'til then, I was sort of hoping it was just a really strong tranq, but even those wouldn't normally have been able to keep one of us down for that long."

"You're Alpha, too, then," Gina said, as if she was just confirming something she already knew. "But I don't recognize your scent."

"*Pantera noir.*" He inclined his head. "It's an honor to meet a Universal. You're my first." The corners of his amazing eyes crinkled with just a hint of amusement. Elaine didn't really follow what they were saying, but filed the conversation away for later examination. Right now, she was feeling more than a little overwhelmed.

"The honor is mine, Alpha. I've heard of your breed, but you guys are supposed to be very rare and always clandestine. Like ninjas of the shifter world." Gina's unmistakable giggle sounded, and suddenly Elaine felt that everything was going to be all right. Gina was her friend. She'd been Elaine's best friend since they were little kids. Gina would never hurt her. And Gina wasn't crazy. She was the least crazy person Elaine had ever known. If Gina believed all this supernatural stuff, then it had to be real.

Holy shit.

"Black Panthers? Weren't they a radical group from the 1960s?" Elaine translated the name Cade had given Gina, puzzling it out.

Gina and Cade looked over at her, both with amusement on their faces. Gina's expression was open and lively, as usual, Cade's more shuttered, but she could still see a trace of humor. It was buried under the same cloak of mystery that surrounded the entire man, but it was there.

"As a clan, and as a breed, we're not affiliated with those guys. They were strictly human."

"And you're not."

"No, ma'am. We're not." Cade's mouth actually angled up in a smile this time, revealing teeth that were sharp in a way human teeth were not.

"Alpha," Gina chastised him, "if you want to frighten my friend, you're doing a good job."

Cade actually laughed, just once, but it was a laugh all the same. "She's not frightened. From what I've seen tonight, it'd take more than a show of teeth to scare off this little warrior."

Gina seemed amazed and looked over with a teasing sort of speculation in her expression, which Elaine studiously ignored.

"So what's the plan?" Elaine wanted to shift the focus and succeeded nicely.

"He'll be out for a while, I think," Gina said, checking Mitch's temperature. "My blood will probably do the trick, but it'll take time. It's good that he's the same clan. That'll speed the process, but I may have to dose him again, depending on how he responds. I'll stay with him 'til he's out of the woods."

"Or back in them, as the case may be," Elaine muttered, drawing a chuckle from Gina and a raised eyebrow from Cade.

Elaine's tabby cat, Chuck, decided to join the party at that moment, prowling into the room and heading straight for Cade. That was odd behavior in itself, but when Chuck sat on his haunches and raised one paw to touch Cade's leg, looking up at him with something like kitty admiration, Elaine was shocked. Chuck was not a very affectionate cat, though he had his moments. Still, he didn't like most people, except Gina, of course. He loved Gina. But he'd bypassed her in favor of Cade, which was downright out of character. The cat followed Gina around purring, every time she visited.

Cade lowered one hand and scooped up the tabby, who never liked to be picked up by strange people, but Chuck didn't object. He was quiet and still for the man. Amazing.

"Chuck Norris recognizes the Alpha," Gina said with a grin.

"Norris? You named your cat after the martial arts champion?" Cade shook his head and that elusive smile almost appeared again.

Elaine felt her cheeks heat. "He was just a kitten when I found him, but he was already a fighter. He wasn't much bigger than a mouse, but he was confronting someone's pet poodle on the sidewalk outside the Downtown Theater."

"Where you'd just seen a Chuck Norris movie marathon," Gina nodded and laughed, revealing Elaine's secrets. "Ellie's big on those old kung fu movies, too. Good thing it wasn't Sho Kosugi week, huh?"

Elaine watched Cade's big hands as he stroked the tabby's soft fur. He caught her looking and the flashing fire in his icy eyes made her breath stutter. He really was the most handsome man she'd ever met, but he was also some kind of...shifter. Elaine didn't know exactly what that entailed, but rather than the expected fear, she felt intrigued. The reaction almost frightened her, but nothing about this man—this *pantera noir*—really scared her.

Oh, he was dangerous. Any idiot could see that. But not to anyone who wasn't his enemy. Elaine didn't plan on getting on his bad side either. No, her inner bad girl wanted to get closer to him in a very naughty way.

Elaine squelched the thoughts, though she knew her pale cheeks were flaming. She could feel the heat, not only from her blush but from his intense gaze. Those silver eyes were heating her from within, like laser beams.

Gina cleared her throat. "I can look after your friend. What's his name, by the way?"

"Mitch." Cade's eyes mercifully shifted to Gina and Elaine felt able to breathe freely once more. "When he wakes, tell him code El Paso. He'll know what it means. Keep him here until I call. Dammit!" Something flared behind his eyes as he jumped to his feet. Chuck the cat spilled onto the floor and took up a vigilant post at Gina's feet while Cade searched the pockets of Mitch's ruined clothes.

"What is it?"

"They took his phone. It's untraceable, and we wipe the memory every day, but a dedicated hacker might be able to retrieve the last few numbers. I have to warn a few people." Cade flipped open his phone and stalked from the room.

Elaine let out a breath she hadn't even been aware of holding. Gina smiled at her with an expression that said it all.

"He's pretty intense." Elaine felt compelled to make some explanation.

"All Alphas are, though I've only known a few. They're the top bananas in our different species organizations—the clans, packs and tribes."

"Gina," Elaine shook her head, "I can't believe you managed to keep this a secret."

The doctor shrugged, looking a little sheepish. "It wasn't easy. And I didn't want to keep it from you, but it was for your own protection. Ellie, when I was six and my folks moved here, it was because we'd been hunted. They killed my older brother. Only the Underground—folks like Harris and others—helped us get away clean and make a new life. I knew if we were found out again, we'd have to run, and some of us would die. It happens every day to members of my Clan and others like them. It's a brutal world, and I wanted to keep it as far from you as possible."

"And here I go, stumbling blindly in where angels fear to tread." Elaine smiled to let her best friend in the whole world know that things would be all right between them.

"Just like you always do, Ellie. Your Alpha was right. You're the most fearless human I've ever known."

Elaine felt the flush rise up her cheeks again as she looked anywhere except at her friend. "He's not my Alpha."

"I think he might surprise you. It's not common for one of us to be attracted to a human, but that one is showing all the signs." Gina's gaze grew concerned. "Watch yourself, El. He's not human. Our ways are different and can be a little more, uh, brutal by human standards."

"Don't worry. I don't plan on any inter-species dating."

Gina turned back to check on Mitch as he moved restlessly. "You may not plan on it. He may not plan on it. But it could happen. When our animal natures rise, we have very little control over our actions. If his cat decides you'd be a tasty treat, it'll be hard for him to control the beast."

"Damn, you really do want to scare me, don't you?"

Gina shrugged. "I want you to understand. To be prepared. He's an Alpha. They're dominant by nature and because we're Other, we can't always fight our natures. When the cat needs to run, she runs."

"Is that why you have that place in the country? Your folks moved there full-time, and I know you visit them a lot. You told me they have a lot of land, but that's about all you ever said. Is that where you run, Gina?"

The doctor nodded. "It's a haven of sorts, which is why I never invited you there, Ellie, though I wanted to share it with you. You'll always be the best friend I ever had, but there was this other part of my life I could never talk about. It's kind of a relief to be able to tell you at last."

"I always wondered. I mean, I went everywhere else with you, and you with me, but never there."

"I couldn't. It was secret. It's a place where our cats can run free, and it had to be kept safe."

Cade came back in, looking grim. "I got to them in time. Anybody Mitch called today is in danger. I put the word out."

"If that's a good thing, and you got to it in time, then why are you scowling?" Elaine felt secure enough to ask.

Cade's chin came up as if amazed someone would question him. Those stormy eyes pinned her in place.

"It's both good and bad. I know a few of the people he called today, but not all. And now anyone those few have called are exposed too, if the numbers aren't wiped in time. And so on down the line. Our enemies could access the phone records and go hunting."

"It's like a tree. I get it," Elaine nodded.

Cade hovered at Mitch's side and addressed Gina. "Is there any way to wake him up? I need to know who else he might've called."

Gina's brow furrowed as she considered her patient. Elaine always knew when Gina was truly worried, and this was definitely one of those times.

"I have something upstairs in my apartment that might rouse him for a short time."

"Good enough." Cade surprised Elaine by reaching down to touch the cat. Chuck blinked once, and took off through the door, looking like he was on some kind of mission. Cade straightened and looked at Elaine, his eyes narrowed. "It occurs to me that someone must've seen you at the *dojo*. The way your car just happened to get stolen at the right time smells bad."

"Do you think they'll come here to check her out, Alpha?" Gina asked, clearly worried.

Cade nodded. "I think it's best if we all lay low for a bit and vacate the premises."

"We can take your friend to my place. It's the same layout. I've got an identical guest room. The trick will be getting through the building unseen."

"That's where our little friend, Chuck, will help us." Cade almost smiled.

Gina's eyes brightened. "Great idea."

Cade turned to Elaine again. "I want you to pack a few things and stay with Gina for a bit. Certain Others can smell a lie, and some can read minds. I don't want you exposed to anyone who might come knocking on your door."

Elaine resented the idea he'd think she'd tell anyone anything, but then, he knew more about this supernatural stuff than she did, so she backed off. Hanging with her best friend wasn't a bad idea. Particularly now that they had all kinds of new things to discuss about these mysterious Others.

Elaine left to pack her bag and threw in some of her few irreplaceable keepsakes without making it too obvious that she'd emptied the apartment of the things most valuable to her. She was ready to go in ten minutes and was amused to find Chuck sitting in front of the apartment door like some kind of sentinel.

The move upstairs was accomplished in short order. Chuck the cat raced ahead to check that the corridors and staircase were clear, reporting to Cade, who seemed to be able to communicate with him. Elaine didn't dare speak while they were out in the hallway, but she was dying to know if Gina could talk with her pet as well. How cool would that be? To be able to communicate with your resident feline and know what he thought?

But Elaine didn't get a chance to ask the questions buzzing around inside her head. When they got to Gina's apartment, the good doctor's attention was focused solely on her patient. Gina looked worried—an expression Elaine had seen only rarely on her best friend's face. Elaine assisted as Gina gave Mitch a shot of something she'd had in her extensive medicine cabinet. The bottle was unmarked and the purple liquid didn't look like anything Elaine had ever seen before in her work as a nurse, but then, she'd never known her best friend was some kind of supernatural creature before tonight either.

Within about five minutes of administering the shot, Mitch stirred. He thrashed a bit, and Cade moved forward to help hold him down. Then fur started sprouting on the man's arms and legs, those sharp claws making a reappearance, but mercifully, he didn't shift all the way to his Other form. Cade was well aware of the risk of reviving a drugged Alpha. Mitch could emerge from his nap in a violent frenzy. It had happened before and the consequences could be dire, but this was a life or death situation for the community of shifters that counted on the few Alphas to help keep them safe.

"Mitch. Come on, buddy," Cade spoke in low, urgent tones.

"I need you here, Mitchell. Stay with me. I need to know who you called today."

Mitch's eyes opened. They were wild and unfocused as he thrashed, but Cade held him. Gina had his legs, holding on with more strength than Cade would have credited for a female, though she was a tiger. Elaine had wisely backed away. There was no way the little human could ever hope to hold a full-grown *tigre* Alpha, though Cade knew she would have given it her best shot had there been room to maneuver.

Slowly, Mitch seemed to settle. His eyes lost the feral glow and began to clear.

"Focus, friend. You were tranq'd and poisoned." Cade pitched his voice in what he hoped were comforting tones.

"Where am I?" Mitch was still out of it, but able to speak. So far, so good.

"You're among friends, Alpha." The woman, bless her, stroked the tiger, her touch soothing. "I'm a doctor. Your associate—" she nodded toward Cade but never took her eyes or hands off Mitch, "—brought you to me when you wouldn't wake up. Good thing, too. I still don't know what they dosed you with, but it would've been lethal to a lesser cat."

"Damn." Mitch tried to sit up but they stilled him. "What happened?"

"The *dojo* burned, but our people got out. Harris was outed. We can't use him again. But the biggest problem is that I haven't located your phone. Who did you call since the last memory wipe?"

"The phone went into a storm drain during the fight." Mitch groaned as he lay back on the bed.

"I'll have someone go fish it out if it's still there. If it's not..." He didn't have to complete the thought. Mitch knew just as well as he did what it could mean.

"I called Amanda and Perkins this morning. Also Bonnie, Ray and Charlie. And the beta safe house landline."

"I got everyone but the safe house. Dammit. The site could be compromised." Cade flipped open his phone again and hit speed dial.

Chapter Three

Elaine watched Cade stride out of the room, already talking in low, urgent tones to whoever had picked up on the other end. He was intense in a way she'd never encountered before. Now that he was awake, his friend seemed pretty formidable as well. He was larger than Cade, but that had been the only thing she really could say about him until he opened his eyes.

Now those sparkly brown and gold orbs were taking in every facet of the room. The man was hyper-alert, sniffing the air. He pinned Gina with his gaze.

"You're *tigre*?" he asked.

Gina seemed to know what he was talking about. She nodded shortly.

"And you're really a doctor?"

Again, she nodded, checking one of the bandages on his brawny arm. "I'm also a Universal, which is the only reason you're alive."

"Blessed Be," the big man said, surprising Elaine a bit with his ardent tone. She didn't think a guy this big or this imposing would care for the blessings of a higher power, but apparently all these shifters felt the way Gina did. Elaine knew from their long friendship that Gina's belief system was a little different, but she believed in her goddess strongly. Stronger than Elaine had ever felt about the church her parents occasionally belonged to, at any rate.

"Whatever they dosed you with, it was lethal. The Lady was

watching over you tonight, brother." Gina agreed as she swabbed a slowly oozing cut.

The man's hand shot out and captured Gina's in a strong grip. "I'm not your brother." Elaine watched, fascinated, as their eyes met and held. The energy of the moment crackled in the room and made her uncomfortable. Was the big guy threatening her friend? He'd better think twice before doing something so stupid.

"Listen up, buddy." Elaine stood at his side, drawing his attention as she stared down at him. "You play nice with the good doctor. She saved your life."

Surprisingly, the man chuckled, but it turned into a cough. He shifted his magnificent tawny gaze between Gina and Elaine with something like amusement.

"Your pet human has claws, Healer. I see now why you're friends." He lay back and seemed to relax a bit. "But you know I'm right, little one. There's something very different about you, and I've never seen you at the Clan meets.

Gina shifted away. "That's because I'm not part of *tigre d'or.*"

"I sniffed that right away." The man seemed a little disgusted by her answer. "But you do have a Clan affiliation, don't you?"

"I have my familial Pride. That's sufficient." A haughty air flowed through Gina's words, surprising the heck out of Elaine, who'd never seen her down-to-earth friend put on airs.

"That's not enough, lone one, and you know it. We tigers need the Clan. You can't go it on your own. Or are you one of those stubborn stray cats?" Mitch's voice was soothing and a bit reproachful now.

"We go our own way, Alpha. It was my father's choice. His bid for freedom." Gina looked as frustrated and annoyed as Elaine had ever seen her. And after a lifetime of friendship, that was saying something.

A cunning sort of knowing entered the big man's gaze. His

focus on Gina didn't waver. "You're not...?"

Gina's head bowed regally in acknowledgement, and no further words were spoken. Mitch had been effectively silenced by whatever they'd just communicated so obscurely.

"Anyone mind telling me what just happened here?" Elaine knew Gina at least would find the humor in her words, but the pale blue eyes turned to her were deadly serious. Elaine sat hard in the chair they'd dragged to the bedside. "What? What's wrong?"

"Nothing's wrong, Ellie. It's just that I'm a little different from the other cats. We live apart from them and have chosen to stay hidden from all Others."

Elaine looked from her friend to the tense man in the bed. "I guess helping this guy let your cat out of the bag, huh?" She tried for humor, but Gina's answering smile was tinged with sadness.

"That's up to him." Gina looked at Mitch. Elaine had seldom seen her friend so fierce.

Mitch seemed to weigh his words before answering. "For now, I'll hold my tongue, but I make no promises for the future. Our people need you and your kind, doctor. Does your sire still live?"

Gina nodded shortly. "He doesn't want anything to do with the Clan."

"But we need him. Especially now," Mitch insisted.

"Why? What's so special about Gina's old man?" Elaine felt like she had to remind them she was in the room. Tempers were flaring in subtle ways she didn't fully understand.

"My dad is the *Tig'Ra*. The Sun King of the *tigre* Clan. Or at least, he was. He renounced his throne in favor of the *tigre d'or* Alpha before I was born."

"Holy crap. Gina, are you saying you're royalty?" Elaine saw a stiffness in her best friend's spine she'd never seen before.

Gina sighed. "I'm *tigre blanche*—a white tiger, Ellie. You

know how rare white tigers are among ordinary cats? Same goes with us, but it's more than a genetic thing. It's kind of a spiritual designation as well. The difference in scent is subtle, but it's telling to one of us. I didn't expect to be able to hide it from this Alpha. My dad's parents were both like him—" she pointed at Mitch, "—*Tigre d'or*—golden tigers. But Dad was born *blanche* and so was I, though mom's golden, too."

"Which means you could be our queen, doctor," Mitch put in quietly.

The enormity of the words hit Elaine, but she just couldn't handle the idea her best friend was some kind of lost princess. She didn't quite believe the thing about shifting form into a big cat either. This was too much for one day. She was feeling overwhelmed, but at least two things were very clear—Gina didn't want to be royalty, and Elaine would stand beside her friend no matter what.

Elaine drew Mitch's attention. "You'd better keep quiet about Gina. She saved your life. You owe her."

Mitch nodded regally. "I see your point and I'm grateful, but I can't make promises about the future. Our people need leaders."

Gina stood and paced softly across the floor at the foot of the bed. "I'm nobody's leader. I'm a doctor and a damned good one. I've never been part of the Clan, never interacted with Others. I'd be the worst sort of role model."

"You're scared."

Elaine wondered idly if the guy in the bed realized the challenge he'd just laid down. Nobody told Gina she was afraid. It was a dare she could never resist ever since they were kids and was the easiest way to piss her off. Sure enough, Gina's chin rose in defiance, and Elaine recognized the signs of anger in her best friend.

"I'm a realist, Alpha. I'm not fit to lead the Clan, and I certainly don't want to be courted and fought over by a bunch of brawny cats with a thirst for power and no regard for me as a person."

Mitch surprised them all by gritting his teeth and sitting up. The rippling muscles of his abdomen fought against the pain of his many wounds.

"I would protect you with my life. Any cat that dared disrespect you would fall to my claws." The fervent ardor in his voice surprised the heck out of Elaine. He really sounded serious. But his words seemed to deflate Gina's anger. She sighed and sat back on the bed, touching the man's bare shoulder with just the tips of her fingers.

"See what I mean? You don't even know me, and you're ready to kill or be killed on my behalf. I don't want that. I'm a doctor. I preserve life. I don't want to be the cause of bloodshed."

Mitch caught her hand and enfolded it in one of his large palms. The man moved silently for such a large guy. Elaine felt a little uncomfortable witnessing the tender sort of understanding in his eyes as he gazed at Gina.

"Don't ask me to forget your existence, doctor. Now that I know, I can do no other than walk beside you and protect your path. It's my calling."

Gina's face went white as a sheet, and Elaine sat forward in concern. "You're not just Alpha, you're Royal Guard, aren't you?" At the man's simple nod, Gina seemed to slump, her energy drained as she turned to face Elaine with troubled eyes. "What the hell did you stumble into, Ellie?"

Cade chose that moment to reappear. The phone was folded and stowed on his belt, and his expression said he'd heard a good portion of the conversation. He'd probably been standing near the doorway for a while before making his presence known by moving into the room. He was so silent, neither of the women would've heard him but surely Mitch had seen him as he'd been the only one facing the door.

"They recovered your phone from the sewer, Mitch. Looks like nobody's messed with it, though all the dialed numbers have been alerted just in case."

The tension in the room eased and Mitch lowered himself painfully back to the bed, letting go of Gina's hand at the last possible moment.

"My apologies, doctor." Cade gave Gina a courtly little nod of the head. "I heard a bit of your conversation and I'm forced to believe the Lady guided us here tonight."

Gina looked troubled still, and Elaine felt a stab of piercing guilt for dragging her friend into this mess.

"I think it's only right to tell you about what brought us here. Mitch and I have been working as a team, safeguarding the travel of the young *pantera* Nyx to her new home." Cade turned to address Elaine, clarifying. "Like the *tigre*, my Clan has a monarch. The *pantera* Nyx is our queen. She's a young, unmated female whose parents were killed several years ago, so her reign started prematurely. She moves every so often for her own protection, since our enemies are well aware of her identifying characteristics. Harris was helping us find a safe place for her when the *dojo* was hit." Cade turned back to Mitch. "They've got her stashed in a safe place."

"So the Nyx is moving to the area?" Gina seemed worried.

Cade nodded. "But now that we know about you, we'll have to rethink the plan. It's not good to have two of you in the same city. Of course, if the Others have ID'd your friend here, your safety may already be compromised. Maybe you should consider moving, doctor."

"Now wait just a minute." Elaine rounded on Cade, but was prevented from venting her opinion as a ball of fur hurtled through the open door and into her lap. Chuck, the tabby cat, was shivering in fear and outrage.

"Something's wrong." Cade stalked out the door on silent, swift feet. Elaine followed, cradling Chuck in her arms, tiptoeing and trying to be as quiet as possible, but Cade seemed to hear her coming a mile away. He hadn't gone for the door, but instead was cautiously approaching the window, angling to look at the fire escapes along that side of the building.

He shook his head at her and jerked his chin in the direction of the bedroom near where Gina was hovering. She could see Mitch trying to lever himself out of bed. Elaine hadn't taken two steps before Cade was behind her, crowding her back into the guest room. It was one of the few rooms in the apartment that had no windows.

Cade shut the door partially, blocking the view of the windows in the other room. "There's a *were*wolf on Elaine's fire escape. No doubt he scented my trail. I was in that same location earlier tonight."

"You were spying on me from outside the fire escape like some kind of pervert?" Elaine was outraged.

Cade shrugged. "I didn't know who or what you were. I was doing my job."

"Being a Peeping Tom is not a job unless you're a sicko." She was working into a temper when Mitch broke in.

"We left traces at her place. What if it's searched?"

Cade held up one hand, palm outward. "I went back after my phone call and sanitized the place. I brought up a garbage bag with anything that might've indicated we were there and sprayed the whole apartment. She might come off as a clean freak, but they won't know we were in there or in the halls leading here. I sprayed anyplace I found traces of scent and a few other areas to decoy, then sent Chuck to prowl around and rub up against the walls, leaving his dander and scent everywhere." Cade reached out to rub the head of the now-purring feline in Elaine's arms. That brought his touch too close to her body and she shifted the cat, placing him gently on the floor where he immediately twined around Cade's legs in an obvious show of kitty affection.

"Good man. But why didn't you do the fire escape while you were at it?" Mitch asked.

Cade sighed and rubbed one hand through his dark hair. "I prowled around most of the outside of the building before settling. It was too much to try to hide. Plus, an Other saw me following her in the park, and we have no way of knowing if he was one of them or not. They probably saw her come and go from the *dojo*, so they knew we had to be watching her too— unless she was one of us. Either way, she's in danger until they know if she saw anything. I'm sorry—" Cade turned his icy gaze on her with what looked like genuine regret, "—but you can't go home for a while. Not until things settle down and we neutralize those responsible for the fire and attempt on the Nyx. You'll have to lay low, or better yet, head out of town for a few days." Cade turned to Gina. "You should go too, Doctor, just in case. We know they're after the Nyx, but if they somehow learn who and what you are, you'll be in just as much danger."

"I'll guard the doctor," Mitch said, drawing all eyes.

"You're not going anywhere in a hurry, Alpha." Gina's caustic words were directed toward Mitch. "In case you haven't noticed, you almost died a few hours ago. Despite the Universal blood I gave you, you're still going to be weak for a few days."

"What about it, princess?" Mitch seemed to have a talent for getting on Elaine's nerves. "If you're heading out of town, I'm going with you."

Gina sighed. Elaine knew that sigh, and it wasn't a good sign. Gina was about to give in to something against her better judgment. It had been the same way when they were in high school and Gina allowed Elaine to talk her in to buying that ugly polka-dotted prom dress. Gina had been the laughing stock of the prom and hadn't let Elaine forget it for years afterward. Gina had that same look in her eyes that said she was resigned to her fate as she regarded the man in the bed.

"Yes, I'll leave and yes, Mitch is coming with me." Gina shut her eyes against Elaine's objections. When they reopened, she didn't look at her lifelong friend. "Frankly, I want to keep an eye on him. I really don't think we'll run into any trouble, but if we do, there's safety in numbers. Which is why I expect you," she looked directly at Cade, "to stick to Ellie like white on rice."

"Why can't I go with you?" Elaine wanted to know.

"Sorry, hun. Where I'm going only cats can follow. You know my parents love you, but I promised them a long time ago I'd never bring you to the family hideaway. I can't break that promise and even if I could, you couldn't make the trek."

"So when you told me the cabin was off the beaten path—" Elaine tried for humor though she was scared for her friend, "—you weren't kidding, huh?"

Gina chuckled. "It's more like over the river and through the woods. I'm sorry, Ellie, but I've heard about these guys—or ones like them—they're the best of the best. Not only are they Alphas, but they're Royal Guards. Cade will look after you, if only because of your links to both the Nyx's safety and mine."

"You've got that right." Cade inclined his head with a bit of respect that surprised Elaine as he agreed with Gina's words. "I'll stash her in one of our safe houses," he said to Gina, talking right over Elaine's head in a way guaranteed to piss her off.

"Excuse me, but what if I don't want to be *stashed* anywhere?" Her ire rose along with her outrage. "I have a job, you know. I can't just call in sick or not show up for days—and don't try to con me into thinking it'll be any less than that. I can put two and two together. I also can tell that if I just disappear, your enemies will definitely know I'm involved. If I go about my normal life, they might just leave me alone."

"No way." Cade's silver eyes sparked with anger but she refused to be intimidated.

"She does have a point," Gina said. Bless her heart. "Ellie's one of the most capable people I know. If she acts like nothing's changed, she could escape this. She's not a shifter, after all. And she can defend herself if she does run into trouble." Gina walked over and took both her hands, holding her gaze. "But you've got to promise me, El, if you *do* run into trouble, you'll call for help. These guys don't play around. If the bad guys think you know anything about any of this, your life would be in more danger than you know."

"So you want me to just let her waltz out of here with a wolf lying in wait and who knows what else looking to find out what she knows? There's no way they won't check her out." Cade looked fit to be tied and his words gave Elaine pause, but she knew she had to at least try to keep her world the way it had been only hours before.

"Yes, that's exactly what I'm asking, Alpha." Gina faced him down, holding herself straight in that queenly way she had. Elaine had always admired the ability. "My friend has a right to live normally. She's human. She was never supposed to know about any of this. And I trust her with my life. She'd never betray me or any of us. I know her as well as I know myself, and I count her as part of my family. I can vouch for her integrity."

"It's not her integrity I'm worried about," Cade admitted grudgingly, finally looking at Elaine, his eyes hot with anger.

"This is my wish, Alpha. We have to try to give her a chance to get out of this unharmed. If things don't work out, she'll run right to one of your safe houses with no complaints, right, Ellie?" Gina turned imploring eyes on her. Elaine had always been a sucker for that look, and her best friend knew it.

"Oh, all right. I'll call Cade if I have trouble."

Cade ran one hand through that long, sexy hair of his in clear frustration. Elaine tried hard not to let him see the satisfaction she felt at his capitulation. She'd bet he didn't give way often, but this really was the best plan. If she just dropped out of sight, she'd never get her life back. She had to at least try to protect herself and her best friend with an appearance of normalcy.

"You're staying here tonight," Cade said shortly, giving in. "I'll help get your friend and Mitch out of town, then come back and watch over you from here while you head back to your place. If—no, make that *when*—someone comes knocking on your door, I want to be nearby in case there's trouble. Once I'm assured you've made it through the confrontation unscathed, I'll be out of your hair."

"That's fair," Gina said before Elaine could get a word in. The look in her eyes said Elaine damned well better agree. Apparently this was as good as she was going to get from the Alpha *pantera noir*.

An hour later, Cade prowled out the door. He was going to scout the route they would take to the basement garage where Gina's car was parked. Luckily the building had decent security and the garage was locked up tight. It was one of the features that had drawn Elaine and Gina to this building in the first place. Both of them worked odd hours at the hospital and needed to feel safe when they finally made it home after a long shift.

"Are you sure about this, Gina?"

"I have no choice, El. I always suspected this would catch up with me someday. Actually, I'm surprised it's taken this long. But if I can get Mitch to safety with my family, and if you manage to get the Others off your tail, I might be able to come back. Right now, they don't know about me, but if that *tigre* stays here long enough, there won't be any way to hide his presence. The bad guys will find him—and me—for sure. I've got to get him out of here."

"I'm so sorry I brought them home with me." Elaine tugged on Gina's hand, near tears. "I never meant to drag you into this or out you. Hell, I didn't even know you could be outed." She laughed nervously, feeling desperate to change things back to the way they'd been just a few hours before, when everything had still been normal.

"It's okay, El. They're the good guys. They're my people, even though my dad decided to leave the Clan a long time ago. He had his reasons, and I respect his choice. I may be *blanche*, but I'm nobody's queen."

"I don't know about that. You did a pretty impressive job of ordering those big guys around. I think they're actually scared of you," Elaine whispered in a conspiratorial tone that made her friend smile. She was glad Gina could see the humor in this horrible situation Elaine had unknowingly created. "Then again, you've always had this certain way of tilting your head that said you expected to get your way. It used to drive me nuts when we were kids, but I think I understand where it comes from now. Your dad can be pretty imperious too."

Gina gave her a dramatic sigh, holding the back of one hand to her forehead. "I'm so misunderstood." They laughed at Gina's antics, and Elaine felt better about the mess they were in. "I'm sorry I couldn't tell you before, Ellie. It was the one thing I most wanted to share with you and the one thing I was strictly forbidden to talk about."

"It's okay. I think I understand. More than just your own safety was at stake. I'm sorry if I messed up by bringing Mitch here. I didn't mean to put you in danger."

"If anyone had to find me, I'm glad it was them. They're Royal Guard, Ellie. That really means something in shifter circles. They're the strongest, the fastest, the bravest...and the most loyal. Neither of them will betray me. They may pressure me to return to the Clan, but I'm pretty sure they'll respect my decision either way. Regardless, you couldn't have left Mitch there to die. You did the right thing. And maybe the hand of fate pushed you along a little." Gina gave her a wistful, slightly mischievous grin. "I'll take care of the *tigre*. You just watch yourself with his *pantera* friend."

"If all goes well, I'll never see him again after tomorrow." Now why did that make her feel so sad? It's not like she was losing her best friend. But wait—if this didn't work out, she might never see Gina again. "Promise me you'll be okay."

Gina smiled. "I'll do my best."

"Give my love to your folks." Elaine hugged her childhood friend close, knowing this might well be the last time. "Take care of yourself, Gina. You know you're the sister I never had, right?"

"Ditto, El." Both of them were tearing up as they let go, only to find Cade letting himself into the apartment with the key Gina had loaned him.

"The path is clear. We should go." Cade scooped Chuck into his arms. "I'm going to ask Chuck to scout ahead when we go down, but I'll send him back. He'll paw the door when he returns so you can let him in. I wish there was another way, but we need to keep Gina and Mitch as safe as possible."

"It's okay. I think Chuck likes helping." Ellie watched the cat, sitting snug and secure in Cade's muscular arms. Just for a moment, she envied the feline.

"He does. He likes you too, Ellie. More than any other human."

The tears that threatened now that Gina was really leaving welled up in her eyes once more. She refused to let them fall. Not in front of Cade and Gina. She would cry in private. As soon as they left.

"I want you to lock the door behind us, then wait by it until you hear Chuck scratch. He's short, so the sound will be low to the ground. Don't make the mistake of opening the door for anything taller." The grim look in his eyes stopped any trace of tears. Just what did he expect to come scratching on the door in the middle of the night? Whatever it was, it couldn't be anything good.

She nodded agreement, swallowing hard around the fear that bubbled out of nowhere. Why now? She'd been so calm to this point, but it all suddenly started to hit home. Gina was leaving. So were the men. Elaine would be alone with God knew what sadistic creatures out there, hunting her.

"I'm going with them to the city limits to make sure they get clear. They'll pick up an Escort from there. I want you to stay here, in Gina's apartment, until I return. Catch some sleep if you can. I'll be back in a couple of hours and then you can go back to your place, pretending like you just spent the night with a friend or something. I expect you'll have a visitor first thing in the morning, nosing around, asking questions. How well you answer them will decide your next move."

"Or my fate," she added. "You said there were Others that could smell a lie and read minds. What happens if they send one of them?"

"If they show up in daytime, chances are they won't be mind readers. That kind only comes out after dark. As for the ones who can smell lies, it all depends on the degree of the lie. Keep your story simple, and you should be okay. Anything elaborate will more than likely trip you up."

"Good to know." She filed that away under useful—if scary—information.

"Here's my number." He handed her a business card that had nothing but a phone number printed on it. Now that was creepy. "If you run into problems before I get back, call me. I can arrange to get help to you, if necessary, even if I'm too far away. I'd have called in someone to stay with you, but we're spread too thin protecting the Nyx, and getting any more watchers on this building might create more of a problem than we already have. They'd be tripping over each other out there." Humor sparked his silvery eyes for a quick moment. "Stay away from the windows and don't answer the phone until you check the Caller ID and only answer if it's someone you know. Use your best judgment but be wary."

"Gina has an answering machine. She always screens her calls anyway, so that's nothing out of the ordinary."

"Perfect." Cade let Chuck go and the tabby cat loped off to stand guard by the apartment door. When Cade moved closer, Elaine had the urge to flee, but she wouldn't be a coward. Still, Cade shocked her when he cupped her cheek with one palm, lowering his head for a quick, stolen kiss.

His lips were firm yet sensuous and her hands rose of their own volition to rest against his powerful chest. He smelled divine and felt even better, but this was crazy. She'd only just met the man—and he wasn't even human.

She drew back slightly, staring into those silver eyes that she could see were flecked with blue and grey. They were gorgeous. *He* was gorgeous. And he was at least part animal. A shapeshifter.

Elaine ordered herself to get a grip—just not a grip on him. She tried to move away, but his arms snuck around her waist and kept her close.

"I don't want to leave you here alone."

"It's for the best," she whispered, her pulse pounding as he held her against his body.

Sighing, he let her go. "You're probably right."

"I'm ready." Gina breezed back into the room, having packed some of her things. She had a knapsack over one shoulder, and her emergency medical kit over the other.

Cade held Elaine's gaze for a long, breathless moment before he turned to the guest room. Gina's gaze followed him, her suspicious expression turning to Elaine when he'd gone.

"You better watch yourself, friend."

"Are you warning me off?" Elaine laughed out loud at the idea. Gina was the least likely woman to get catty about a man.

"Just hoping you keep a level head where that Alpha is concerned. That kind of man is walking, talking temptation, but he's not for you, El. You're human. A mating between one of us and someone like you rarely works. And the few that do take human mates and succeed aren't Alphas. He could really hurt you, El, and I don't mean just by breaking your heart."

"All right already. You've made your point. Besides, there's nothing happening. He's going to make sure I'm in the clear, then he's going to disappear. We'll never see each other again. No harm, no foul."

"I hope you're right, El. I don't want to see you hurt." Gina didn't get to say more because Cade walked back into the room with Mitch in his arms. The tiger shifter was unconscious again. Cade carried his big friend as if he weighed nothing, and Elaine was impressed by his strength.

Sending Chuck ahead to scout, Cade went out the door first with his burden, followed closely by Gina. They couldn't chance making any noise now that they were in the hallway, but both women had silent tears running down their cheeks as the elevator doors closed.

This was it then. Elaine was alone. Until Chuck got back from his super secret spy mission, she didn't even have her cat to console her. Elaine sank to the floor near the door and let a few tears fall. It felt good to let go a little, but she'd feel better when Chuck came back. She'd know then that they'd made it to the car safely and at least she'd have company. Even if he couldn't talk...to her at least. Elaine wondered if shifters could actually talk to house cats and thought it would be cool to be able to communicate with Chuck. If she ever saw Gina again, she'd have to ask her about it.

When the scratching sound came near the bottom of the door, Gina was happy to let the orange tabby into the apartment. He bounded into her lap as soon as she sat after locking the door tight. She petted him, praising his courage and rubbing her face in his soft fur.

After a while, she decided to clean Gina's apartment. Cade had told her to erase any traces of the men's presence as best she could. She stripped the sheets off the guest room bed and started the small washer in one corner of Gina's well-equipped home. She remade the bed and flopped down on it with Chuck, deciding to just close her eyes for a few minutes.

Chapter Four

Elaine awoke to kisses. A hot mouth trailed wet, licking kisses down her arm and while the tongue was a little rough, it was way too big to be her cat's.

"Cade?" Her sleepy voice was rough to her own ears.

"You're safe, Ellie," he whispered into her ear, his mouth trailing over her neck and onto her other arm.

Safe? She wasn't so sure. "Uh...did Gina and your friend get out of town okay?" Elaine rose up on one elbow blinking awake, then pushed herself up to a sitting position.

Cade gave her only a little room as he sat on the edge of the bed, looking at her with those almost reflective silvery blue eyes. They disconcerted her. They distracted her. They turned her on.

"The Escort met them just outside of town. They should be okay." Cade trailed the fingers of one hand down her arm, raising goose flesh.

"Stop that." Elaine moved away, but he stalked her, not letting her put space between them.

"Stop what?" He moved closer.

"You know what you're doing. Knock it off." Her voice was a breathless whisper as he closed in on her.

She scooted backward against the headboard, unable to move farther away. Cade prowled forward, hovering over her, his breath warming her cheek as he lowered his head.

"Just give me one kiss, sweetheart. I want to taste you."

Something rippled to life within her womb as he came closer. His hair draped forward a tad, framing both their faces in darkness as his lips grazed over hers.

She was a goner at the first brush of his lips. She succumbed with a gasp of pure desire. He took full advantage of the small opening. His talented tongue dipped into her mouth, drawing out her response, making her surrender her pleasure. She'd never felt anything like it. He commanded and coaxed in equal measure and beyond the startling sensations coursing through her body, she couldn't focus on anything else.

When Cade lowered her to a reclining position beneath him on the soft mattress, she went willingly. His arms boxed her in, but she reveled in his possession. The soft ends of his hair trailed over her cheeks adding their own caress to the harsh male demand of his body over hers.

Cade's muscular body hovered over her, his chest rubbing against suddenly sensitive breasts. His hips found the cradle of her thighs as if he'd been made to fit there, and the way he rubbed against her from head to foot drove her out of her mind.

All this, from just a kiss. They were both fully clothed, but she didn't dare give in to the temptation to tug at his shirt or reach for the button on his pants. She wasn't that brave.

A rumbling started deep in his chest, vibrating against her most sensitive places, shooting a dart of pleasure that danced in her tummy. He was purring.

The thought shocked her out of the sensuous daze he'd held her in, and she pulled back. He let her go after a tense moment where she wasn't sure if he was completely in control of his beast nature, but in the end, he moved away. But he didn't go far. He watched her with hooded eyes, now the color of blazing steel, impenetrable and strong.

"As I suspected, you're pure catnip, baby." His lazy smile fired her senses in a way she was unable to deny. He lifted one of her hands in his and brought it to his lips. "I want to lick you all over." He put action to his words, placing a kiss on her hand that ended with a broad swipe of his tongue. It tickled...all the way to her womb.

Elaine tugged her hand away from him, trying desperately to regroup. "You shouldn't have done that."

Cade's eyes fell and he seemed to retreat both mentally and physically as he stood from the bed. He sighed long and hard, running one hand through his sexy hair before meeting her eyes once more. The fire in his gaze was banked for the moment.

"I couldn't help myself. To tell you the truth, your scent has been drawing me toward you since the moment we met outside the *dojo*. I don't understand it, but you're potent stuff, Ellie. I've been wanting a taste of you for what feels like my entire life."

"Wow." Elaine could read the honesty of his stark words in his expression. He seemed just as befuddled by their explosive response to each other as she was. He stared into her eyes for a long moment as if searching for answers, but finding none. Cade finally blinked and moved another few steps toward the door.

"You'd better shower. I rubbed all over you and to any sensitive nose, you'll carry my scent. Gina's too, since you've been touching things in her apartment. Put your clothes outside the bathroom door, and I'll wash them while you're in the shower."

He left, and she was finally able to take a deep breath. Cade was such a strong presence it felt like he sucked all the air out of a room just by being there. Once again he was ordering her life, but she complied with his wishes easily. He was the expert on this crazy situation and the players and skills involved. She'd do whatever he thought would work to help fool those he thought would check her out the minute she returned to her own apartment.

With a weary sigh, she went into the bathroom to wash off his scent. Too bad she couldn't erase the memory of his kiss as easily.

Cade ran his hand through his hair again in building frustration. He was reeling at the revelations of the past minutes. Could it be possible? Could that little *human* woman really have made him purr in his man form?

Legends abounded about the mating of his species. Cats often knew their perfect mates by the way they could make them purr even when not wearing their fur. It shouldn't be possible, but for each cat shifter, it was said, there was one woman who could inspire such a thing.

Could Elaine Spencer be his perfect mate?

The thought should have alarmed him even more than it did. But as he opened Gina's refrigerator and set about making a very early breakfast for them both, he couldn't seem to focus on anything other than Elaine and the danger that might be stalking her. He'd feed her well, he decided. They'd need their energy to deal with the trials yet to come this day.

Cade worked on autopilot, gathering ingredients until he heard the bathroom door open and close. That was his cue to pick up Ellie's clothes for washing. He went into the small hall and found a neat little pile of folded pants and top, but nothing else.

Biting back a grin, Cade rattled the knob on the door. It was locked, but it was one of those little push button locks that could be easily sprung from the outside. He popped it with little remorse, hearing the strong swish of water from within the tiny bathroom. He licked his chops at the idea of catching a glimpse of the troubling human woman in the buff. He'd bet she had pretty pink skin—just right for licking.

"I'm coming in," he warned a split second before he pushed the door inward. He had to bite back a laugh at her shriek. She really was the cutest thing as she stood there, grasping the almost translucent shower curtain against herself.

"What the hell are you doing?"

"I need your undies too." He leered at her, snapping his

teeth in her direction even as he snagged her sports bra and surprisingly naughty lace panties from where she'd hung them on the towel rack.

"Why? You didn't touch them." She eyed him accusingly, holding tight to her dignity and the shower curtain that preserved it...somewhat.

"That doesn't mean I didn't want to." He winked at her, betting it would drive her nuts. For some reason he didn't care to examine, he enjoyed teasing her. "Best to be thorough on a job like this. Leave no stone unturned, no panty unsniffed."

"You're disgusting." Her words were probably meant to be harsh, but the rosy flush rising up her cheeks said something very different to him. As did her eyes, following the progress of her panties in his hand as he brought them to his face and took a deep breath.

He'd done it to tease her, but he ended up torturing himself. If he'd thought her skin smelled like heaven, her intimate fragrance was designed solely to drive him out of his mind. He threw the fabric into the hallway with her other clothes and stalked forward, facing her. Only the thin fabric of the shower curtain stood between them as he wrapped his arms around her.

She was wet, but he didn't care. The shower sprayed in the background, causing droplets of water to adhere to his forearms and her back. Even so, nothing mattered but the feel of her slick skin and the slight weight of her body against his as she surrendered.

Her head dropped back on her shoulders, and her mouth opened in anticipation of his kiss. He liked that she knew what he wanted. He dove in, capturing her ripe lips and bringing them into a fast, deep, intimate embrace.

One of his hands slid downward, over the taut swell of her shapely ass, his fingers teasing the cleft there before delving lower. She gasped and arched against him, offering even better access.

His fingers found the moist heat he'd been searching for and pride filled him at the slippery slickness he found there. She was wet with more than just water as she panted against him. The undeniable evidence of her body said she wanted him. The beast within growled in triumph.

Cade lifted her, wanting to pull her out of the shower, but the loud pop of shower curtain rings roused him out of the Ellie-inspired stupor that had claimed him. A plastic ring bouncing off his forehead only added insult to injury. He let her go with a sheepish grin, looking at the half-destroyed shower curtain with one raised eyebrow.

"Honey, you bring out the barbarian in me."

Thankfully, Elaine laughed at his words. The drooping part of the shower curtain covered her luscious breasts, but just barely. Cade's mouth watered as he looked at her.

"I'd better get out of here before I forget all my good intentions and destroy your friend's bathroom."

"Yeah, maybe that's a good idea." Her eyes lit with mischief, and he breathed a sigh of relief that she had a good sense of humor. He'd need that in a mate.

The unconscious thought stopped him cold. *Mate?*

Damn. He was going to have to watch those kinds of thoughts. It was difficult for any shifter to take a human mate—doubly so for one like him. Alphas needed strong partners. But if any human female was up to the challenge, Cade had an idea it would be this one.

It wouldn't be an easy road. It would be fraught with danger to her, disapproval from most of his people and no doubt disappointment for them both. He wouldn't do that to her. Other than a few uncontrollable kisses, he had to leave her alone. It would be one of the hardest things he'd ever done, but he'd have to walk away once he was sure she was out of danger. And he could never look back. He wouldn't be strong enough to let her go twice.

"Scrub hard, baby." He backed toward the door. "Use the

perfumed soap. Your safety depends on them not being able to smell me on you."

But oh, how he wanted to leave her marked for any shifter to sniff. The impulse was nearly undeniable, but he had to be strong. Her life was at stake. That was the only thought that made it possible for him to leave her in that damned shower where he knew she was erasing any trace of his claim. The very idea of it made him want to claw something.

Cade shut the door behind him and leaned back against it, gathering his wits and his strength. He had work to do this morning. He had to clean her clothing with the scented soap powder Gina favored, fix breakfast for them both and sanitize the apartment of his presence.

He was becoming very domestic, he mused, as he loaded the small washer again. Gina had the supplies he would need to mask his scent. She seemed very good at hiding herself among humans and unless they caught her unawares, as he had, most Others would never even know she was a *tigre* in disguise. Even if they did recognize her as another shifter, only a precious few could discern the differences between the *tigre d'or* and the *tigre blanche*.

Few would believe the heir to the *tigre* throne would be allowed to live so freely in the human world, without even a modicum of protection. No Guards. No other shifters near her home at all. As long as she kept a low profile, Gina was safe and had years of living this way to prove it. The knowledge gave Cade hope for the mission he was currently working on for the Nyx.

Elaine's blood simmered as she showered off—again. She'd been almost finished with her lightning quick shower when Cade accosted her. She was angry at him, but even angrier at herself. It seemed she had no strength at all to resist him. She hated any weakness in herself and especially this one. She'd never been foolish enough to pant after a man. Not after her doomed relationship with Bob.

Bob was the one who'd first sparked Elaine's interest in martial arts. They'd dated in college and when he left for grad school, he'd left her with a crushing let down. She'd thought they were in love. That he'd take her with him or at the very least, propose. He'd done neither. Leaving her instead with a resounding chorus of nothing. Nothing to show for the years she'd put into a relationship that was completely one-sided.

In the end, she realized she'd meant nothing to him, while she'd built her dreams of the future around his broad shoulders. The golden boy had broken her heart, and she'd been wary of men ever since. But Cade...well, he was something else.

She wondered idly as she rinsed off for a second time, if being a shifter gave him some sort of animal magnetism. Otherwise, she couldn't explain her mind blowing reaction to the sexy *pantera noir*.

Elaine shut off the shower and wrapped herself in a clean towel. Luckily Gina had those giant bath sheets that she could wrap around herself in a toga and still be somewhat presentable, because Cade had stolen all her clothes.

She opened the door slowly, aware as never before of the slight click the metallic handle made as it opened. The scent of bacon hit her nose, and her stomach rumbled in hunger.

"I left one of your friend's robes outside the door. It was in the dryer and she hasn't worn it, so it's clean of any scent," Cade called from the kitchenette just a few yards away. "I'm making breakfast. Your clothes should be ready after we eat."

Well wasn't he Mr. Efficient Domesticity? Elaine grabbed the robe and closeted herself back in the bathroom, glad he'd thought ahead. She hadn't felt particularly safe parading around the apartment in just a towel. Of course, when she got a look at herself in the mirror on the back of the door, she wondered if this flimsy robe was any better.

Still, she had precious few alternatives. She had to go out

there and face the lion in its den—or rather, the *pantera noir* in Gina's kitchen. She wasn't looking forward to it, but another part of her wanted to see him. A forbidden part wanted to drink in his presence and memorize everything about him against the time she knew would come soon, when he would leave her life for good.

Admittedly, he was a fascinating creature. Even if he'd been a regular human man, he would be stunning. Those silver-grey eyes were startling, and he had the most masculine physique she'd ever seen. And she'd seen quite a few good-looking male bods in her martial arts classes. Cade had them all beat as far as symmetry and sex appeal went.

His hair was the kind that made women want to run their fingers through it. It was just a little long—not feminine in any way, but temptingly silky and black as night. She knew from first hand experience how soft it was when it brushed over her skin. A shiver raced down her spine at the memory of how he'd awakened her.

The man should be outlawed. Really.

All that, and he could change into a black panther. She'd seen the animal version on television and always thought they were beautiful and fascinating. Elaine wondered what all that power would be like when driven by a man's intelligence—if he retained his human intellect while in his beast form. That was just one of many questions she wished she could ask him, but doubted he'd answer.

Elaine steeled herself and walked down the short hall toward the kitchen area. Gina's small table had been set with two plates, glasses of orange juice and silverware. A heaping platter of eggs and bacon steamed in the center of the table, and Cade was hovering over the toaster in the corner of the kitchenette. He looked up when she entered, and she could have sworn his eyes glowed for a shocking moment.

Her steps faltered, but Cade looked away and she felt like she'd been released, free to make her way to the seat waiting for her. She didn't want to analyze the moment of stark heat she'd felt when their eyes locked. This man was entirely too dangerous to her self-control.

"This looks great," she said with false cheer. "Can I help with anything?"

"Just waiting on the toast. There's coffee on the counter right next to you."

Elaine turned in her seat, glad to have something to do while the toast popped up and Cade whisked it onto a plate. When he sat at the small table, she felt crowded by his heat, surrounded by his masculinity. It could have made her feel claustrophobic. Instead, it made her feel safe.

She started at the thought. Since when did Elaine Spencer, advanced *jiu jitsu* student, need a man around to make her feel secure? One of the main reasons she liked martial arts so much was that learning the skills of self-defense made her feel safe in her own skin. This was a dangerous world. Being able to at least hold off an attacker, if not always best him, made her feel safer than she'd ever felt. It gave her confidence.

Now, suddenly, a man was giving her those same feelings of safety and security, when she hadn't leaned on anyone that way in years. It was disconcerting to say the least.

"Dig in." Cade pushed the platter in front of her, motioning for her to take a portion first. She picked up the serving spoon, annoyed to find her fingers shaking. He really had the most unnerving effect on her.

She served herself in silence then pushed the platter back a few inches toward him. Cade took twice as much as she did, nearly clearing the plate. She was pretty sure he'd left a little in case she wanted more and the polite, thoughtful gesture touched her.

"You might as well polish that off," she told him. "I already have more than I usually eat."

Cade eyed her plate with a frown, then without even asking, slid half of the remaining food on her plate and put the rest on his own. "You'll need your strength today. Eat up."

She didn't argue, eating in silence for a few minutes as she realized she was famished. She'd only had a light dinner the night before because she'd learned never to eat heavily before a class. In the normal course of events, she would have eaten when she got home after class, but things had been too crazy to think about food last night.

"So what's our next move?" Chuck padded over and curled into a warm, furry ball by her feet. She'd noticed the plate of tuna he'd been munching on when she came into the kitchen and was glad Cade had taken care of Chuck's needs. To her shame, she'd been too frazzled to even think about her cat since Cade had woken her up.

"Eat first, then we'll get your clothes out of the dryer. You should dress and leave quickly to avoid picking up any scents from here. Gina lives as fastidiously as any cat and has a lot of perfumed cleansers to mask her scent, but we need to be sure there's no trace on you when you leave. When we get into the hall, I'll give you the sniff test." His eyes lit with humor as her eyebrows shot up.

"What's the sniff test?" she asked with growing suspicion.

"Just what it sounds like. You're going to stand in the hall and let me sniff around you to see if I can discern the scent of shifter. Believe me, that's what those bastards will be doing when they check you out."

"They're going to sniff me?"

"If you let them get close enough, you bet."

"Well, you can rest assured I usually keep people I don't know at arm's length."

"You may not have a choice. It depends how they play it. If they want to be low-key, they'll send a minion to knock on your door under some pretense. If they've got some kind of agent with a connection to you, they may get close without you even realizing, so beware of any acquaintances who try to visit you in the next day or two. And worst-case scenario, if they want to play hardball, they won't give you a choice. They'll come at your fast and furious, and you probably won't know what hit you."

"I'll fight back." Her lips thinned as she clenched her jaw.

"You won't win. Harris can hold his own against a skilled shifter, but he's one of the most cunning of human fighters. You're only a student. You're good—and if they've done their homework, they'll expect you to fight—but you won't win. There's no shame in that. Stay as calm as you can and don't make them hurt you. As long as they can't scent shifter on you, chances are they'll leave you alone after the initial inspection."

Elaine dropped her fork. "This sucks."

Cade eyed her. "I know, but it's the only shot you have at keeping your life the way you've always known it. You were right about that last night. If you run now, they'll know you're involved with us. If you pass this test, you'll probably be left alone. Gina too. They don't know about her. The only link to her is you. If you're found out, they'll start looking around at your friends."

"Shit."

"That about sums it up." He nudged her plate toward her. "Eat up. You need the energy."

"Why? If they're just going to sniff me from afar or kick my ass and sniff me up close, it doesn't really matter either way, does it?"

"Look, you've probably still got a *were* in wolf form waiting on your balcony. I doubt he could get in that small window, but you need to be careful. Don't go near it. And didn't Harris teach you to always be prepared? Eat. You need the calories."

Giving in, she picked up the fork and shoveled some scrambled egg into her mouth, but something about what he'd said bothered her. She thought it over as she chewed, then realized it was the wording that threw her off.

"Why is the wolf a *were* and you're a shifter?"

"Semantics, really." He shrugged and bit into his toast. "Our Clans see ourselves as different from the *were* because our animal nature is considered more exotic. We're snobs, I guess. But there's a definite separation—at least in our minds—between ourselves and the *were*. There are fewer of us, for one thing. Wolves are a dime a dozen, though there are exceptions like *were*bears. There aren't that many of them, I don't think." He seemed to reflect as he continued to eat. "The exotic predators tend to be more rare. *Lionine, pantera, tigre* and all the variations, gather in small familial Prides and then into Clans, Tribes or Packs who each have separate leaders. The *were* seem to band together more under twin lords who govern each generation. We respect their authority, but we go our own way most of the time. They live in the countryside. Most of us like city life." He shrugged again. "It's complicated, but somehow it all works."

"I bet. Just thinking about it gives me a headache." She finished the last of the food on her plate and helped Cade clean. She still wasn't entirely comfortable with him, but she did her best to ignore the tingling sparks that ignited every time he accidentally brushed by her as they worked together in the small space.

Dawn was breaking as they finished. Soon it would be time for her to return to her own apartment. The thought distressed her more than she expected. They'd go their separate ways and—if things worked out well—she would never see him again.

Even touching was off limits. Those accidental brushes would hopefully not cause any of his scent to linger on her, but she'd have to undergo the sniff test he insisted on, even though just the thought of it made her want to giggle.

"What happens if I don't pass the sniff test?"

Cade held up a spray bottle that contained liquid freshener—the kind that was supposed to take odors out of fabric. Elaine recognized it from the time she'd nearly burned down her own kitchen and needed to treat the curtains and other fabrics to get the stink of smoke out.

"Your friend Gina is well supplied. We can try a few sprays

of this. It should be enough to mask any casual contacts. But if that doesn't work, we can try a few other things."

They finished putting the small kitchen to rights, and Cade motioned for her to precede him out into the living room. Cade bent to give Chuck one last stroke before spritzing the feline with the odor eliminator. Elaine was surprised the cat stood there and allowed it. He was usually the friskiest when she tried to get him anywhere near water. That he'd sit still to be sprayed was truly a miracle.

"Nothing can fully mask a feline but hopefully this will confuse any scent that I might have left on him. I checked and this stuff isn't toxic to him. He should be okay when he grooms. Your friend Gina bought the expensive stuff." Cade sent her a smile as he finished with the cat.

As he stood, their gazes met and held. Both knew this was it. She'd be out that door in a few minutes and hopefully, on her way back to her old life.

"I can't thank you enough for helping us. Mitch would have died if not for you and your friend, Gina."

"If I were a believer in coincidence, that certainly would be a doozy."

"So you think it was fate?" One raised eyebrow challenged her.

"I think 'there are more things in heaven and earth, Horatio, than are dreamt of in your philosophy.'" She accompanied the famous quotation from Shakespeare's *Hamlet* with a lopsided grin. "So, I guess that's a yes. Too many things are chalked up to coincidence when I think they really should be described as fate. Why else would you literally run into me— a trained nurse who just happens to have a doctor friend who unbeknownst even to me, is one of you guys? I mean, what are the odds?"

"Pretty low, I'll give you that." Cade tilted his head as if considering her words. "For what it's worth, I think you're right about fate. She can be fickle and she can be fair, but she definitely plays a role in our lives. Otherwise, I never would have met you."

Cade leaned in and placed a gentle kiss on her lips. He was careful not to touch her anywhere else, she noted, to avoid leaving any more traces of his scent on her. It wasn't enough, but it would have to suffice. There was danger awaiting her, and he knew better than anyone else what it would take to keep her safe. As much as she wanted to burrow into his arms and stay there forever—a strikingly odd thought to have about a man she'd only met hours before—he had managed to convince her how important it was to erase all traces of his presence.

She knew he wasn't for her. She just had to convince her body of that. Too bad it didn't seem to want to listen.

Cade drew back, holding her gaze for a long moment.

"You're a beautiful woman, Ellie. I'll never forget you."

She felt the blush rising in her cheeks. She'd never been so touched by a compliment before in her whole life. Then again, she'd never really believed in compliments. Too often, she thought they were passed out too freely with very little sincerity, but when Cade spoke with that look in his eyes, she felt the honesty in his words down to her soul.

"There's no way I'll ever forget you either, Cade." She laughed to lessen the impact of that life altering statement. "It's not every day I learn about the existence of a whole new species living side by side with my own. Or that my best friend has been keeping it a secret my entire life."

"Yeah, I can see how that might be memorable." Cade's grin put her at ease even though she was about to face one of the most important trials of her life. "Let's get this over with."

He motioned for her to precede him to the door. Cade sent Chuck out first, probably to scout around. Then Cade stuck his head into the hallway and had a look around before he allowed her to exit the apartment. He'd explained that they had to do the sniff test, as he called it, outside of Gina's apartment where his nose wouldn't be influenced by the residual scent of her lair.

The hallway wasn't ideal, but it would have to do.

Gina's place was the last at the end of a long, thankfully dim hall. The next apartment's doorway was yards away and no one was about at this early hour. Cade placed her before him and leaned toward her, sniffing near her ear, then worked his way down her body and back up the other side.

The act itself was one of the most erotic things she'd ever experienced with her clothes on. Elaine closed her eyes to block him out, but it did no good. She felt every nuance, every air current as he worked his way around her body—never touching but making her aware of him in every cell, every breath, every thought.

Oh, this man was dangerous, indeed.

"You'll do," he said at long last, spritzing her shoes with a little of the odor removing spray. "You have my number. I'll be watching until I'm sure you're in the clear, but if you have problems later, don't hesitate to give me a call."

She nodded, trying for bravery. If everything worked out as planned, this was the last she would see of him.

"You'll be the first to know if I run into trouble. Make sure your friends take good care of Gina. Tell them I'll kick their asses if they let anything bad happen to my best friend."

He smiled, as she hoped he would, as she walked down the hall. Chuck led the way to the elevator, and Cade gave her a little wave as the doors opened with a soft chime. She stepped inside and that was the last she saw of her *pantera noir*.

Chapter Five

Elaine let herself into her apartment with little fuss. A quick glance around told her everything looked as she had left it, so she tried to be as nonchalant as possible, yawning as she started making coffee. Trying not to show her anxiety to possible watchers was more nerve wracking than she would have believed. It was going to be a long day.

Since it was her day off, Elaine started the usual chores—laundry, dishes and generally cleaning the entire apartment. Her work was made considerably easier by the fact that Cade had already done much of it when he'd erased all traces of his presence. Of course, she didn't let that slow her down. Cleaning was a good way to get her mind off the startling events of the night before. It also helped distract her from the possibility that a werewolf was watching every move she made.

She tried her best not to look toward the window, but even the idea that someone—or something—could be out there, watching her, gave her the creeps. The confrontation Cade expected couldn't come soon enough for her peace of mind. Not knowing whether she could go back to her normal life, or whether she'd have to flee her home with bad guys on her trail was making her crazy. She wanted it settled one way or another so she could get on with her life, and try to forget about Cade.

Yeah, like that was even possible. The man disturbed her on every level, but not necessarily in a bad way. She'd never felt so alive as when he'd kissed her, and she'd never been so attracted to a man. She made a mental note to ask Gina—if and when they spoke again—whether shifters had some kind of magic mojo that made them irresistible. If so, Elaine had most definitely felt its effects.

Just after noon, someone knocked on Elaine's door. Steeling herself, she took a deep breath before looking out the peephole. A middle-aged man in a suit stood in the hallway. Next to him was a younger man, in dark dress pants and a blue uniform shirt with some kind of insignia she couldn't make out through the distorting lens of the peephole. If they'd come looking for a fight, they were dressed all wrong. That thought gave her some small amount of comfort.

She opened the door and tried to look inquisitive rather than fearful. The older man flashed a badge at her, much to her surprise.

"Ms. Spencer? I'm Detective Figueroa, this is Sergeant Bimley of the fire department. We're investigating a suspicious fire that occurred at a martial arts studio last night. It says here..." He consulted some papers in his hand. "I have a report that you phoned the precinct to report your car stolen from the front of the same building a few minutes before the fire alarms went off."

"Yes, my car was stolen last night, but I didn't know anything about a fire. Was anyone hurt?" She and Cade had agreed that she shouldn't let on she knew about the fire. Better she chance a lie than open up a line of questioning that could cause her even bigger problems.

"Yes, ma'am, I'm afraid there were some fatalities. May we come inside? We'd like to get a statement from you."

"Oh, my goodness! Of course. But I don't know how much help I'll be. I was only there for a few minutes before my car was stolen." Elaine showed concern as she let the two men into her apartment.

For all she knew, these guys could be exactly what they claimed—investigators following up a lead. They might not be *were* at all. Other than their amazing physiques, she had no way of distinguishing shifters from regular people. And guys who were employed by the fire and police departments were usually in pretty good shape physically anyway.

The fireman was a reasonably good-looking guy. He was tall and very fit with sandy brown hair and eyes. His nose was kind of narrow which gave him an unfortunate pointed look to his angular face. If either of these men was *were*, he would be the one she picked.

The detective was less attractive and had a very large nose. His complexion was dark, and he had black hair and dark brown eyes. By his surname she guessed he was of Latin descent. He wasn't much taller than her, and not particularly fit either. She didn't know what to make of him. All the shifters she'd seen so far were much more muscular and taller than this guy.

"Now, Ms. Spencer," Figueroa began after he'd been seated in her small living room. "What brought you to 121 Water Street last night?"

"I'm a student there, at the Silent Tiger *dojo* located on the lower floor. We were supposed to have class last night, but it was canceled at the last moment. There was a sign posted on the door when I got there."

"Did you go in?" the firefighter asked.

Elaine knew she would have to stick as close as possible to the truth. If these guys were part of the group that had attacked those people in the *dojo*, they probably already knew she'd gone inside and come right back out a few minutes later. Cade had been pretty sure the bad guys have been watching for some time before they launched their operation. Heck, they'd probably even orchestrated the theft of her beloved VW bug. The bastards.

"I was in a hurry." She tried for a self-deprecating smile. "I turned to chirp my car alarm and totally missed seeing the note on the door. I was halfway down the stairs when I met *Shihan* on the way up. We talked for a few minutes, and he told me that class was canceled for the night. I felt like such a dope. I hope he's all right. Was he caught in the fire?"

"By *Shihan*, do you mean Mr. Harris, owner of the Silent Tiger Martial Arts School?" Figueroa asked.

"Yes. *Shihan* is his rank. Above *sensei*. He's more than a teacher. He's a master. Is he all right?"

"He escaped without injury."

The fact that Figueroa didn't look too happy about Harris's survival clued Elaine in. These guys were more than likely the ones Cade had said would pay her a visit. The fireman looked downright hostile, but the detective was better at hiding his thoughts.

"Thank goodness." Elaine made a show of relief. She had to tread carefully with these men. Her future depended on it.

"Did you know any of the other people in the *dojo*?" the sergeant asked. His way of speaking was rapid fire and intense, almost like he was barking. If this guy wasn't a werewolf, she would be surprised.

"I only saw *Shihan*. Like I said, we met on the stairs and he told me about the note I'd missed on the door. If anyone else was down in the *dojo*, I didn't see them."

Elaine could have sworn the fireman was grinding his teeth. He did not look like a happy camper, even as he moved closer to her on the couch. She'd known about the sniffing, but it still startled her when he began breathing deeply around her. He was subtle about it, but since she'd known what to expect, she recognized his behavior for what it was. The bastard was sniffing her out.

Fat chance he'd find anything incriminating. Cade had sniffed much closer than that, and he'd said she was clean. Thoughts of the *pantera noir* alpha brought a pang to her heart. If this kept going so well, she'd be in the clear. No reason to call that super secret spy number on the card he'd given her. No reason to get back in touch with the sexy panther.

Except that she wanted to. She tried not to give in to that thought. Down that road lay trouble. Life was unfair sometimes, she thought with rising annoyance at being subjected to the sniff test. Here she'd finally met a guy that pushed all her buttons and there was no way they could possibly pursue a relationship. So not fair.

"What did you do after you left the building? Did you see anyone lurking in the parking lot?" Figueroa asked sharply.

The look in his eyes told her he knew damned well what happened next. Elaine did her best to hide her anger. These jerks might've been the very ones who set the fire, but she was powerless to do anything about it. At the very least, they were in league with the bastards who'd tried to kill Mitch last night. They were scum, but she had to be polite. Her happy, normal life—and Gina's—depended on her acting skills.

"As a matter of fact, I ran into a creepy guy just as I came out the door. He really scared me, especially when I realized that not only was my car gone, but my cell phone battery was dead. He didn't have a phone so I got out of there as quickly as I could. I walked all the way home and called the cops from here."

"Can you describe the man you ran into?" Elaine got the distinct impression that Figueroa asked for a description for form's sake, not because he really needed one.

Elaine dutifully described Cade's appearance, being certain to dwell on the fact that he was a very scary guy. She wasn't entirely sure, but she thought she had both these men convinced. She just had to get through the rest of this interview. Hopefully, once she'd satisfied their curiosity, they would leave her alone.

"Did you see anyone else?" Bimley growled, still sniffing discreetly every once in awhile.

"No. Like I said, it was dark, and even with my martial arts skills, I wanted to get out of there and away from that scary dude as quickly as possible."

"No doubt that was the wisest course," Figueroa agreed, closing his small notebook. She hadn't seen him take one note. "Here's my card. Please give me a call if you remember anything else." He stood, and she reached for the card, only to be pulled toward him when he didn't release it. She heard a loud inhale and knew he was doing the same thing his partner had done. Not giving in to her anger, Elaine covered the strange moment with nervous laughter.

"Sorry, I didn't get much sleep."

"Why's that?" the firefighter asked with suspicion in his tone.

"I loved that car, sergeant. I'm taking its loss pretty hard. I spent the night with a tub of ice cream, a couple of chick flicks and my best friend in the whole world, trying hard not to think about the fact that I'll have to walk everywhere until the insurance comes through."

"I'm sorry for your loss," Figueroa said in a placating way. It was obvious he didn't give a damn one way or another about her beloved bug.

She was ushering them to the door, when Chuck decided to make an appearance. He hissed at both men, clearly detesting them both on sight. Such a violent reaction was usually reserved for dogs. Elaine had to hide her amusement. Chuck the cat was probably right. At least one of these men was probably the werewolf who'd been hounding her fire escape. What the other one was, she had no idea.

"I'm sorry," she tried to hurry them out the door. "My cat doesn't like most people. He's very territorial."

Figueroa spared only a disdainful glance at the cat before heading into the hallway. His fireman friend actually bared his teeth at Chuck and the quick glance she got of pointy canines only confirmed her suspicions. That guy was some kind of cur dog, but Chuck, bless his little feline heart, didn't back down one inch.

They left without further ado, for which Elaine was grateful.

Today had been full of ups and downs. Really, from the moment she'd entered the *dojo* last night, her life had taken a turn for the strange. She felt as if she'd been in the Twilight Zone for the past twelve hours or so. Thank goodness things might actually be getting back to normal.

Hopefully, she'd seen the last of the detective and sergeant. She didn't think she'd said anything to incriminate herself or her new shifter friends, but only time would tell for certain.

Elaine went to work the next day, glad for the chance to get out of her apartment. She'd never felt so claustrophobic in her own space. Even Chuck's antics couldn't cajole her out of the doldrums. It felt creepy to think that at any moment she might be watched. That shifters were silent enough to creep around on fire escapes she didn't doubt. Cade had admitted to spying on her from the fire escape, and she hadn't known a thing. She dreaded the idea of looking out her window at night only to see glowing eyes staring back at her from the darkness.

By the same token, she couldn't leave her blinds drawn all the time. That would only serve to raise suspicion. She had to carry on her life as normally as possible, even though nothing was truly normal anymore.

The hospital seemed the same as always, hectic but soothing in its familiar routine. Of course, Gina wasn't there, which was something that stood out in Elaine's mind. Gina had arranged to take time off and a few people asked about her absence. Elaine fobbed them off as best she could, using the excuse that Gina had finally taken some time to go see her family. Most people seemed to take that at face value, but Elaine couldn't help wondering if some of those people were really shifters in disguise.

Still, Elaine didn't think Gina would have taken the chance of working in close quarters with anyone who could have discovered her secret. So chances were, the hospital was a safe place to be. Safer than her apartment at least.

Things rolled along calmly for a couple of days before the other shoe dropped. Elaine had really thought she was in the clear and had finally stopped jumping at every noise when suddenly all hell broke loose.

Dropping into a weary sleep, Chuck curled up at her side, it seemed like only moments had passed when the cat started punching her arm with his paws. Annoyed at first, she tried to push him away, but Chuck would have none of it. He persisted until she sat up in bed and finally noticed the unearthly flickering orange light coming from the living room.

The apartment was on fire!

She threw on her sneakers, which were near her bedroom door and peered cautiously out into the living room. One glance told her there was no way she could stop the flames. She had to get out of there or die.

Elaine made a grab for the bag she'd kept packed, ready to go in case she had to leave fast. She thanked whatever benevolent powers had led her to stay prepared as she slung the knapsack that held all her most prized possessions—a few mementoes, from her family and friends—over her shoulder. She headed for the fire escape, shooing Chuck out before her, but the tabby cat stayed at her side, guiding her through the smoke, as if he was watching over her safety.

He really was the most remarkable cat.

"When we get out of this, Chuck, I'm buying you a whole salmon," she promised him under her breath as she grabbed for the metal stairs leading downward.

The old metal creaked and groaned as she pounded down the stairs. She was one of the few tenants on this side of the building, so she wasn't surprised to be alone except for her cat. She wasn't sure, but it looked like the fire was limited to her place. She'd have to hit the fire alarm when she got to street level, she thought, to warn the rest of the tenants if the alarms in the building hadn't gone off by then.

The alleyway below her was dark, but the flickering orange

light from above grew stronger with every passing moment. She was almost all the way down when she caught sight of a man waiting, arms folded, calm as you please, below the fire escape. Her steps slowed. She thought she recognized the guy. He looked a lot like Sergeant Bimley, the werewolf fireman who'd stalked her in her own apartment.

Instead of the fear, which she recognized would have been the sane response, Elaine felt her blood boil with anger. In all likelihood, this so-called fireman had probably started the blaze himself, hoping to flush her out. Why else would he be lying in wait for her?

Even as she moved, Elaine strategized her best mode of defense. There was no doubt in her mind that Bimley was waiting for her—and he didn't have a social call in mind this time. No, this time, he'd probably try to either kill or capture her. Either way, she was in big trouble.

A normal guy his size would have given her pause, but this guy was almost positively a werewolf. Who knew the kind of strength, agility, skills or even claws he could bring to the fight. Elaine had one shot at this. She was as good as dead if she messed it up.

Taking a deep breath, she launched herself from the fire escape. It was the one thing she could think of to give her the advantage of surprise over the man waiting below.

It worked, to a point. She managed to knock him down, but he popped back up again, much to her dismay. The fight was on, and it took all her skill to defend against his lightning fast strikes. This guy wasn't going for capture, she realized in the first few exchanges. He was out for blood.

Elaine put up a good fight, but she knew she was outclassed when it came to sheer brute strength and brawn. She retreated farther and farther back into the alleyway, blocking for all she was worth while getting off very few punches of her own. But she did have one advantage. The firefighter was top heavy. He relied almost exclusively on his upper body strength, sending jab after jab toward her.

She was much shorter than he was, and easily able to duck and weave around his straightforward and somewhat unimaginative attack. He also didn't expect or count on her creative use of leg work. Having studied ballet as a child, Elaine had always had great flexibility and extension on her kicks. Few men gave such skills much thought because like the firefighter, their strength was mostly in their arms and upper body.

When she'd backed up as far as she could go, she bided her time and waited for the perfect moment, watching for an opening. It came when the werewolf moved in for the kill. He got too close and too overconfident. She used that to her advantage, sweeping down and out with her leg to trip up his feet and knock him flat. Her luck held when he cracked his head on a discarded brick and lost consciousness.

Elaine didn't wait around to see what would happen. She ran back up the alley, pausing only to grab her knapsack and her cat who had stood guard over her possessions while she'd fought for her life. Cade had done something to Chuck. She just knew it. The cat acted more like a protector than a companion since meeting the *pantera noir*.

Elaine fished her cell phone and Cade's card out of the front pocket of her pack as she ran for the front of the building. There were fire engines pulling up, and tenants spilling out into the street as the fire spread. It would be easy for her to slip away in the confusion. She just had to hope Sergeant Bimley didn't have any furry friends like him waiting on those fire engines.

She kept to the shadows as much as possible while running as fast as she could with a knapsack on her back and her cat trotting alongside. She didn't know how long the werewolf would be out or how hard he had cracked his head. She prayed it would be long enough for her to get away.

When Cade's phone rang he knew instantly something was

very wrong. The ring was that of a strange number, and he'd only given his card to one stranger in recent weeks.

Elaine was in trouble.

Cade's heart raced into fight mode as he touched the switch on his receiver. He liked using the wireless earpiece, except when he was expecting a fight. Then it would get in the way.

"Are you all right?"

"Cade! The fireman came back and set fire to my apartment. He was waiting for me at the bottom of the fire escape." She was sobbing for breath, trying to keep her voice down, but Cade could hear her feet pounding the pavement in the background. He realized she was running for her life. He ran for the door, keys already in hand.

"Where are you?"

"I'm just passing Pine Avenue. I got lucky and knocked him out, but I don't know for how long."

"What street are you on?" Cade was already on his motorcycle, pulling out into traffic.

"Pullman. I'm heading north."

"I'm close. I'll meet you coming down. Stay on Pullman if you can and keep the phone connection open. Don't talk. Conserve your energy. I'll be there in two minutes. Look for a motorcycle. You'll probably hear me before you see me."

Precious moments sped away as his wheels turned, bringing him closer. He'd resisted every temptation to call her or go by her apartment, just to see her face again. He'd held strong, but fate seemed to have other ideas.

"I hear a motorcycle." Her feet continued to run, though he could hear her pace slowing as she tired.

"That's me. Hang on, baby. I'm almost there."

He saw her a moment later jogging down the road, her tabby cat pacing along beside her. Chuck was a trooper; there was no doubt about that. Cade pulled up beside her, angling the bike so she could get on. He wanted nothing more than to pull her into his arms and assure himself she was okay, but time was against them. At any moment, their enemies might find them, and he had to get her to safety. The scent of smoke clinging to her clothing brought home the danger she'd been in.

"Hop on." He scooted forward to make room for her on the narrow seat.

"What about Chuck?" Elaine slung her knapsack across her shoulders, securing it to her back.

"No problem. He can ride on my lap." Cade patted his leg and the tabby cat jumped up. "Put your arms around my waist and cup your hands around Chuck. It's not the safest thing in the world, but it'll have to do."

Elaine followed his instructions without argument, and he revved the motorcycle into motion seconds later. The cat was effectively in his crotch, which didn't make for the most comfortable ride, but Elaine's fingers weren't too far away either. The thought of how close he was to feeling her cupping him instead of the cat had him breathing hard as he negotiated turns and watched his mirrors for signs of pursuit.

Cade tried not to think about her touch as he maneuvered the bike through the city streets. He was taking a circuitous route to a safe house they kept prepared for any contingency.

When he was certain they weren't being followed, he took them into an alley behind a row of houses. There was a matching row of garages in back, and he pulled in to one, latching the door shut behind them.

This location in particular had a feature he would take full advantage of this night. There was a secret entrance from the garage to the basement of the house. But first things first.

Cade let the traumatized cat off his lap. Chuck bounded down, away from the bike, heading for a dark corner to curl up in. Elaine climbed off next, and Cade wasn't far behind.

He pulled her into his arms for a hard embrace, allowing the emotion he'd felt over the past minutes to spill over. He

Bianca D'Arc

rocked her in his arms, thanking the goddess over and over in his mind and in his heart for keeping Elaine alive long enough to call for help.

"God, baby, you gave me a scare." Cade looked down into her eyes, cupping her cheeks in his hands.

"I was so frightened, Cade. Thanks for coming to get me."

"I'll always come for you, El. No matter what." He couldn't wait any longer. He had to taste her, to assure himself that she was all right, to know again the flavor of her passion.

Cade captured her lips with his, putting all the pent-up longings of the past days into the kiss, feeling all of it returned and then some. It was like coming home after a long time away. The welcome of her arms warmed him right down to his soul.

He drew his hands down her body, pulling her closer. She was trembling, but he knew it wasn't in fear. Still, she'd had a rough night. He should be taking it easy on her, but the time apart had only made him more desperate for her touch, her taste, her scent.

Cade made himself release her, but he couldn't break their connection completely. He kept her in a loose embrace, resting his forehead against hers as their harsh breathing slowed.

"I'm not letting you go this time, Ellie. Don't ask me to."

He hadn't meant to be so frank. He didn't want to scare her off, but he'd had some time to think about it and knew if he ever saw her again he wouldn't be strong enough to let her go a second time. This time, she would be his.

For how long? Only the goddess knew for certain. As far as Cade was concerned, he'd keep her as long as he possibly could, though he feared circumstance might eventually drive them apart. Humans and Alpha shifters were a difficult mix.

"That fireman was trying to kill me, Cade. I think I'm better off with you than trying to muddle through on my own."

"That's not what I was talking about, baby, and you know it." She drew back from him as his tone hardened. He held her gaze, willing her to understand—to accept.

94

She watched him with steady eyes. "I had an idea what I was getting into when I dialed your number, Cade." She stepped into his embrace, and he knew a moment of joy, feeling her acceptance of what fate had handed them both. "As crazy as it sounds, I've missed you."

"It's not crazy at all, sweetheart. My panther's been pacing, trying to break out and find you. He wants you. And I want you. Like I've never wanted anyone or anything before in my life."

"Oh, Cade." She rose on tiptoe this time, bringing her lips to his in a kiss that went on and on.

A noise in the yard broke Cade from his reverie. He lifted away from her kiss reluctantly, but he had to get her to safety. This garage was defensible, but not the best place to be caught by a band of rogue *weres*. The house was much sturdier and close enough that he could placate his inner cat with the idea that he'd have their woman prone on a bed soon enough.

"Let's continue this inside," he whispered in her ear as she snuggled into him.

Turning, he guided her to the hidden trapdoor and the stairs that led down one level to the newly extended basement. A quick look to the corner of the dark garage summoned Chuck, who padded down the cement steps ahead of them like a good scout should.

Bonnie and Ray met them at the basement door that led into the house. They'd no doubt heard the bike as he pulled in. The electronic sensors he'd tripped as soon as he opened the garage door would have helped too. It was their job to protect this safe house, preparing it for use by the Nyx, if necessary. Right now, the house was empty except for Bonnie and Ray, a mated pair of tigers who were also semi-retired Royal Guards.

"Who's your little friend?" Ray asked, blocking the door.

Cade wasn't sure if the tiger referred to Chuck the cat or Ellie, but either way Ray's tone was insulting. Cade bristled. Both the tabby and the human woman had proven their mettle again and again. They didn't deserve the tiger's disdain.

"Watch it, Ray," he warned. "This is Ellie. Some rabid werewolf just tried to kill her, so cut her some slack." Cade muscled past Ray, pushing Ellie along ahead of him.

"You're the one who helped save Mitch, aren't you?" Bonnie asked, clearly as curious as the cat who lived inside her.

"She is," Cade confirmed, unwilling to prolong this meeting or satisfy the tigers' curiosity any more. Ellie was physically beat. She needed TLC, not twenty questions. "She's had a hell of a night, guys. She needs rest and quiet. We'll see you in the morning. *Late* in the morning."

"You're staying then?" Bonnie's eyebrow rose in question.

He stared her down, his mouth set in a firm line. She had no right to question him. He held the higher rank among the Guard and was answerable to no one but the Nyx. This was a private matter, of concern only to his familial Pride. Bonnie dared much to challenge him, and he wouldn't stand for it.

"I'm staying. Deal with it, Bon. I let her go once, and she almost died tonight because of it. I'm not letting her out of my sight again."

Cade knew he was being more than a little heavy handed, but he couldn't help himself. He'd known Bonnie since he was a cub and knew how she felt about human-shifter relationships. It would take some convincing to get her to accept even having Elaine stay in the safe house.

Bonnie was one of those shifters who looked down on humans, and her mate Ray was almost as bad. Too bad they had to be the ones on watch at this house, but there was really no alternative. This house was the only one not occupied at the moment that was close enough to get to quickly.

Chuck the cat trotted at their side as Cade guided Elaine through the house. He knew the layout well, but had never stayed here more than a day or two. They'd bought the house through shell corporations only a few months before and had their own work crews gut the inside and reconstruct it from below ground all the way to the attic. The result was a nice place to share with Elaine while she recovered from the ordeal of the fire and he finally got to spend time with her. He wasn't going to leave her on her own like last time.

No, this time would be different. He didn't know where this would all lead, but he knew one thing for certain. He wasn't letting Ellie out of his sight. Not any time in the foreseeable future, that is. Not until he had to.

"I don't think that woman liked me very much," Elaine observed as they walked up the stairs to the main floor.

"She's a snob about humans, but she'll come around."

"What? She doesn't like anyone who can't turn furry? Why'd that guy sneer at Chuck then? Or don't they like housecats?"

"Some tigers are just assholes," Cade grumbled, holding in his laughter. He loved the way she defended her little pet.

"Chuck saved my life, you know. He's the one who woke me when my apartment was on fire. And he was so brave, leading me down the fire escape. Even when I was fighting that werewolf, Chuck guarded my knapsack. He's such a good cat." She was near tears, and Cade realized it was delayed reaction from all she'd been through that night. She was about at the end of her rope, but he would catch her when she fell and help her climb back onto solid ground. He would be there for her.

"He deserves tuna for a week, at least," Cade commented as they climbed another flight of stairs to where the guest bedrooms were located in the house. Bonnie and Ray had the master suite on the ground floor, and Cade chose the guest suite on the opposite side of the house. He didn't want them listening in through the walls if he and Ellie happened to get loud.

"I promised him I'd buy him a whole salmon," she admitted with a little hiccupping laugh. She was on the verge of tears, and he wanted to be in a comfortable place when she finally gave in to the wash of emotions running through her overtaxed system.

"I'll see what I can do on the salmon, but I'm sure we have something in the cupboards for him to eat while we're here."

He pushed open the door to the bedroom suite, and Chuck prowled in ahead of them. The bed was huge and the attached bath had a Jacuzzi tub, another reason he'd chosen this particular suite.

Cade closed the door and turned to her. She looked like a forlorn waif standing there, her eyes filled with tears she refused to let fall and her shoulders slumped with fatigue. She'd been through hell tonight, but Cade was just the man to help her feel better.

He approached slowly, helping her slide the knapsack down over her shoulders. He let it drop gently onto the floor. Next, he brushed her hair back from her face with his fingers. He could smell the smoke clinging to her skin and the scent of the werewolf she'd fought, which was strongest on her badly bruised arms.

"Why don't I run you a bath? You need to relax, El, before we go to bed."

"We?" That woke her up. Her big eyes blinked up at him in surprise.

Cade placed his palms over her shoulders. "I'm going to hold you all night, Ellie. Nothing and no one will get near you while I'm here." Her lips trembled, and her eyes filled, shining bright with tears until they finally spilled over. "Come here, baby." Cade tugged her closer.

She clung to him, weeping into his chest. Her façade of calm had finally crumbled. He didn't blame her in the least. She'd been strong when she'd needed to be and gotten herself out of a mess few people could have handled. Now reaction was setting in, and she needed comfort. Cade was thankful he was there to offer it—and doubly glad she was alive to accept it.

From what he could tell, it had been a very close thing. The thought scared the hell out of him. He'd almost lost her.

"It's all right, Ellie. I've got you. You made it. You got

yourself clear."

"I almost didn't." She hiccupped. "That fireman was stronger than anyone I've ever sparred with. He kept coming and coming, and I had no way to stop him. He had me backed against a wall."

"How did you get free?" Cade could see the desperate situation clearly in his mind.

"I used a leg sweep. He went down hard and hit his head on a brick that was lying in the alley. I don't know how bad he was hurt, and I didn't stick around to find out. I ran away and called you."

"You did the right thing, baby." He held her close, stroking her hair as she gathered herself. "Now, how about we get you cleaned up a bit, and then you can try for some sleep. Things usually look brighter in the morning."

He coaxed her toward the bathroom and turned on the hot water tap. While the tub was filling, he reached into the floor to ceiling cupboard next to the door and pulled out three big, fluffy towels. Two, he left on the warming rack for her to use after her bath and the third he unfolded and rolled up into a little nest for Chuck, who'd followed them into the bathroom.

Elaine was busy petting the cat who twined around her ankles, and Cade had to smile at the scene they made. It was so obvious they loved each other.

"Will you be all right?" he asked on his way to the door.

"I can handle a bath. In fact, it sounds like heaven right about now. Thanks." She gave him a weak smile as he stepped through the doorway.

"I'll be right outside. Call if you need anything. Promise me."

She nodded solemnly, though her eyes held laughter. "I promise."

He tugged the door almost shut behind him, leaving it the tiniest bit ajar so he'd hear if she needed him.

Chapter Six

"Silly man," Elaine talked to her cat as she undressed. "But I'm glad he answered his phone, Chuck. I don't know where we would have gone otherwise."

She was still in her pajamas—a loose T-shirt and lounge pants that had seen better days. Suddenly it hit her—those were the only clothes she had left. Everything else had gone up in smoke earlier that evening.

Elaine refused to give in to tears. Once had been enough. She wasn't normally a weepy sort of person, but she figured she was allowed a little human weakness considering she'd not only lost her home and had to fight for her life to get away. If not for dirty alleyways with discarded bricks strewn around, she'd probably be dead. So she cut herself some slack.

The bath felt like heaven, even more so when she discovered the switch that turned on the Jacuzzi jets. She stayed in there longer than she probably should have, but it felt glorious after the night she'd had. Without meaning to, she drifted off, fatigue claiming her.

A soft touch on her arm roused her minutes later. She was in the big tub, her head thrown back to lean comfortably against the rim. Cade was inspecting one of her arms and the dark bruises that were beginning to form. She looked downward, glad the bubbles from the water jets obscured most of her body. Still, she was naked in the bath and Cade's presence disturbed her on many levels.

"There should be some liniment in the medicine cabinet." Cade stood fluidly from his crouch and walked the short distance to the vanity area. He rummaged around in the big medicine cabinet hidden behind the mirror, pulling out a few supplies that he placed on the countertop.

"We keep these places stocked for just this kind of situation, but I don't think we have any kitty litter in the house for Chuck." He turned back to her with a smile and a tall bottle in one hand, cotton balls in the other. "I gave him a box for tonight. I've already left a note for Bonnie and Ray to get some supplies for him when they go to the store in the morning. They'll need to buy more groceries to feed all of us." He glanced at Chuck, fast asleep on the towel near the radiator. "Make that five of us." Cade had placed a box with some torn up newspaper near the toilet as a makeshift litter box, and she was touched he would go to such lengths.

She loved his thoughtfulness about Chuck, but was increasingly aware that he was fully clothed while she was naked except for some very half-assed bubbles from the Jacuzzi jets. She shifted around in the tub, trying to hide from his probing gaze.

"Come out of there, Ellie." His tone was one of command that when combined with the smoldering look in his eyes made her breath catch.

"Um..."

"Come on, baby. You know I'll take care of you. You have bruises all over your arms. It's killing me to see them forming right before my eyes. Where else are you hurt? Come out of there and let me see."

She would have laughed, but she suspected it wasn't a line. He really did seem worried about the extent of her injuries. That didn't make her comfortable parading around in the nude in front of him, but a combination of factors made her want to comply with his request.

First, she was just too damned tired to fight anymore. She

knew Cade wouldn't try to hurt her physically. No, the battle with him was completely emotional. It was a battle to protect her heart. Second, she'd been attracted to him from the moment they met. His gaze heated her blood and his kisses fired her senses. She wanted more of him—as much as he'd give her—but fear had held her back.

Facing death last night had brought a lot of things into sharper focus. Life was short, and her life in particular had gotten increasingly dangerous since she'd stumbled on to the secret about shifters. She wanted to enjoy what she could because she didn't know what would come tomorrow. Being with Cade was one of those forbidden things she wanted to experience now that her life had so drastically changed.

Breathing deep for courage, she stood from the water. Cade stood there, watching her for a long moment, but he didn't touch. Not physically, at least, but his eyes burned a path down her body that made her stomach clench. Ripples of awareness shivered over her skin everywhere he looked and when his gaze finally met hers, the current passing between them was downright combustible.

"You're gorgeous, Elaine. If you weren't banged up, I'd lay you down and ride you until you couldn't walk straight."

Her breath caught at the heat in his voice, the glow in his eyes. He meant every word. Of that she had no doubt. She shivered, and he visibly shook himself, withdrawing some of the heat, though his eyes continued to rake over her body.

Cade scaled back. He tamped down the fire, put away the flames for later. She felt him retreat both physically and emotionally as he reached for one of the big bath towels he'd left on the warming rack. Shaking it out, he held it open for her to step into. The move brought her into his arms at the same time.

He wrapped her in a fluffy terrycloth hug that warmed her to her soul. He took his time, surrounding her in his warmth before setting to the mundane task of drying her skin. But nothing was mundane or commonplace about his hands roaming over her body, covered with a thin layer of terrycloth. The soft, damp cloth paused over her breasts, his hands shaping the points of her nipples through the terrycloth. She stifled a moan that wanted to come out, but his wicked grin told her he knew damned well what he was doing to her. His hands roamed downward, over her hips. One hand roamed over the curves of her ass while the other delved between her legs from the front, the towel draping below one of her hips as he stood at her side.

His head lowered, his lips nuzzling her ear as his hands met in the middle, between her legs. Only a thin layer of damp towel kept his fingers from moving where she most wanted them. The hand in front rubbed light circles over her clit while the hand that attacked from behind pushed upward, between the swollen lips of her pussy.

A cloth-wrapped finger pushed slightly inward, into her wet core. This time, she couldn't hold back the little moan of desire that broke from her lips. Cade's purr at her side warmed her.

"You like that?" His voice teased her, and she was unable to answer except with a little whimper as he rubbed her clit faster. "Oh, yeah. I can tell you like that a lot."

He pressed her harder until she came against his hand, the thin towel the only thing keeping her skin from his. He nipped her earlobe and held while she shuddered through her climax in his arms.

As she drifted down from a lovely orgasm, he removed his hands from between her rubbery legs and wrapped the towel around her. He pulled her into his arms, looking deep into her eyes.

"You're beautiful when you come for me, El. Next time you come, I'll be inside you."

She didn't know how to respond, but her body wholeheartedly endorsed his ideas. Her tummy clenched in renewing desire. She wanted to feel him inside her. Desperately.

"First," he drew back, "we need to see to your bruises." He

sat on the commode lid so he could make a more detailed inspection of her arms and legs. Opening the liniment bottle released its pungent odor.

"This stuff smells like hell, but it's the best thing for bruises."

He was right on both counts, she knew from past experience with the stuff. It was a favorite remedy of martial arts students who habitually returned from class bruised and hurting.

Now that he'd made her focus on it, she started feeling the ache of her bruises. They were worse than anything she'd ever received in class but she supposed that was to be expected, considering this fight hadn't been for practice.

"Do you have any Tiger Balm in that medicine chest?"

Cade gave her a sly grin. "Where do you think it got its name? One of the *tigre d'or* invented it, so of course we have some." He reached up and snagged the little bottle of red goo and tossed it to her.

She rubbed some into her overtaxed thigh muscle while Cade soaked a few cotton balls with liniment. Surprisingly, the strong scents complimented each other. She finished with the Tiger Balm and recapped the small jar, placing it on the countertop with Cade following her every move.

He took each of her arms in his hands, one by one, stroking the cotton ball over every little bump and forming bruise, leaving a streak of brownish red behind. The scent was overpowering to her human nose. She could only imagine how the stink of it assaulted his more acute shifter senses.

When he finished with her arms, he dropped to the floor to inspect her feet and legs. She'd only been wearing pair of old sneakers when she made her escape, so not only did she have a bruised instep from taking down her opponent, but also a nice set of raw blisters from running without socks. Cade used the liniment on top of her abused foot, but switched to ointment and bandages for the blisters.

Her shins got a light stroke of liniment too. She'd blocked the werewolf's punches and kicks with everything she had. Luckily, he hadn't been much of a kicker, so the bruising on her legs wasn't as bad as her arms.

To her credit, her opponent hadn't managed to land any punches to her midsection. Being a small target, combined with her blocking ability and speed, had saved her from any worse injury. Cade dropped the wet cotton into the trash and sat back on the commode lid, wrapping his arms around her waist. He pulled her close in a move that stole her breath, resting his cheek against her abdomen, his hands wrapped tight around her.

It was a silent show of the concern she'd felt in every stroke of cotton against her skin. If this man didn't care about her in some small way at least, she'd be surprised. She rested one hand on his shoulder and stroked his soft black hair with the other, offering him comfort even as he comforted her.

He pulled back after a long moment and rose to his feet. He scooped her into his arms and carried her as if she weighed nothing at all, impressing her with his incredible strength. He took her straight to the bed, and laid her gently upon it.

Cade sank onto the bed at her side, resting on one elbow above her. His gaze held hers, and what she read there gave her pause. In his silver eyes she saw a reflection of the feelings burgeoning in her own heart. It was complicated—deliciously so—but troubling at the same time.

"You're a dangerous woman, Elaine Spencer."

The unexpected words startled a laugh out of her. "Dangerous? I don't think so. I barely managed to escape with my life. You're right about *were* strength. That guy could have crushed me like a bug."

"You were smart enough to evade him and had enough foresight to be ready. You did well against a superior opponent, and you should be proud of the way you handled yourself."

"I wish I felt that way." She looked down, unable to hold his gaze, but he was having none of it. He used one finger to tip her chin upwards and forced her to meet his gaze once more.

"Believe it. You did as well as anyone could have expected considering the circumstances tonight. I'm only sorry that I wasn't there to protect you. I shouldn't have accepted that they'd give up and go away so easily. I should have known better than that, and I'm sorry for putting you in even greater danger."

"Cade, this wasn't your fault."

"I'm glad you think so, but I know the truth." He flopped back on the bed, resting beside her, staring up at the ceiling. "It's my job to prepare for all contingencies. I'm the one who's trained to keep people safe, and I let you down. I couldn't be more sorry or ashamed. I let my personal feelings—and inability to control them—interfere with my duty to you. I'll never forgive myself or forget how close you came to paying for my mistake."

"Don't be so hard on yourself, Cade. I was sure I'd convinced those guys I didn't know anything about shifters. When they didn't come back, I assumed I was in the clear."

Cade sat up again, looking down at her, his eyes sharp. "There was more than one? How many came to see you? How many questioned you?"

"Two that I know of. The werewolf fireman—he said his name was Sergeant Bimley—and the detective. He was older and less noticeably *were*."

"How so?"

"Well, the fireman was really obvious about sniffing me. He sat next to me on the couch and did all this heavy breathing. The other guy sat across in the armchair. He didn't do any sniffing until right before he was about to leave. It was kind of freaky, but I tried not to let on that I knew what they were doing." Her hands dropped against the towel that was still wrapped around her. "I guess I was wrong. They had to have known, or figured out later, that I was lying to them."

"What was the detective's name?"

"Figueroa. At least that's the name he gave me. I didn't get a close enough look at his badge to know for certain."

Cade looked away, his expression pensive. "Did Figueroa do anything else to make you think he was *were*?"

She thought back. "Just the sniffing thing, really. Otherwise, he was pretty normal. A little creepy, but normal."

"Creepy in what way?"

"Well, my hand tingled when he shook it, and his eyes were like laser beams. The blue was really intense, almost cutting, if you get my meaning. Why?"

Cade returned his attention to her. "He might not have been *were* at all. I've suspected for a while there was a magic user in the mix of this somewhere. Figueroa might be the one. Too much has gone wrong with this operation for it to just be the result of a couple of rogue *weres*. I'd suspected bloodletters, but they came to you during the day, right?"

"You don't mean—" The implication of his words made her gasp, but the possibility was undeniable. "You're saying that vampires really exist?"

He gave her a small grin and raised one eyebrow. "If I can exist, why can't they?"

"You're kidding."

"Afraid not." He winked at her. "But for the record, they don't like the term vampire. We call them bloodletters. We don't mix with them much, but it's best not to insult them. They can be...unpredictable."

"You're on speaking terms with vampires?" Her voice rose along with her incredulity.

"Not all of them. In fact not many at all. We supernaturals tend to go our own way, but every once in a while, our paths cross. We've learned to respect each other, when possible. It's the only way to share a territory as big as a city. Bloodletters, like shifters, tend to enjoy city life."

"So they're good guys?" She was confused.

Cade shrugged. "Some are. And some are downright evil. Like any race, they have good and bad among them. Unfortunately, quite a few of them see shifters as inferior, and a small number want to kill us all."

"My God!" Elaine couldn't get over the casual way he spoke about rogue vampires plotting to destroy him and everyone like him.

"Don't worry, baby." Cade cupped her cheek in one hand, leaning in to place a sweet kiss on her lips. "We've got it covered. This has been going on for centuries, and I can't see anything changing the balance of power at this point."

Cade settled back on the bed, pulling her into his arms so she rested comfortably against his chest as they talked. One of his hands stroked her shoulder—one of the few places not covered in bruises and liniment.

"There haven't been any major inter-species conflicts for a few years," Cade reassured her. "The leaders of our respective peoples tend to frown on anything with the potential to blow up in our faces. Wildcats fighting fanged guys in the middle of the night on a city street could expose all of us to discovery and none of us want that. So the bloodletter Masters keep their people in line, as our leaders do for us."

"I'm not going to wake up and find this is a dream, am I? You're really serious."

"Afraid so." He placed a kiss on the crown of her head, soft and comforting. "Don't worry, I'll be here when you wake up. We have a lot to discuss and a lot to settle between us, El, but we both need to rest and recover. I, for one, lost a couple of years off one of my nine lives when I got your call," he teased her, making her feel warm inside. She genuinely liked this man—his sense of humor, his integrity and the brave way he faced the world.

She'd fought against the attraction and lamented the fact that he hadn't called or stopped by to check on her, but she'd understood. Now everything was changed. She was in his arms, in his bed, and in his life—as he was in hers. They might even get a shot at happily ever after this time. She'd do anything for a chance at that with him.

She put her hand on his leg, meeting his eyes.

"I think I owe you something for before."

She saw the flare of heat in his silvery eyes before he tamped it down.

"You owe me nothing, El. What I gave you was freely given. I don't expect payback."

She leaned up on one elbow. "It wouldn't be payback. Okay, well, maybe a little." She grinned as she moved her hand higher.

Before he could speak again, she had him in her hand. Through the fabric, she could feel his arousal. She held his gaze as she slipped her hand beneath the waistband of his pants and then he was in her hand and she could tell all thoughts of objecting went completely out of his mind. Daring greatly, she moved closer, leaning over him while her other hand moved his clothing out of the way. She looked away from his face to see what she'd uncovered.

He was magnificent. Thick and long and hard as steel in her hands. She wanted a taste. She wanted to know his texture, his scent, his flavor. Her head dipped, and her tongue stroked outward. He jumped just a bit when she touched him.

As she'd suspected, he tasted good. She didn't have a lot of experience with other men to compare him with, but she knew he liked what she was doing as she lowered her mouth over him, taking him deep. The tension in his muscles gave him away even before the low, deep groan issued from his throat. The sound had an animalistic quality to it that was unique to him. Probably because he was a shifter.

She wondered what else would be different with him than with the few other men in her past. With an inward grin, she set about finding out.

She hollowed her cheeks, sucking as she used her tongue

on him. He growled again, and she redoubled her efforts. She hadn't thought he could get any harder, but somehow he did. His balls drew upward in preparation for unloading even as she fondled them gently with her fingers.

"Oh, baby. I'm gonna come." His voice was guttural and so intimate it made her shiver. His hands went to her head, not to imprison, but to lift her away. She resisted. She wanted to taste him, to swallow him down.

After a momentary tugging match, he got the upper hand, lifting her head away. She was disappointed, but not for long. He growled again with what sounded like satisfaction as her fingers continued to stroke him, her grip tightening in an undulating rhythm. He brought her face closer to his as she felt his body tightened in preparation.

"El, you feel so good," he whispered in that low voice that made her insides quiver. "Damn, baby. I'm close." His silver eyes flashed with desire as he lowered his lips to hers, crowding out all question, all hesitation.

He purred as their tongues met in a fierce, frenzied battle. And then he came in long torrents of hot release over her hands. Creamy streams of come covered them both as he grunted in satisfaction, releasing her mouth as his head dropped back and his eyes closed in ecstasy.

When he was done, she raised one hand, intending to lick the essence of him into her mouth, but he grabbed her wrist.

"No, honey. Not yet," he whispered so low, she wasn't sure she'd heard him right.

He used the sheet to gently wipe her hands in a gesture that seemed strange at first but oddly tender. They lay back on the bed, and he tucked the remaining bedding around them. She liked the way he moved, boneless as a well satisfied cat. She met his sleepy gaze with a mischievous grin, snuggling into his side.

"Now we can both sleep."

"Give me a minute and I'll make it good for you too, El."

"You already did, Cade. Remember? Now go to sleep."

A mix of satisfaction and fatigue caused her eyes to flutter closed as the enormity of the night's events caught up with her. She was safe. Safe with Cade. That was all that mattered.

Cade felt it the instant Elaine fell asleep in his arms. Deep satisfaction rumbled through him at the trust that simple act implied. That she'd turned to him when she was in trouble touched him on a visceral level. Instinctively, she'd known he would come to her rescue and keep her safe from harm, if possible.

He would do anything it took to honor the trust she'd placed in him. For the first time in his life, his duty as a Royal Guard conflicted with the innate need to take care of this small human woman lying so peacefully in his arms.

He'd almost lost her, even before they'd had a chance. He'd been on the verge of denying himself—and her—the chance to be together, but tonight had brought home the need he felt deep inside for her, and only her. No other would do.

The panther paced in his soul, keeping watch over the female it insisted was his mate. As a man, Cade didn't see how it was possible, but the beast inside knew better. Cade suspected the panther always knew better than the man, but they would both have to live with the results of their actions, so he would tread lightly.

One thing was certain, before they left this bed, he would take her. It was the first step on the path to marking her and making her his in the eyes of other shifters. This first time wouldn't create a permanent mating bond, but when he marked her gently tonight, it would grant her some protection as she walked among his people. Not that they'd try to harm her, but there were bigots in every group and shifters were no different. They'd think twice about messing with her if she wore his love bites on her neck.

That thought firmly in mind and the knowledge that he

would soon claim her luscious body, Cade finally fell into a light sleep.

It seemed like only moments later, the sun woke Cade from the most restful sleep he had ever experienced. It streamed in through the blinds, illuminating their entwined bodies with slanted golden shafts. Elaine's towel had come loose in the night and lay discarded at the foot of the bed. Cade's shirt was unbuttoned and her hands lay palm down against his chest, her cheek resting over his heart.

He couldn't remember unbuttoning his shirt so Elaine must have done it in her sleep. The thought of her fingers working the small buttons jumpstarted his libido. Even unconscious, she wanted him.

Her skin was the softest thing he'd ever felt. Cade slid his hand down her back, cupping her rump with satisfaction. She was curvy, round and womanly, but fit and muscular in a way that made his mouth water. She had the softness of a human female and a physical glory that matched any shifter female he knew. Add to that her courage and wit and she was perfect for him.

Elaine had thrown one leg over his, curling into his side as she slept. He liked being her pillow, but he liked the way her breasts pressed into his ribs even more. The only thing better would be if she were on top of him—or under him. He wasn't picky. He wanted to feel her hot body pressed against every inch of him in the very near future. He could barely wait.

All he had to do was wake her up.

Cade was eager to see what she would do when she realized she was wrapped around him like colored paper on a present. Would she be shy or bold? Would she respond to him right away or would she need to be coaxed? He couldn't wait to find out.

He squeezed her hip with one hand, stroking her soft hair with the other as he bent to place a kiss on her temple. She stirred, but didn't wake immediately.

"Come on, kitten, wake up," he whispered, stroking his hand lower, delving between her thighs from behind, unable to wait much longer. He was a desperate man.

Her eyes blinked open, and a smile touched her lips even before she was fully awake. He liked the way she responded to him, loved that she couldn't hide her response to his touch.

"Cade?" She stretched a little and stroked his chest. "Mmm. If I'm dreaming, don't wake me up."

He chuckled at her response. Totally unexpected. That was his woman.

"We're not dreaming, Ellie." He slipped one finger into her folds, startling a squeak out of her as she moved to accommodate him. She certainly wasn't pushing him away, and her headlong response sparked his own. Encouraged, he moved his fingers downward and inward, sliding through her moisture.

"Cade, please," she gasped as he grew bolder.

"Mmm. I like that. I like the way you beg for my touch." His fingers found that special spot that made her squirm. She rubbed against him like a cat—his very own pussy cat. Cade tried to suppress the smile that thought brought to his lips but was unsuccessful. She was satin and silk under his hands, her body responding to his lightest touch.

He moved his other hand in front to rub her clit and she went off like a rocket for him. As she had before. He loved how ready she always seemed to be for him. Dipping his head, he kissed her lips as she came off the small climax. She tasted like his own personal catnip and he suspected his touch was something special to her as well.

Cade removed his hands and rolled, flipping her onto her back in a sinuous move that put him above her, his knees between hers. Sitting back on his haunches, he held her sleepy, aroused gaze as he unbuttoned the cuffs of his shirt. He shrugged the whole thing off and threw it across the room. He liked the way her eyes flared as she saw his chest for the first time. He also liked the way her body responded, her nipples tightening into sharp points as her excitement mirrored his.

His fingers went to the closure of his pants, daring her to join him in the sensuality of the moment as he pushed the fabric away but not completely off. He'd gone too long without touching her, and he was a starving man. Starving for the feel of her skin, the taste of her kisses, the sound of her sighs.

Cade leaned over her, trailing nibbling kisses up her ribcage, pausing at her breasts, biting gently on the generous undercurves before taking the weight of them in his hands, angling for better access to the taut peaks. The gentle, sexy scent of her skin drove him wild and seeped into his pores as if it belonged with him always. He licked one hard nipple into his mouth and sucked, groaning as she gasped, loving her response to his every touch.

"Do you like that?" he asked, watching her. Elaine's head thrashed lightly from side to side as she moaned. "I'll take that as a yes." Joy followed him as he treated her other breast to the same and more, sucking harder, licking longer, driving her as wild as he felt.

"Cade!" She sounded desperate and Cade felt like a million bucks, having driven her passion upward again with a few simple touches.

She had no idea what she was in for, but he'd show her what to expect from his lovemaking. She'd match him stroke for stroke by the time he was through with her. But he had to take it slow. She was human. He couldn't forget that. He had to rein in the beast that wanted to mark its woman in the most feral way. Time enough for that later—if he didn't scare her off first.

Cade continued to play with her nipples even as he moved upward, claiming her mouth with his. The kiss was tempestuous, hotter than anything that had come before, and he found he needed it like he needed his next breath. She was everything to him in those moments, his air, his pulse, his very life.

He couldn't wait much longer. Desperation was setting in. Cade pushed his pants down far enough to free himself. He positioned himself between her splayed legs and took a moment to touch her, stroking her clit until she writhed under him again. He loved the feel of her slick heat against his fingers and the way she moaned his name. She was ready, but was he? Could he be gentle enough to take a human when his heat was so high?

He'd give anything not to hurt her. Not now. Not ever. But he couldn't wait.

Cade slid forward, touching the tip of his aching cock to her wet opening. At the very last moment, he met her gaze, trying to calm himself enough to be careful.

"I'm coming in, baby. Are you ready for me?"

"It's okay," she gasped. "I'm on the pill."

Those words were so unexpected, he almost laughed, but her worries brought home to him as nothing else would, the glaring fact that she wasn't a shifter. He wanted to reassure her, and himself as well, but nothing could change the facts. She didn't know much about his people. It would be up to him to teach her if he wanted a shot at keeping her for any length of time.

"Don't worry. Shifters don't carry human diseases, and you're not in heat. I'd know."

"How?"

"Your scent, baby. Women are the most alluring to my kind when they smell ripe and ready for conception. You smell fantastic, don't get me wrong, but the pheromones you'd be releasing if you were in heat would drive me even crazier."

"You can *smell* that?" She seemed both fascinated and outraged. He loved to tease her, but he was treading a knife's edge. He needed her, and he needed her now. This was no time to talk.

"I can't take much more, sweetheart. Do you want me?" He dared her to say no, enticed her to say yes. He'd do whatever she wanted—even if it killed him.

"Come inside, Cade. I need you." Her words were music to his ears. Not only was she accepting him. She was spurring him on. Her legs wrapped around his hips, her heels digging into his ass, pressing him forward in an emphatic demand.

"I can't go slow, Ellie." He gasped as he pressed inward just a short way. He pushed into her by slow degrees to ease his way. She was tight, and he was bigger than the average human male, so he had to be careful.

It was sheer heaven, even though Cade was definitely no saint. He slid into her delicious warmth inch by inch. A feeling of homecoming came over him as he joined with her. It was both ecstatic bliss and insatiable hunger rolled into one—like nothing he'd ever experienced before and suspected he never would again with any other woman.

Chapter Seven

Cade joined with her in one long, slow, gliding sweep that drove all conscious thought from her mind. He was so overwhelming, so...big...all over. So masculine and so perfect in almost every way. His height complimented her shorter lines, his muscular physique made her mouth water and his masterful possession made her want to surrender, body and soul.

"Cade, please!" She didn't know what she begged for, but she needed it. Whatever it was. And she knew he could give it to her. It didn't make any sense, but then, nothing she'd experienced since leaving the *dojo* had made sense. Her world had been turned upside down, but if the result was having Cade in her life, she knew it was worth every last terrifying minute.

She thought it couldn't get much better, then Cade started to move. Slow at first, he moved with feline grace over her and inside her. His hips undulated in a way few men could match, driving her higher with every last motion. He couldn't make a wrong move.

Elaine had never experienced sex like this before. It was as if Cade had been made specifically to her requirements. She hadn't known what she'd been missing all these years, but the point was driven home tight, hot and hard within her, never to be forgotten.

Cade was an imposing figure of a man. His height and the

muscular width of his shoulders should have intimidated her, but she could only find desire in her heart to be possessed by this male animal. She couldn't even think about his *pantera* side, although the idea of his ability to change into a giant predator was as tantalizing as it was terrifying. It was almost more than she could handle having the man side of Cade in her bed and in her body.

"Are you with me, baby?" His voice was rough and growly above her as his pace increased.

"Yes," she moaned. "Oh God, Cade." She was barely coherent as he drove her higher than she'd ever flown before.

"Then come with me, El. Come with me now!" The command in his voice did things to her she never would have believed. He buried his face in her neck and Elaine thought she felt the harsh sting of his teeth against her skin, but was too far gone to worry about it.

Cade's hips slammed into hers, but there was no pain— only pleasure. The greatest pleasure she'd ever known as he came deep, hard and fast within her body. His explosion ignited her own, sending her into a stratosphere of bliss she'd never seen before and knew she would never experience again with any other man.

Cade was a master. She accepted that, even though she sensed there was much more to being involved with a shifter than he'd been able to show her so far. She was an eager student, willing to learn from the only man who'd ever mastered her pleasure.

He held her securely in his arms as their ecstasy unfolded, both shaking and clinging to each other while their bodies floated down from the pinnacle. She loved the feel of his hard body against her, the slight roughness of his skin and the soft hair on his chest rubbing her breasts. He was the most beautiful specimen of manhood she'd ever had the good fortune to lure into her bed.

Not that there'd been all that many men in her bed, but of

the few she'd elected to go all the way with, Cade was without doubt the finest of the fine. Elaine felt a little thrill of pride that he wanted her. Cade could have any woman he wanted, and probably had. Tomcats were notorious for their conquests and she assumed *pantera noir* males were no different considering how appealing they were to the female of any species.

But Cade was in *her* bed now. He'd chosen her, for the night at least. It was an oddly old-fashioned thought for a modern woman to have, but the giggling schoolgirl inside couldn't help herself. It was as if the star quarterback had singled her out and asked her to the prom—something that had never happened back in high school.

Hell, nothing like that had ever happened at any time in her formerly dull and boring life. But that had all changed. Her best friend was a shapeshifter, the possible queen of her species, and Elaine was living on the lam with a dominant male panther who managed to raise goose bumps just by looking at her.

"Mmm," he grumbled in her ear. "That was a great way to start the morning." Cade pulled back to look at her. Elaine couldn't help the flush that rose in her cheeks as their eyes met. "I didn't hurt you, did I?"

"I don't think so," she hedged. To be honest, she couldn't feel anything other than pleasure coursing through her body. The aftershocks of Cade's loving were as potent as the act itself.

He bent to lick her, where her shoulder met her neck and the action made her aware of a sore spot, but his licking kisses made her dismiss the little pain from her mind. She was much more interested in what he was doing. She hadn't thought it possible, but her body sparked to life, responding to his renewed passion as if the huge orgasm she'd just experience had never even happened.

"Come on, let's make use of that Jacuzzi tub." Cade slinked off the bed in one sinuous move, taking her with him. He stood with her already in his arms and carried her into the bathroom.

Chuck greeted them at the door, twining around Cade's legs. Only Cade's surefootedness saved them from a fall and thankfully he laughed at the cat's antics.

"He's probably hungry," Elaine said. "It's not every night he saves someone's life."

Cade lowered her to her feet, then crouched down to look at the cat, scratching him behind the ears.

"He's been such a good kitten, I'll go get him a can of tuna." He looked up at her, and her breath caught at his masculine perfection. "Maybe I'll sneak a little something up for us too. How does a Continental breakfast sound?" Her stomach growled in answer, and they both laughed. "Hop in the shower and rinse off the liniment. Then run a tub. I'll be back in a couple of minutes, okay?"

He left her breathless. He had so much energy and seemed to have such a joy for living. His enthusiasm was contagious.

"Hurry back." She tried for a saucy grin as she stepped into the separate, spacious shower and turned on the water. He winked and left. Only then did she become aware of the lingering aches from her encounter the night before. The liniment had done a good job at limiting the bumps and bruises before they could fully form, but she did hurt in places— especially her shoulder. Elaine lathered the liniment away, glad to see the icky brown stains on her skin disappear and take the lingering smell with them.

Finished, she stepped out of the shower. As she looked in the mirror she saw the half moon of a bite mark high up on her shoulder. Son of a bitch! Cade had bitten her.

She didn't know what that meant exactly, but it was startling to come face to face with the reality that her new boyfriend—if that was even the right term to use—wasn't human. The bite was a half-moon of round dimples where human teeth would have left a totally different pattern. This looked like a cat bite. She remembered the look, on a much smaller scale, from Chuck's kitten days when he'd chewed all her shoes before she could break him of the costly habit.

Elaine shook her head in bewilderment as she put on a short terrycloth robe she found hanging behind the door before starting the water running into the big tub. A hot soak would do her body good and the Jacuzzi was pure decadence. She'd always loved the idea of having her own hot tub, but living in an apartment on a nurse's salary, she could never afford one.

Chuck twined around her legs, pawing her toes. She loved this cat. He'd been her companion and friend since the moment she'd found him as a feisty kitten, soaking wet on a street corner. She sat on the edge of the tub as it filled and scooped him into her arms. Like most cats, he wasn't thrilled being near so much water, but he knew she wouldn't dunk him. They'd built up trust over the years.

"I love you, Chuck." She hugged him close, kissing his head. "You saved my life."

A comforting meow was her only answer.

"He loves you, too, you know." Cade's voice came to her from the doorway. He had a bowl in his hands and the wafting scent of tuna fish reached her nose. "Come on, Chuck." He coaxed the cat off her lap. Chuck jumped down, following Cade out of the spacious bathroom.

When he returned a few minutes later, the cat was nowhere in sight.

"I figured we could do without the smell of fish in here." Cade turned off the taps. The tub was full, and she hadn't even noticed. Cade was too distracting. "Hop in the tub while I shower off the liniment. Some of it transferred from your skin onto me while we slept and...did other things." His wicked smile teased her. "I'm not complaining, but that stuff is pretty strong."

"And you have such a sensitive nose." She quipped back, knowing full well that he could smell things she could not. "Thanks for putting up with it last night. It really helped keep the bruising under control."

He eyed her critically, taking a seat next to her on the rim of the big tub. He took one of her arms in his hands and pushed the sleeve of the robe to her elbow. His fingers were gentle as they traced over the lingering bumps and dark spots, some of which were black and blue with traces of purple and red, not to mention the lovely putrid yellow and green around the edges. She was a wreck. Her arms were a mess, but it could have been so much worse. She'd been lucky to escape with just a few bruises to show for her first real run in with a werewolf.

Cade placed a tender kiss on the worst of the bumps, and the look in his eyes touched her deep inside. He was such a gentle, caring man, yet she knew he held a beast inside that could rend and tear as easily as the man comforted and cuddled. She didn't know how she might react if he changed to his beast form in front of her. She wasn't clear on how it worked and wasn't sure she really wanted to know. It was easier on her nerves to block that aspect of his personality out for now, even though she suspected she'd have to face it sooner or later if they continued being together.

For now, she was happy being an ostrich with her head buried in the sand. More detailed knowledge of shifters would come—or not—in time. First she had to figure out how to stay alive and salvage what she could of her life. Luckily, today was the first of two days off from the hospital, so she wouldn't have to worry about dealing with her job until the day after tomorrow.

"We may not like the smell of it, but we always keep liniment stocked in our safe houses and in our homes. Shifters get banged up a lot both in our fur and out of it, so it comes in handy."

He held her gaze, and she knew he was deliberately pointing out the differences between them. It was as if he sought her acceptance, but she didn't think she could give it to him at this early stage.

"It came in very handy last night. Thanks for taking such good care of me."

"It was my pleasure." He gave her a comical leer that made her laugh.

"Mine too," she admitted but then she remembered something. "You bit me!" she accused, poking him in the chest.

For the first time, she saw him blush. Heat rose in his cheeks as he ducked his head, caught.

"I wish I could say I was sorry about that, but being an honest man, I have to tell you I loved every minute of it. And if you're being honest, I think you did too." He looked back at her, and his expression smoldered. "Shifters have a tendency to want to mark their partners. It's an erotic act in itself—as I believe you experienced—but it also leaves a clear sign for others of our kind to read. Effectively, I put you under my protection, and anyone who sees that bite will know if they mess with you, they're messing with me."

"You're kidding."

"Afraid not. Big cats are very territorial and now that you're with me, I want the other shifters you're going to come in contact with to know it. I'm not letting you go, Ellie." He shifted closer, wrapping one arm around her waist as he pulled her in for a quick kiss. "You're mine," he whispered against her lips. "For as long as possible."

When he finally drew back, Elaine's head was spinning. He really gave the most devastating kisses she'd ever experienced. His eyes flared with possession as he watched her.

"Are you all right with that, Ellie?"

Swallowing hard against the fear her life had just taken another turn for the strange and exhilarating, she nodded. "I think so. I like being with you."

"Just like?" Cade laughed, drawing her to her feet with him. "I think I'm going to have to work on that. Hmm, I love a challenge."

He planted a kiss on her that made her dizzier, but he released her just as fast. Turning her, he slipped the robe off her shoulders and threw it over the towel rack before she even knew what he was doing.

"Get in the tub, Ellie." He patted her on the butt, making her jump. "I'll be right with you."

Left with little choice and enjoying his playfulness, Elaine stepped into the huge Jacuzzi tub. The water was toasty warm and felt good against her continuing aches and pains. She heard the shower go on as Cade rinsed off the liniment, and she leaned back and switched on the jets, awaiting his return.

The shower shut off and a moment later water lapped at her skin as Cade slipped into the giant tub. There was plenty of room for two in the decadent bath.

"Miss me?" His devilish smile dared her to play as he positioned her against his chest, sitting behind her in the water so he leaned against the back of the tub.

"Yeah. I definitely need someone to scrub my back." She sent him what she hoped was a coquettish smile over her shoulder.

"I think I can oblige, but I'd like something in return."

"Really? Do tell." Her hands were drawn to his thighs, resting beneath her in the water. He was already hard at her back, ready for action and she wasn't very far behind.

"I need some help with this." He lifted his hips, leaving her in no doubt about what he meant. A blush stole up her face as fire raced through her veins.

"I think that could be arranged."

Water splashed as they tussled and played in the water, but neither of them cared. All that mattered was each other and the moment. Cade spun her around so she faced him, straddling his lap. His fingers zeroed in between her thighs, rubbing with a circular motion over her clit that drove her crazy. He knew where to touch to bring her the maximum pleasure.

"Do you like that, kitten?" he asked when she moaned.

"You know I do," came her breathless reply. She gasped

when he thrust one long finger inside her, never letting up the caresses with the palm of his hand. "Cade, don't make me wait."

"Do you think you're ready for me?" His words challenged her while his fingers tormented. Couldn't he see she needed him?

Frustrated passion made her bold. Elaine slipped her hand between them, taking hold of what she wanted most. She stroked him, enjoying her chance to turn the tables as he growled deep in his throat, the sound rumbling through his chest.

The reminder of his other form made her hotter. Cade was hands down the sexiest man she'd ever seen, and she'd bet in panther form he'd be just as gorgeous.

A purr rumbled though his torso as she positioned herself over him. She couldn't wait any longer. She had to have him.

Holding his gaze, she slid onto his cock, pushing him inside her desperate core. He groaned as she took charge sexually for the first time with him. She watched closely for any sign of annoyance—she'd run into that once before in a short-lived relationship with a man who thought he had to be dominant in all things.

But she should have realized that Cade didn't just play at being dominant. He was and always would be an Alpha male. Such a secure man wouldn't feel threatened by giving power to a woman sexually from time to time. He was probably enlightened enough to realize that letting her have her way every so often could bring him a whole new kind of pleasure to them both.

He grinned with satisfaction as she began to move on him. His hands were free to cup and shape her breasts as they hovered over the water. Their skin was slick and wet as they slid against each other. His powerful thighs cradled her as she rose and fell against him, over and over.

She arched as a small wave of pleasure broke over her,

then threw her head back as the pleasure began to build once more.

"Stay with me, babe," Cade ordered softly, cupping her head and drawing her gaze back to his. He pulled her against his chest as he kissed her and began to thrust up into her at an increased pace. "I want to look into your eyes as you come for me, Ellie. I want to see it happen."

"Cade!" He reduced her to one-syllable sentences and most of them consisted of her crying out his name.

"That's it, baby. Almost there." His breath came in hard pants against her sensitized skin. Unlike the last time when he'd bitten her at the end, this time he watched her, holding her gaze with his own as he seemed to measure her pace. One hand held her hips, assisting her movements even as he guided her into his rhythm.

The illusion of her being in control was well and truly shattered, but she didn't care. All that mattered was the pleasure they were creating together, the ecstasy waiting around the next bend. It was close now. She could feel it building, even bigger than before as he powered inside her.

When the wave broke it took everything she was with it, washing over her and through her, only to return even stronger than before. She held Cade's stormy silver gaze and watched as his eyes glowed for her, his beast nature reflected there, in the magic that made him what he was.

She felt him come inside her at the same moment rapture claimed her, over and over again. She was shaking by the time the climax loosed her from its claw-like grip, letting her tumble free into the abyss, but Cade was there to catch her. He held her close, sharing those moments out of time with her, intimately locked together in body, mind and soul.

It was a turning point. A beginning of something new. An ending of her old way of life and the things she'd accepted as normal in her past. Cade was making new rules for her future. He'd already showed her pleasure beyond anything she'd ever dreamed of and proved to her that almost anything was possible.

After him, she'd be ruined for all other men, but at the moment, she couldn't work up the energy to care. All that mattered was being here with Cade. Everything else would work out in time.

She must have dozed because the next thing she knew, Cade was lifting her out of the cooling water. He'd already turned the jets off and had towels warmed on the rack for their use. He was handy to have around, and he seemed to think of everything she'd need even before she knew she needed it.

"Mmm," she mumbled against his chest as he wrapped her in a heated towel and began drying her off. "You have the most delicious way of pampering a woman."

Cade chuckled as he turned her around so her back was to his front. He dried her off with long sweeps of soft terry cloth over her skin. His face nuzzled into her neck, his tongue licking over the still-sensitive spot where he'd bitten her that first time they'd come together.

"I don't go this far for most ladies," he admitted. "You're special."

Her breath caught. "Because I'm human, you mean?" She was fishing for information, pure and simple, but she couldn't help herself.

"Yes, in a way," he agreed, nipping her earlobe. The simple act sent shivers down her spine. "But you're also the first woman I've ever marked. The first one I've ever wanted to mark. For a variety of complicated reasons." She heard the thoughtfulness in his voice. "You're human, and my mark is a simple way to put you visibly under my protection, but even more, I like you, Ellie. I liked you from the moment we met, and I admired you even more after the way you stuck your neck out to help Mitch. You're one in a million, babe, and I plan to keep you chained to my bed for a long time to come."

"That sounds kinky." She shivered again, but not with cold.

"And serious." She dropped the teasing tone. "Are you sure, Cade?"

"Honey." He turned her back to face him. "I've never been more sure of anything in my life. I can't explain it and frankly, I don't want to try to analyze any of this, but I want you in my life for the foreseeable future. Is that okay with you?"

His almost obstinate tone dared her to say no, but there was no danger of that. A grin stole over her face, but her buoyant mood was tempered with caution.

"It's more than okay, Cade, but you'll have to bear with me as I learn my way around this strange new world."

He hugged her. "I can do that. You've already passed the first few tests with flying colors."

She held up one bruised arm. "Lots and lots of colors," she joked.

He kissed her bruised and colorful arm. "Never again, El. I don't like seeing you in the line of fire. No more frantic phone calls in the middle of the night. From now on, you stay with me, where I can see you at all times."

She was surprised by the possessive tone in his voice and more than a little startled by the vehemence behind his words, but for the most part she agreed. She didn't ever want to be in a life or death situation like that again. One time through the wringer had been enough to last a lifetime.

"I'll do my best, Cade."

"See that you do." His smile turned daring. "Now there's one more thing I want you to do for me."

"What's that?" She liked the sexy purr in his voice.

"Kneel." His eyes glowed as he spoke the single word that made her belly clench.

He held her gaze as he threw a folded towel on the floor in front of him. She sank to her knees, the cushy towel padding her skin against the hard tile floor. That wasn't the only thing that was hard either. His cock stood out proud and long, seeming eager for her attention.

She opened her mouth to speak but he placed one finger over her lips.

"No talking."

She shut her mouth and nodded at him. She liked this game. This was the Alpha male in his prime, commanding his mate. The thought sent a shiver down her spine. It was a shiver of anticipation.

He moved his hand away from her mouth with a gentle caress, then stepped closer, positioning his hard cock in front of her. Suddenly, she wanted it more than anything. She wanted to know the feel of him against her tongue, the taste of him on her lips.

"Now suck." He placed one hand on the back of her head and drew her closer. She willingly came to him, taking the head of his cock into her mouth and running her tongue over the cap and down below to the sensitive spot that made him shiver.

"Yeah, baby. Just like that," he rumbled, thrusting shallowly as she took more of him in.

He was everything she'd dreamed. Salty and sweet, ridged against her tongue and strong as he thrust more deeply. She worked to take more of him as he thrust increasingly deeper into her mouth.

"Look at me, El."

She looked upward, meeting his gaze and the glow was back. It sustained longer than she'd ever seen it as she raised her hands and began working him in a steady rhythm. One hand cupped his balls, rubbing gently as her other hand took the root of his cock, fisting around him as she lowered over him and withdrew helped along by his shallow thrusts. Between the two of them, she took him deep, keeping the pressure on him with her fingers.

He growled low in his throat as she hollowed her cheeks and sucked strongly over the head of his cock on each stroke. The sound turned her on. He was close, she could feel the almost violent tremble in his limbs as her pace increased.

"I'm going to come, kitten."

She blinked up at him, staying close as the pace picked up again. She felt his body preparing itself to erupt and craved it. She wanted to taste him, to swallow him, to take him inside her body in every possible way, but he moved away. Instead of filling her mouth with his hot seed, he spurted his come all over her breasts.

He held her gaze as he came, covering her with his creamy spurts of come. He groaned, but it sounded more like a growl. She loved the sound and let it wash over her. He held her gaze as he dipped low and lifted her upward so she was standing in front of him.

"Now you."

Oh, man. The low-voiced command made her quiver as he sat her on the vanity and spread her legs wide. One toe dragged the folded towel over for him to kneel on. He dropped down and licked his way up her dripping folds, homing in on her distended clit. He sucked it between her lips as two long fingers pushed into her channel.

She moaned as he brought her to a fast, shuddering climax. He wasn't much for finesse at the moment, but she didn't care. The hard, rough edge to his passion sent her right over the moon with a keening cry that made him purr in satisfaction. The added vibration of his purr against her most sensitive skin drew out the orgasm and made it even more memorable.

Damn. The man knew just how to touch her to drive her wild. He smiled smugly as he rose from between her legs and gathered her into his arms.

"Thank you, El. That was beautiful."

"Mmm. Yeah. For me too." She was dizzy with satisfaction.

Placing a quick kiss on her lips, he tucked her into a terrycloth robe and took her into the bedroom.

Cade had set up the promised Continental breakfast while she was in the shower, so it was waiting for them when they emerged from the spacious bathroom. Chuck the cat had finished his bowl of tuna and was sunning himself in the window, batting lazily at the feathers hanging off what looked like a piece of Native American art.

"Is this a dream catcher?" Elaine greeted Chuck with a tummy rub as she looked at the intricate design.

It reminded her of the circular ornaments she'd seen in stores, but the workmanship was more exquisite than anything she'd ever seen. It had beads and shiny shells and stones worked into the webbing, and what looked like real hawk or eagle feathers dangling from ribbons on the sides and bottom of the decorative hoop.

"You'll find them in most shifter homes. It's something we've adopted from the native people of this continent. It's one of the few things that's come to us from the *were*. Very potent magic to help guard our sleep and protect our homes. A few of the raptor Clans make these." Cade fingered the dangling feathers.

"Then those are real? I thought only Native Americans were allowed to have real eagle feathers."

"And only shifters can have real *were*eagle, *were*hawk and *were*owl feathers." Cade sent her a knowing grin.

"They pull out their own feathers?" Elaine was appalled by the idea.

Cade laughed, and she hoped he was going to tell her she was wrong. It seemed kind of sick to mutilate yourself to decorate someone else's house.

"They molt," he explained. "What you see here are probably juvenile feathers. Their adult feathers are much bigger. From what I understand, starting when they're in their teens, every few years they have to stay in their bird form a few weeks until the new feathers are fully grown. New feathers grow in and sort of push out the old ones. It depends on their age and species how long the molt takes and how often they have to suffer through it. They collect the old feathers and use them for all kinds of things. Making these is one of the more profitable uses, and takes advantage of the magical nature of shifter feathers. Even the old, discarded ones hold some of the magic of the shift and make these dream catchers magical, beautiful and very useful too."

"That's fascinating. I didn't even know such creatures existed. It's daunting enough when I remember that you and Gina can turn into big cats. I had no idea there were others out there that could shift shape into something that can fly. That must be so cool."

"I agree." He seated her at the small table by the window. "Flying must be awesome, but I'd rather do it from the protection and comfort of an airplane." They both laughed as he poured coffee.

"So what other kinds of shifters are there? You've mentioned wolves, bears, eagles, hawks, owls and big cats. Are you all predators?"

"For the most part. There are varying schools of thought on why that is, but I personally believe that to pair with a human soul, an animal predator is the most sensible combination. After all, humans are at the very top of the food chain thanks to our ingenuity and creativity. We have our moments of compassion and complacency, but underneath it all we are still predators. Only now we hunt the next big deal, the next corporate merger, the next hot stock, or whatever field of endeavor we choose. Very few humans in the developed world are still in touch with their predator nature because they no longer have to hunt for food or protect their homes and families from being hunted."

"I never thought of it that way. When you put it like that it makes sense that the other part of your nature renews those ties to the predator within. Of course, I'm kind of glad to be sitting down to breakfast with the man, not the scary big cat."

Cade laughed as he sat opposite her. He'd cleared a vase of flowers off the small, round table and replaced them with a tray holding bagels, lox, cream cheese, butter and assorted jellies, along with two plates, silverware and a thermos carafe.

"Lox and bagels?" Elaine shot him a questioning grin.

"Hey, what can I say? Chuck isn't the only one who likes fish in the morning."

They shared a laugh as Cade saw to her every need. He was so solicitous she felt like she was eating in a five star restaurant instead of somebody's guest room. Cade gave her a plate and let her choose what she wanted from the serving tray first.

"How'd you get Chuck not to pounce on this?"

"I asked him nicely and bribed him with a portion of the lox in his bowl. He seemed content to leave some for us."

Chuck picked that moment to stretch hugely, yawn, then curl up in a furry ball and close his eyes. After such a rich meal, Elaine wasn't surprised that he'd fall asleep. They'd both been through a lot over the past week.

"So what's on the agenda for today?" Elaine asked, unsure where she stood in the larger scheme of shifters, *weres* and humans. She had a vague notion that Cade, or one of his people, would probably try to track down the men who had questioned her and especially the one who tried to kill her. She wasn't sure how they'd go about it, but wanted to help in any way she could.

"For you? Healing," Cade said shortly. "For me? I'm free until later tonight. I called in while you were in the shower and explained the situation. I'm sure Bonnie and Ray reported in last night after we got here, but they didn't have all the particulars. The Royal Guard has a vested interest in trying to identify exactly who the players are in this town. I'd like you to think more about that detective, Figueroa, and talk to some of my people. Any little identifying characteristic you can remember might help us figure out just who this guy really is."

"And when you know that?"

"We'll know what we're up against. It's never good to go into a battle without understanding your opponent. I bet Harris taught you that."

"Speaking of *Shihan*, is there any news on what happened at the *dojo*? It occurred to me the two fires were probably set by the same guy, or group of guys. My bet is on Bimley, the fireman. It wouldn't be the first time a firefighter turned out to be a fire bug in disguise."

"Maybe," Cade's eyes narrowed as he ate his breakfast. "But a better bet would be Figueroa. If he really is a magic user, he might also be our arsonist. Some mages specialize in fire."

"You mean like that kid in the old horror movie?" Elaine was fascinated by the idea.

"Something like that, I guess. I've only known a few mages and none of them were firestarters, so I'm not sure how dramatic they get."

"You've actually known people who can do magic?"

"A few. Like I said before, it's not common for shifters to mix with other supernaturals. Every once in a while we work with Others, but not often."

"Still, that is so cool."

They lingered over their meal, enjoying the blessedly quiet morning. The bagels were fresh, the coffee hot and the company better than any she'd shared in a long time. Come to think of it, the company was hot too. There was no man who appealed to her more on a physical level than Cade, and she was fast coming to appreciate his appeal on other levels as well. For one thing, he had a wicked sense of humor. She loved that about him...and so much more. If she wasn't very careful, she'd find herself loving everything about him, and then where would she be?

She turned away from those dark thoughts, resolving to focus instead on the moment. She'd almost died the night before. Today was a day to live.

She was already off to a good start. Experiencing more pleasure than she'd known all year was a good way to wake up any day of the week.

Chapter Eight

"What's it like?" She hadn't meant to ask the question. In fact, she'd hoped to ignore the panther side of Cade until it became absolutely necessary to acknowledge it, but the words just popped out.

"What's what like?"

She felt heat rise on her cheeks as she turned back to the remains of her breakfast. "Never mind. Forget I said anything."

"No," he touched her hand. "What did you want to know?"

Emboldened by his gentle tone, she thought how to phrase such a delicate question.

"Well, I was wondering about...you know...when you shift."

"Yeah?" His expression encouraged her curiosity.

"I told myself not to be so nosy but that's obviously not working. So what's it like to be a panther? Can you shift at will or is it a full moon kind of thing? And do you know who you are when you're a panther or does the cat take over?"

"You're curious as a kitten, aren't you?" His tone was teasing, but she feared there might be annoyance veiled by the laughter.

"You don't have to answer. I know I'm being rude."

"Not at all," he assured her and this time, she believed him. "After all, I think you're more than entitled to know something about the man who's sharing your bed, don't you?"

"Well, when you put it that way." One side of her mouth

lifted in a cautious smile.

"To answer your questions in random order…" He sat back and sipped his coffee, watching her with sexy, hooded eyes. "I'm me when I shift, and I can shift anytime I want. Too many shifts too close together can be dangerous because they're taxing, both physically and magically, but as an Alpha, I have a little more power than the ordinary shifter. And being the panther is…exhilarating, electrifying, amazing in a way I can't describe, yet at the same time, it's just me. I was born a shifter and always knew I'd be a panther when I got old enough. I looked forward to my first shift the way most teenagers look forward to their first car or the first time they make love."

"That good, eh?" She challenged him with a frisky grin.

"Better." He sipped coffee, holding her gaze in a way that made her think they weren't talking about shifting anymore.

"Can I see it?" She couldn't help but tease him.

Cade lowered his coffee cup. "Just what are we talking about here?"

"You," she drew the word out, "turning into a panther."

He burst out laughing. "You had me going there for a minute, Ellie."

Cade stood and discarded the towel he'd wrapped around his hips. Her mouth watered at the sight of his amazing body. He was male perfection in the flesh.

"I'll satisfy your curiosity this time, El, but when I shift back it'll be your turn. Are you okay with that?"

"More than okay," she answered without hesitation.

The promise of pleasure was enough to make her want to jump his bones. Forget about shifting. She wanted the male animal, not the beast, but he began to shimmer, his eyes glowing bright with the power of his change. His entire form blurred, bones shifted, fur sprouted and hands and feet became paws—all in a matter of seconds. Before she could blink, a sleek black panther stood before her. He was as gorgeous as she'd imagined and absolutely huge.

He sat on his haunches, looking at her with his head tilted as if waiting for her make the first move. She saw Cade's startling silver eyes were the same when he was the panther. They were filled with intelligence as he watched her and when she didn't move closer, he took the choice out of her hands, lowering his head to her lap and nuzzling her thigh. His fur tickled and scraped across her sensitive skin, the sensations sending shivers down her spine.

This was no mere cat. His fur was different than say...Chuck's. It was sleeker, the hair longer and thicker. Cade's nose sniffed delicately at her as his whiskers trailed over her, igniting sparks wherever they touched. She dared to touch his head, stroking his ears as his eyes closed in pleasure and a rumbling purr came from his chest.

Chuck's eyes blinked open at the deep sound, and he answered with a short meow of greeting, lifting one paw in the direction of the giant black cat. Cade returned the gesture, lifting a paw that was as big as Chuck in return, and Elaine had to stifle a laugh at the irony of the situation. Her new boyfriend was a cat.

Her friends had warned her she'd wind up an old single lady with a bunch of cats, but she'd bet they never had this scenario in mind. Neither had she, come to think of it, but she'd take Cade over an apartment full of housecats any day. His kind of kitty came with some amazing fringe benefits if this morning's performances were anything to go by.

When Cade lowered his paw, it came down gently on her thigh. He flexed the paw, giving her a glimpse of some wickedly sharp claws. Elaine gasped. He nudged her hand, and she sensed he was inviting her to inspect his paw—his hand, really. Elaine traced the contours of surprisingly soft flesh, fascinated by the long ebony claws he showed her. They had to be lethal, but she knew in her heart he'd never hurt her.

Apparently satisfied with her reaction, Cade lowered his paw to her side, putting his weight on the chair as he moved closer once more. He lifted his head, running his muzzle up her body, into the curve of her neck. She jumped when he licked over the spot where he'd bitten her earlier, his raspy tongue making the fine hairs on her arms stand on end.

His touch was electric. He was magic made flesh. He was amazing.

Losing her fear, she stroked him, rubbing her hands along his flanks, loving the feel of him. Cade sat back, then stood on all fours, nudging her with his jaw.

"What? You want me to stand?" His furry black head nodded, and she got to her feet. He got behind her and herded her toward the bed. She wasn't sure exactly what he wanted, but she'd play his game—to a point.

Elaine didn't argue when he pushed her down on the bed, but she was a little concerned when he jumped up beside her and stretched out. He didn't make any further moves toward her, so after a short time, she relaxed enough to pet him. He really had the softest fur, and he moved with a sexy, sinuous stride that made her mouth water when she realized he was also a man—a man who'd already made love to her twice that morning, and who'd indicated he wanted to do it again as soon as he changed back.

She couldn't wait.

"You're beautiful, Cade. I really appreciate your sharing this with me," she whispered to him as he lay beside her in the big bed, his cat eyes following every move she made. "Change back so I can show you how much.

The process she'd witnessed only minutes before reversed. His entire body shimmered as he shifted, the air around him vibrating with something she could only describe as magic. She had no idea what it really was, but it felt like electricity wrapped in velvet.

She blinked, closing her eyes against the strange feeling and when she looked back, the sultry black cat had been replaced with an equally sexy man. Cade grinned at her as he moved closer.

"So you like my wild side?" He rose on one elbow, leaning over her.

"You know I do."

She wrapped one hand around the back of his neck, drawing him down to her lips. She nuzzled him as he moved closer, using one hand to remove the towel that covered her body. He threw it behind them, off the bed. She vaguely heard it land some distance away, but she didn't really care where it went or if it broke anything in the room when it landed. All that mattered was Cade, over her, soon to be in her. She hoped.

"I like the way you show your appreciation, baby." He captured her lips with his.

The kiss was shattering, earth moving and totally undeniable. He licked inside, making her want him even more— if such a thing was possible. She didn't think she could get any hotter, but Cade had a way of making her surpass all of her prior experiences. Everything was new with him. Fresh and clean, and perfect in every way. It was a far cry from what she was used to in her dealings with the opposite sex.

Cade eased up, rolling over her. He pinned her with both his body and the wicked gleam in his eye.

"Let's try something a little different this time. Are you game?"

She couldn't resist the dare, though she wasn't sure what this wild man might have in store. Still, he hadn't done anything but protect her from the moment they'd met. Judging by their encounters to this point, she seriously doubted he'd do anything she wouldn't enjoy.

"Do your worst, big boy."

He took one of her wrists in each of her hands, raising them upward until they rested on either side of her head, above her ears. His sexy smile warmed her as the feeling of being exposed and under his complete control nearly overwhelmed her.

"This is a game of trust," he said, lightly holding her wrists in place. "I just showed mine by shifting in front of you. Now it's your turn."

"Does trusting you not to eat me alive count?" she quipped.

His eyes glowed as he looked at her. "But that's just what I want to do to you. And you'll love every minute of it. I promise."

She realized they were talking about very different things, and her pulse leapt at the images his words conjured in her mind.

"Leave your hands exactly where I put them, Ellie. No matter what. If we were in another place and time, I'd tie you to the bed while I had my wicked way with you, but this will have to suffice for now." He leered at her in an almost comical way, diving in for a quick kiss before he released her hands and moved downward.

He paused at her breasts, giving them each the attention she craved. He teased her with his mouth, tongue and even his teeth. His touch was alternately demanding and gentle, and incredibly arousing. By the time he moved on, she was gasping for air.

Cade leaned back and spread her thighs as far as they would go. He grinned up at her, displaying his sharper-than-human teeth. The sight sent a shiver down her spine of mixed excitement and the most delicious sort of danger.

"You're a flexible little thing, aren't you?" His growly voice said he approved.

"I took years of ballet before I ever started doing martial arts," she admitted, her voice sounding breathy to her own ears.

"Mmm. A dancer. No wonder you're so graceful and strong. Will you dance for me sometime, Ellie?"

She had to bite back a laugh at the leering look on his face. "I did ballet, Cade, not exotic dancing."

"Anything you do is exotic to me, baby." He leaned in and blew a breath of warm air over her exposed body, reminding her of their intimate position. She'd never been so turned on before—or so comfortable with a man in any and all situations.

141

With her hands up around her ears she was utterly exposed to him, vulnerable in the most basic way, but she knew he would never take advantage—not in a bad way, at least—of her vulnerability. No, Cade was an honorable man. He might make her scream, but it would only be in ecstasy. She trusted him that far at least.

Trusting him with her heart was another matter entirely. She didn't trust her own judgment when it came to taking that final headlong leap from lust into love. Her track record wasn't stellar where relationships were concerned and this one had all the earmarks of a disaster waiting to happen.

He'd just shown her why. Could a *pantera noir* shifter and a regular girl really make a go of it on a permanent basis? And for that matter, did Cade really want her for a lifetime? He seemed possessive, but maybe that was just a big cat thing. He might be thinking in terms of weeks or maybe even months—not years or lifetimes. Elaine had to tread lightly and try to protect her heart as best she could.

It wouldn't be easy, but she had to at least try. For both their sakes. She knew him well enough by now to realize he wouldn't enjoy breaking her heart, but he'd do it if he had to. He'd already turned away from her once by leaving her after that first night. She would never have seen him again if not for the arson happy fireman and his friend.

But depressing thoughts of the future went up in smoke the moment Cade touched her. His fingers framed her as his head dipped to place nibbling kisses on her tummy, then farther down.

He licked her folds, lapping at her like the big cat that hid inside him. Her breathing hitched as Cade's motions hit her with a blast of sensation that made her whole body tremble. Her muscles quivered, and she longed to move her arms, but he'd told her to keep them where they were.

She feared if she disobeyed and clutched at his soft hair the way she wanted, he'd stop. And that would kill her. She knew it. Nobody could live through that kind of torment—or this kind of pleasure.

Cade played her body like a master violinist played a Stradivarius. He made her moan and pant, and when his fingers joined the action, dipping inside her thrust and rub against her most sensitive places, she went off like a rocket. Pleasure rose to a crescendo within her spilling outward as her body vibrated and shook with release.

She screamed his name as he rode her through the peak and subsequent lull, only to bring her back to trembling need faster than she thought humanly possible. She felt the rumble of his purr against her thigh and heard the deep, rich sound that made her feel a kind of feminine satisfaction. She'd done that to him. He purred for her. She'd heard it before and it never failed to turn her insides to molten lava.

She didn't quite know what it meant, but it had to be a good sound. After all, even Chuck purred when he was happy. Not that Cade was anything like her housecat, but he *was* a cat and maybe the two very different breeds were similar in this small way at least.

She was fully recovered and getting into the swing of things again when he lifted his head. She bit back a curse, knowing he probably had something even better in store for her now, though how he could top what he'd just made her feel, she had no idea.

"I see you kept your hands where I wanted them." He licked his lips with a satisfied grin. "For that, you deserve a reward."

She nearly came when he stalked up her body, crawling over her inch by inch as he sought her mouth. She could taste the faint echo of herself on his skin, and the very idea of it made her feel naughty and deliciously hot.

"What do you want for your reward, baby?"

"I want you, Cade. Now!"

He reared back, a dangerous smile lighting his face. "I think that can be arranged."

Cade laced his fingers through hers, aligning their bodies perfectly on the first try. He was so ready, he didn't need anything to guide him inside. He surged forward, his gaze holding hers. His eyes glowed with mesmerizing desire as they became one. Elaine couldn't look away, he held her enthralled even as he started to move.

"Wrap your legs around me, El. Show me how much you want this."

The silky ends of his hair drifted forward to frame his face, swaying with his thrusts as he increased his pace. Elaine did as he asked, thrilled by the feel of his muscular body against her thighs. He was all lean muscle and hot kinetic energy as he took her in the most primal way.

"Harder, Cade," she begged, and he immediately gave her what she wanted. He was an intuitive lover. A spectacular lover.

She writhed under him, meeting his thrusts with upward pulses of her hips. Anything to bring him closer, to drive them both higher. They were almost there.

Cade leaned down and kissed her, swallowing her moans of desire as he pushed her higher. He broke the kiss, trailing his lips down her neck.

"I'm going to bite you again," he whispered in her ear, his hot breath skating over her sensitive skin. "Do you want it? Do you accept me?"

"Do it, Cade. I want it."

"Do you want me?" He held out, demanding her answer.

"I want you. Cade. Please."

Her cries finally got through to him. He bit down on the place where her shoulder met her neck as he thrust high and tight within her. The world exploded around them as she screamed. She could feel Cade's body tense above her and within her as his warmth filled her, renewing her, drowning her in the pleasure he created and controlled.

She still couldn't move her hands, but it didn't matter. He held her, he guided her, he was in charge and she loved every minute of his mastery.

It was a long time before rational thought was restored. She floated on a sea of clouds, pleasure her only sensation, Cade her only companion. That's all she needed. Cade and the pleasure he gave her.

They drifted together, joined in sensation for endless minutes before Cade finally moved away. He rolled to her side, gathering her close, his strong arms a little wobbly as he licked the new marks he'd made on her neck. She was wobbly too. Cade was that good.

"I didn't mean to get so rough, Ellie. I'm sorry."

The contrite tone touched her heart, and she rushed to reassure him.

"You don't have a single thing to be sorry about, Cade. I loved what we just did. Couldn't you tell?"

She felt his smile against the skin of her throat.

"I had a small inkling. You're sure you're okay?"

"Better than okay." She turned to face him, stroking his cheek with her fingers. "I don't have words to describe how okay I am."

He turned his head, nibbling on her fingers. "I'm glad. I feel the same way."

Her breath caught. He hadn't spoken of love, but she knew with every touch, every caress, he told her how much he cared. It might not be the forever kind of love she'd dreamed of since she was a child, but it was more than she'd ever had before and it meant something. Never one to jump into bed with a man, Elaine needed to know the man cared before giving herself. She felt that with Cade and longed to feel more even though she knew their relationship was probably doomed from the start.

"Let's sleep for a while. We had a long night and nobody expects to hear from us today. I took care of all that earlier."

"You're a genius," she said on a sigh, snuggling close to lay her head against his chest. He seemed to like her there, and she loved the way they fit so perfectly together. Plus, she was too weak from pleasure to move too far away. Better to snuggle with her *pantera noir* lover while she could.

She fell asleep with a smile on her face and tiny wrinkle of worry on her brow.

He woke her twice more during the day as they dozed lazily in the big bed. Once was a slow, languorous loving and the second was a quick, tempestuous romp that would've knocked her socks off if she'd been wearing socks. After the rough quickie, Cade took her back into the luxurious bathroom where they lazed in the big tub again.

He washed her hair with gentle fingers, stroking her like she was the cat in this relationship. She had to chuckle as the thought crossed her mind.

"What puts that sexy little grin on your face, my lovely?" Cade didn't miss a thing.

"Just enjoying the attention. I've never had a man wash my hair for me before."

"Mmm. I'm glad to be your first." His chuckle rumbled against her back as he spooned her from behind in the giant tub. "It's a first for me too. Now I wonder why I deprived myself of this pleasure for so long."

She reclined against him after he finished rinsing her hair with the hand sprayer. There were bubbles all around them from the shampoo but neither of them cared. The scent it gave off was subtle and clean, sort of woodsy, like herbs. Whatever brand it was, she liked it.

His hands skated over her body, the slick water adding something to the experience. He cupped her breasts through the bubbles, and her breath caught. He spent a long time playing with her nipples, sending her temperature and her passion soaring.

He moved his caress lower, one hand claiming her pussy, the other reaching around between their bodies to tease the cleft of her ass. She squeaked when he pressed inward on the tight rosette there, while his other hand played with her clit.

"Ever done it this way, kitten?"

"Um...no." Was that anticipation in her voice? She'd never done it, but she'd thought about it a time or two.

"Is that interest I hear in your voice?" He pressed in deeper, making her squirm as she felt new, forbidden things that made her want more. She didn't dare answer as he moved deeper. The slickness of the water made his entry easy. It almost seemed too easy.

"What's in this water?"

"You found me out. The shampoo as well as the bath oil I put in the tub are made by one of our herbalists. It's good for your skin and will ease your muscle aches. I put some in our last bath too, but this time I added an extra dollop." Cade's dark chuckle only made her hotter.

"You planned this?" The words came out in a gasp as he added another finger in her bottom.

"Not this exactly." His words rumbled near her ear. "I only wanted to soothe your body." He nipped her ear with a little more force than he had before as he stretched her wider.

"I wouldn't say this was soothing, exactly." She murmured as he began to gently move his fingers in and out. The sensation was...well, it was indescribably delicious. Better than she'd expected, in fact. She couldn't wait to learn the way his cock would feel inside her.

So far, everything she'd done with Cade had brought her incredible pleasure. He'd been rougher with her than any other man, but she loved it. What she probably would have objected strongly to with the few men she'd bedded in the past, only drove her higher with Cade. She wanted it all with him. Everything she could imagine and anything he could introduce her to as well.

"I want you, Cade." The words ripped from her lips as he withdrew his fingers, allowing the magic potion in the bathwater to soothe her skin.

"You've got me, kitten. Anywhere and everywhere." He repositioned her in the tub, sliding her slick limbs over his.

The position was a little awkward but it worked. Cade made it work. He lifted her over his hard cock and let her take him in small degrees. The entry was shallow at first, which allowed her time to get used to the girth of him inside her.

"Okay, baby?" his words whispered past her ear as he pushed down on her hips, driving himself deeper.

"Yes." She was beyond words of more than one syllable as he began to move.

Whatever was in that bath oil, it eased his way, allowing him to thrust easily into a place that had never been invaded in such a way before. The pleasure struck hard and fast, driving her to a small peak of pleasure that made her cry out.

"You ain't seen nothing yet, kitten." Cade's mouth nuzzled her neck as he increased his pace. One hand guided her on his hips, the other reached around and toyed with her clit, sliding and rubbing until she began to pant. He nipped her shoulder, biting down as her passion rose again.

"Cade!" She was so close. She cried out his name as she neared another devastating peak of pleasure.

"Come with me now, El." He ordered, and she complied. She went off like a rocket, reaching for the stars as he pressed deep, pulsing and straining within her. She felt his cock spurt its release and she screamed his name, riding him as the water sloshed against the sides of the big tub.

The pleasure lasted for long, long minutes while their pleasure peaked, and Cade held her, supporting her. He was there for her. Taking care of her. When they began to descend from the high point of passion, he gently nibbled on her earlobe, sucking and nipping.

"Are you okay, kitten?"

"I'm good." She loved the sexy purr of his voice.

He pulled out in a gentle slide that was soothed by the heated oil in the bath. That stuff was pure magic as far as she was concerned. She'd never have been able to do this so easily otherwise, she was sure.

"How are you?" She turned her head into his neck, lolling all over him as he spooned her tired body in the still warm water. She felt like she was floating, supported by his strength. It was a heady sensation.

"Never better." He growled. Actually growled. "I mean that. I've never had better, Ellie. And I suspect I never will." His words drifted off as she did, a pleasant fatigue claiming her in a light doze. She slept, secure in the knowledge that Cade would take care of her.

Chapter Nine

When Cade and Elaine finally emerged from their bedroom suite around dinnertime, the house was in an uproar. Bonnie and Ray had been joined by several other shifters. Cade recognized Charlie, one of the leading Escorts in the shifter underground. He'd done good work ferrying people to safety over the years and was well respected. Molly and Steve—both sporting bandages and looking pale—were there as well. Both were Royal Guards, Alphas in their own right and dedicated to their cause. They'd been inside the *dojo* when the attack went down and both had been injured while taking on the enemy.

Cade was glad to see them up and around, looking a little frail, but on the mend. Of the two, Steve was hurt worse, but both had broken bones and had suffered blood loss. Cade greeted them with genuine warmth but was concerned by their presence at the safe house.

"What's going on?" he asked as soon as they'd all settled around the dinner table.

Molly spoke first as they passed plates around the table. "The Nyx wants to meet your new friend."

Cade's stomach flipped. The Nyx was young, but extremely powerful. She had all the abilities bred into her line for generations, in addition to what Cade could only describe as psychic ability. She *knew* things. Not always and not often, but every once in a while, she definitely knew what was coming next. That surprising clairvoyance had saved her life more than once, so Cade and all the Royal Guards had come to respect it, even if they couldn't quite understand it.

"She's coming here?" Cade asked.

Molly nodded. "As soon as we can arrange it. She insisted."

The Nyx arrived later that evening, against her guardians' better judgment. Ellie listened to Cade and his friends complain all through dinner about security concerns.

Bonnie caught her by surprise when the tigress unbent enough to loan Elaine something to wear after dinner. They weren't close in size, but Bonnie had a lovely caftan that looked well enough on Elaine's shorter frame.

What had come to mid-calf on Bonnie touched Elaine's toes, but she thought she looked good in the shimmery fabric. It had an Egyptian motif that appealed to her, and she was grateful when Bonnie said she could keep it. The older woman probably realized Elaine had no clothes left after the fire.

Elaine didn't know exactly what to expect of the royal visit, but the young woman that held court in one of the basement rooms was well beyond the realm of her imagination. On the way in, Elaine hadn't paid much attention to the expanded basement area. It went well beyond the boundaries of the house above, out into the yard area and what she imagined was under the frontage street.

There was a long hallway leading from the secret garage entrance to the door going upstairs, but there were many other doors along the hall she hadn't noticed before. Judging by the position and distance between the closed doors, some of the rooms were smaller and a couple were very large indeed.

When Cade led her into what looked like the largest of all the subterranean rooms, Elaine expected anything other than what she found. The walls were covered in marble and granite and a small, ornamental pool complete with fish and a fountain gurgled in the center of the room. Lighting was dramatic and plentiful, allowing for the greenery of many potted plants and even one or two small trees.

In this underground Eden, Elaine didn't see the woman at first but when she finally noticed the Nyx near the back of the chamber, she thought she understood why everyone was so protective of her. It wasn't anything physical or obvious, but there was an air of fragility about the young woman whose dark eyes held deep and lasting sorrow.

"Welcome, Elaine," the *pantera noir* queen said as a smile lit her face. She had black hair like the panthers Elaine had met so far and perfect porcelain skin.

Elaine wasn't sure what the proper etiquette was when meeting the leader of a species. She tried for a friendly smile.

"Thank you. It's a pleasure to meet you." And right there Elaine realized she had no idea what to call her.

The Nyx seemed to realize it because she laughed and came forward to sit on the edge of the pool. "Call me Ria. Have a seat." She indicated the wide stone rim of the pool opposite her, and Elaine was more at ease.

Cade prowled around near the door, talking to Steve who'd been stationed inside when they entered. The two men looked like slightly blurred carbon copies of each other. Both had lustrous black hair and lithely muscled physiques. Both were tall with light colored eyes, but where Cade's eyes were silver, Steve's were a bright blue. Steve also had a soft cast on his left arm supported by a sling around his neck. He'd been badly hurt in the attack preceding the fire at the *dojo*.

All of that seemed so long ago, but it had really been less than a week. So short a time for such a huge upheaval in Elaine's life. It was really remarkable how quickly things changed.

"I'm sure you're wondering what this is all about," Ria began, gesturing with graceful hands at the opulent décor. "It's mostly tradition, but it seems my people think that wherever I go, I need to be surrounded by fountains and the Hanging Gardens of Babylon. It's beautiful, of course, but it gets a little annoying now and then. If I let them, they'd make me wear togas all the time." Ria rolled her eyes, and Elaine joined in her laughter.

Ria wore blue jeans and what looked like a Cashmere sweater. She looked like any audaciously beautiful young woman except for her striking jewelry. Ria wore a lovely scarab pendant around her neck carved from gleaming lapis lazuli with flecks of gold. A matching ring graced one of her fingers. The precious metal setting glittered in the light, and the stone was so expertly carved it looked almost alive.

"I see they got to you too." Ria pointed at the caftan Elaine wore, and it took a moment for her to realize the Nyx was talking about her somewhat Bohemian dress.

The caftan had an Egyptian motif, which Elaine hadn't questioned originally because it was so pretty. Looking at it in conjunction with Ria's scarabs—the ancient Egyptian symbol of resurrection and eternal life—Elaine had to wonder if there was some kind of connection as she fingered the silky material.

"Well, beggars can't be choosers. Bonnie was nice enough to give this to me. All I had when I got here were some ratty old pajamas. Everything else I owned was probably lost in the fire."

Ria looked immediately contrite. "I'm sorry. They didn't tell me you'd been in a fire." She shot a look toward the door where the men stood talking casually. "Did you live with other family members? Did everyone get out all right?"

Elaine was touched by her concern, but a little puzzled by her words. "It was just me and Chuck—my cat," she clarified when Ria's brows rose in surprise. "He's the one who woke me up, actually. Otherwise I would have been in real trouble. He saved my life."

"You have a cat?" Ria looked like she wanted to giggle but was controlling herself by supreme effort. "How...appropriate. Considering my cousin is grumbling about leaving the Royal Guard, you're going to need a lot of patience if you mate with him. Having already shared your life with one feline might give you an edge."

"Wait, Cade's your cousin? And what's this about mating?"

"Our mothers were sisters. My mother was the older sibling, so she inherited the title of Nyx. I was her last child, and the only one to survive. I had a sister and a brother. Both were killed by our enemies, so I'm the last of my line. If something happens to me, Cade's sister or one of our other cousins would have to take my place for the continuance of our Clan."

Now Elaine understood some of the sorrow she saw in this young woman's eyes. She'd known horror and loss in her life.

"I'm so sorry."

Ria smiled gently. "Fate determines a large portion of our destiny. I've come to believe that during my time as Nyx. But there are turning points along our paths where we get to decide—for good or ill—which direction to take. I believe you're at one of those places now, Elaine. You'll soon have to choose whether or not to accept a life with my cousin or go your own way in the human world. You've already taken the first step, whether you realize it or not."

"How so?"

"You let him mark you." Ria eyed the fresh bite on her shoulder. "That act has great significance among our kind. Didn't Cade tell you?"

Elaine looked toward her lover, standing so casually by the doorway. He grinned when he saw her looking his way, all predatory male, secure in his conquest.

"No, he didn't. The first time, he just bit me and I didn't even realize it until I looked in the mirror later."

"He's done it more than once?" Ria leaned in to inspect the small wounds.

She sensed Cade prowling closer. Apparently Ria's interest in the bite marks was something he wanted to monitor for himself. If he'd been holding out on her, she wasn't surprised he'd want to hear what the Nyx told her.

"He did it a couple of times."

"The second time, did he ask? Did you agree?"

Elaine thought back to those tempestuous moments and knew the answer. "Yeah. I agreed." She didn't add that she would have agreed to anything at that particular moment. She'd been a desperate woman.

"Didn't you explain anything to her?" Ria's gaze focused over Elaine's shoulder, up to where Cade now stood protectively behind her.

"There hasn't been much time or opportunity, Ria. Things have been a little...tense around here since a certain Nyx decided she wanted to pay us a state visit."

Elaine liked the way they interacted. Alarmed at first by his casual tone and chiding words, she quickly realized they were nothing more than family members hassling each other. Or at least Cade was hassling Ria. Elaine couldn't wait to see the young woman turn the tables on him.

"All right. I'll cut you some slack, Cade, but you need to fill her in on what that mark means. She's human."

"I haven't forgotten, Ria." Cade sounded annoyed at the reminder.

"I didn't mean it that way," she backpedaled, her eyes losing their accusatory glitter. "She doesn't know our ways, Cade. You need to explain things. She needs to know."

"And she will," he promised, relenting. "As soon as we have a chance to talk privately. I really prefer not to discuss what should be a private matter in front of everyone."

Ria looked pointedly from Steve's guard position at the door and back again. "It's just us *noir* here, Cade," she chided him. "But I get your meaning. Promise me you'll have your private conversation tonight—before this goes any further."

"Yes, oh mighty Nyx. Your wish is my command."

"Laying it on a little thick, cousin, but thank you." Ria turned her attention back to Elaine. "Don't let him bite you again until he explains things. The more he does it, the more bound you will become."

Alarm raced through Elaine's mind, but she didn't want to get into what Cade seemed to think was a private matter in public any more than he did.

"I will, Ria. Thanks for clueing me in."

"Now, about why I wanted to meet you." Ria changed the subject. "Did Cade mention that I sometimes...um...see things?"

"You mean like you're clairvoyant? No, he didn't mention it." Elaine shot him a mock accusing look.

"You don't seem too surprised that I'd claim to have foresight." Ria looked intrigued. "Why is that?"

Elaine shrugged. "My grandfather was psychic. He used to call and warn us when something bad was about to happen—like when my brother was planning to take a leap off the garage roof with a bed sheet tied around his shoulders. Instead of a broken neck, he ended up with a severely tanned hide." Elaine chuckled at the memory. "There were lots of little things gramps could do. He'd call the night after I took a big test in school and congratulate me, telling me how I did before the teacher even gave back the papers. He was a sweet man."

"I wish I could have known him," Ria commiserated with a gentle smile. "It sounds like he could have taught me a lot. As it is, I had to figure most of this out on my own. The ability hasn't manifested in a few generations, though it goes back to the oracle on the acropolis of Megara or earlier, if you believe the writings of Orpheus. Megara's oracle was Nyx in her time, as were her daughters after her."

"Orpheus. Isn't that a figure from Greek mythology?" Elaine was confused. First ancient Egyptians and now ancient Greeks. These *pantera noir* seemed to have strong ties to both ancient cultures.

"Our clan history traces back to the time of the ancient Greeks, but our people come from all over. Among big cat shifters, black cats are rare so we banded together early on for protection and mutual aid," Ria said. "But it was Michelangelo who organized all the cat shifter Clans."

"Michelangelo, the renaissance artist?" Elaine's eyebrows rose in surprise.

"And *tigre d'or*," Cade rumbled from his place behind her. "He was a shifter of many talents, and from all accounts had a personality strong enough to forge an alliance of sorts between the various big cat shifter Clans of his day."

"He's the one who orchestrated the first conclave. He got us to start working together and since his time we have grown stronger, working together and sharing resources." Ria had a right to the look of pride that settled over her expression, Elaine realized. Michelangelo had been a genius by anyone's measure. That he was one of their people was something very special indeed. "He was born to a Pride of Tuscany *tigre d'or*, but joined a Clan in Rome when his work took him elsewhere.

It wasn't common in those days for people to travel around. So it was a big deal when the Roman Clan accepted his bid for membership, and an even bigger deal when he rose to a position of great power within their ranks, but he was a visionary. Sort of like me, but they say his ability to see the future was greater. He could see the distant future and helped created our system of government to deal with what he knew would come. I only see events unfolding in the near future, but in greater detail. As I saw you, Elaine."

"You had a vision about meeting me?" Elaine wasn't sure whether to be flattered or alarmed.

"More of a premonition. I hate to say this, but our mutual enemy isn't done with you yet. Not if what I'm seeing comes true. Cade," she turned her focus upward, her expression imploring. "You have to work together to avoid some really horrific results. If you don't stick together, Elaine could die. In fact, you both could. I saw it."

"How? What did you see?" Cade's hand rested on Elaine's shoulder and she could feel the increasing tension in his grip.

"Fire."

A shiver of fear coursed down her spine. She'd seen enough fire to last a lifetime.

"Someone burned her apartment to try to get her already." Cade's tone held intensity and growing concern. "Could that be what you saw?"

"No. I'm sorry." Ria's sympathetic gaze turned back to Elaine. "What I saw was definitely in the future and it wasn't an apartment building. It was a man—throwing fire."

"A magic user?" Cade growled in question and Elaine felt his tension rising higher.

Ria squinted as if trying to see something in the distance. "I'm not sure. Could be. I don't know what other explanation there could be for such an image. The man had fire in his hands and was throwing it at Elaine. I wasn't absolutely certain who she was until I saw her face. That's why I insisted on coming here."

Cade surprised Elaine by crouching down in front of the Nyx and giving her a hug. "All is forgiven, Ri. I'm sorry I gave you a hard time. I should have known you had your reasons."

The strength of his reaction made Elaine think that he'd had words with Ria about her visit in the short time Elaine had been with Bonnie looking at clothes. It felt strange to see Cade hugging another woman, but these two had a history Elaine wasn't part of. They were cousins. Family. She wouldn't begrudge him that closeness. She had no idea what they'd been through together to get to this point.

When he pulled away, Cade urged Ria to her feet. "I think the team needs to hear this. Let's go into the conference room so you can tell everyone what you've seen and correlate that information with what they've been able to find out the old-fashioned way."

Elaine stood and walked with them to the door. Steve checked outside before he would let either Elaine or Ria pass, then Cade led them to one of the many rooms down the long hall.

The room they entered looked very much like a traditional conference room complete with audiovisual equipment, flip charts, white boards and the like, but with a twist. The fabrics were softer and the colors more vibrant than any office conference room Elaine had ever seen. A gorgeous tapestry covered one wall, depicting several species of big cats seated together in a circle. The symbolism wasn't lost on Elaine. This was a place where all different kinds of big cat shifters could meet and work things out between them.

When everyone was seated around the table, they began. Molly spoke first, outlining the security measures that had been put in place upstairs.

"Bonnie and Ray are guarding the house, the security system is armed and we have a few people outside watching the perimeter." Elaine hadn't gotten much of a chance to speak with Molly, but she seemed a capable, competent and almost scarily powerful woman despite the bandages and air cast on her ankle.

"Good work," Cade complimented her as he took charge of the meeting. "I've suspected for some time that there was a magic user involved in this mess. Of late there have been too many suspicious fires for my comfort, and now the Nyx has had a vision of a man throwing fire. I think the mage is a fire starter."

"That could fit with what I found out about the guys who visited Miss Spencer," Charlie put in. Elaine had learned at dinner that Charlie was an Escort.

Despite the unassuming name for the job, being an Escort was one of the most highly respected positions within the shifter underground organization. Escorts were top men and women who led others to safety. They had to be nannies, companions, protectors, assassins, fighters, strategists and whatever else the job called for. The people they escorted could be any age, in any physical or emotional condition. Escorts had to be able to work well under the worst possible circumstances to keep their charges safe.

Charlie Gantry had a near perfect record, Cade had told her, and was considered one of the best of the best. Before he'd retired to do Escort work, he'd been some kind of operative for the government. Elaine had been surprised to learn that some shifters were utilized in key positions throughout human society.

"I did a little checking after what you told us at dinner." Charlie nodded in Elaine's direction.

They'd asked her questions about the men who'd come to her apartment, but she hadn't thought there'd been enough time to really do anything with the information she'd provided. Apparently she'd been wrong.

"I've got a friend with a small *bodega* near Elaine's apartment building. I asked him to check his security camera footage. Do any of you recognize this guy?"

Charlie passed around a grainy black and white blown up picture of two guys walking down the street in front of her building. Elaine could tell right off that he'd isolated the right men.

"That's them. Figueroa and Bimley." She fingered each of their images as she spoke the names.

Cade took the photo from her and swore. "Is this who I think it is?" His finger poked at the man Elaine knew as Sergeant Bimley. "Tell me I'm wrong. Please."

"You're not wrong. It's Billy Bob all right. Son of a bitch was supposed to be dead." Steve cursed as the photo was handed to him.

"Who's Billy Bob?" Elaine asked.

All eyes turned toward her, but it was Ria who spoke. "At one time, he was a friend. An emissary from the *were* Lords who preferred city life and decided to stay. We took him in when he ran into trouble from some rogue wolves who'd already staked out his chosen territory."

"We even helped him find a part of the city that wasn't already claimed by canines of any kind," Cade added. "We went out of our way for the bastard, and then he betrayed us. Hell, he's *still* betraying us!" His fist pounded on the table making it shake. "Why isn't he dead?"

"I have no idea," Molly spoke from the other side of the table. "I swear to you, I saw him go down. Nobody could have lived through that. His throat was ripped out. I can't believe he's not dead."

"Who took him out? Do you remember? Did you see?" Steve bombarded her with questions.

"Matilda. She shifted and knocked him down before he had a chance to shift. You know how fast she was," Molly said. "She had his throat in her teeth before anyone could say boo. She trashed him. I saw it."

"She died a few weeks later as I recall, in an accident. She was run over by a truck on her way home from a local bar. I was always suspicious about that," Charlie put in. "She was too fast to get hit by anything, even if she was drunk."

"Hell!" Cade muttered curses under his breath. "Matilda was sleeping with Billy Bob. I confronted her about it once, and she got defiant with me. She swore they were mated, and they loved each other. I relented when I realized the little fool actually believed it. She wouldn't have killed him. She had too soft a heart."

"So you think she only wounded him to get him out of the fight?" Steve asked sharply.

"Come to think of it, there wasn't any time to clean up the bodies. We took our wounded and ran once the fighting ended," Molly clarified. "I guess we assumed they'd done the same. Nobody ever saw Billy Bob again."

"Maybe Matilda took him home and nursed him. It certainly would fit the timeline," Cade said. "She went into hiding for a while after the blow up. I always assumed it was because she was embarrassed she'd been duped so badly by her lover."

This casual talk of some past battle confused Elaine, but she caught the gist of what they were saying. Sergeant Bimley was really a traitorous werewolf they'd known as Billy Bob. One whom they'd thought was dead.

"So if he knew you guys so well," Elaine dared to interrupt. "Doesn't that put you all at a disadvantage?"

"A huge one," Cade agreed, covering her hand with his on top of the conference table. "But after that last big battle we changed our locations. We got new safe houses, encryption, passwords, vehicles, communication devices...everything. All the places and numbers he knew were changed."

Molly picked up the explanation. "We knew we had a leak, but we didn't know who it was until Billy Bob very publicly went over to the dark side during the fight. Little bastard almost got away with it, but Matilda was at his side and faster than any of us. She tackled him and put the odds back in our favor."

"And more than likely paid the ultimate price for her soft heart," Ria said in a sad tone, reminding them of what had probably happened to Matilda after Billy Bob was well again.

The room was silent for a moment as everyone digested that information. Finally, Charlie took hold of the photograph again, drawing attention back to it.

"I'm glad we figured out what happened to Matilda. She didn't deserve to die for her compassion, but even more distressing is the identity of this other man."

"What have you been able to find out about him?" Cade was instantly on alert. Elaine felt tension in the hand that covered hers, their fingers intertwined.

"I ran his face through some databases I used to have access to." Charlie winked, and Elaine understood from his sly expression that he'd probably hacked in. Very little surprised her where mild-mannered Charlie was concerned. She'd realized at some point during Cade's explanation of his Escort job that Charlie had to have more than a little James Bond in him. Cade seemed to think he could do just about anything.

"And?" Steve was as impatient as Cade.

"He's known by more than one name." Charlie consulted some papers in the file before him. "The one alias that he seems to favor most is Fidelio."

"Isn't that the name of the only opera Beethoven ever wrote?" Elaine asked, hoping to lighten the suddenly dark mood. They looked at her as if she was crazy. "I took some classical music courses in college," she explained, uncomfortable under the weight of their collective stares. "So sue me."

"Miss Spencer is correct about the opera," Charlie allowed with a slight smile. "But the somewhat distinctive name, Fidelio, also correlates to a known magic user. I hacked the *Altor Custodis* database for the rest of the information since this kind of data isn't in any of the regular civilian repositories." Charlie shuffled some papers. "Fidelio—if this is the same guy the *AC* are watching—is supposed to be a high-level mage. His element of choice is fire."

"Son of a bitch!" Cade cursed.

Charlie went on despite the upset around the room. "Fidelio's been credited with dozens of kills in arson fires all over the world. Most recently, the *AC* thinks he's been operating in the U.S., with confirmed sightings in Florida, Utah and New York."

"And I had this guy in my apartment?" Elaine felt her knees tremble.

"He was probably scoping you out," Steve said. "Learning the layout of your place and the building for when he sprung his trap."

"If he's not *were*, then why was he sniffing me?" Elaine asked, puzzled by that. "And what's this *AC* thing you're talking about? Can their information be trusted?"

"The *Altor Custodis* is an organization that has been watching supernaturals for as long as we've been keeping records. They predate Michelangelo's time, but how far back they go is anyone's guess. They watch and record anything about us we let them see. And actually a lot of things we'd prefer they not see," Charlie answered with a rueful grin. "Their resources are far reaching and better than almost anything we have, I'm sorry to say. Their field reports have to be witnessed by two of their brethren, co-signed and cross-verified, so the information is usually as solid as it comes."

"Are they magicians too?" Elaine asked, astounded by the idea that someone was watching and recording the doings of so many people who remained hidden from the rest of the world's population.

"They're not supposed to be," Ria said, drawing the attention of the room. All eyes rested on her, alert and questioning. "They're supposed to be a strictly human organization, but I've seen things lately that worry me. It's nothing specific, but I can't help the feeling that their time as impartial observers might be at an end. Somehow *weres* are involved and I don't know who, or what, else."

Elaine could feel the tension level rise in the room. Although she didn't fully understand the implications of what Ria had just revealed, Elaine sensed the others were alarmed by the Nyx's words. Silence reigned for a long moment as the information was digested. Finally, Cade spoke, his voice low, strong and reassuring in the pall of swirling uncertainty.

"If the rules have changed, we need to adapt. The *AC* has information sources we can only guess at, but from anecdotal evidence, we need to assume they're watching everything we do and everyone we're associated with. If our enemies have somehow infiltrated the *AC*, we have to believe they'll have access to those same databases Charlie has found a way to hack—and more. I'm not doubting your skill, Charlie, but I've never been comfortable with how easily you get to their data. An organization as old and complex as the *AC* has got to have more than just the layers of protection you've been able to compromise. I think there's got to be a deeper level of security—

quite possibly eyes-only hard copy records somewhere that can't be hacked."

"Your instincts are good, and I'm inclined to agree with you," Charlie admitted. "I've noticed curious gaps in the data stream as if certain records and cross-references had been deleted, or more likely, banned from the beginning. Still, what I have managed to glean over the years has been helpful."

"I'm not disputing that," Cade agreed. "I'm just saying there's probably more we don't have a way to see, and we have to contemplate the idea that our enemies might have infiltrated far enough into the organization to be one up on us."

Steve cursed under his breath, and Elaine could see the sentiment was shared by everyone at the table. They wore expressions with some mixture of fury, frustration and determination.

"It might explain some of their recent successes." Molly's tone was both angry and forlorn.

"So if I'm following you," Elaine spoke when the silence had stretched long enough to make her uncomfortable. "This guy Fidelio the fire freak and his furry friend might have access to information from the *AC*. This is bad. I get that. However, I don't understand why he was sniffing me. Could someone be both *were* and a magic user?"

"Not likely," Ria answered. "I can only guess that he's one of those mages that can smell magic. Some can, from what I've heard. Maybe he was checking to see if you had magic of your own."

That made a weird sort of sense to Elaine.

"So how do we deal with these guys? And is there any chance I'll ever be able to go back to my old life?" Unspoken was her worry about Gina.

If Elaine was now on the *AC*'s radar because of this mess, would they discover Gina's secret? Had Elaine outed her best friend to a group that might harbor a nest of killers in its ranks? The thought was too terrible to contemplate, and Elaine didn't want to talk about Gina in front of these other cats. Cade knew Gina's real identity, as did Mitch, but beyond those two and Elaine herself, Gina was still an unknown shifter who just happened to be available to help Mitch out when he needed it.

Elaine would do everything in her power to keep it that way. Gina didn't want to be found. That much was obvious. And it wasn't Elaine's place to tell the world her best friend was some kind of tiger queen. Gina would come forward—or not—by her own decision. Elaine hoped. But if these *AC* guys already knew about her, all bets were off.

Cade turned Elaine's hand over in his, gripping it tight, drawing her attention. "*You* stay safe while *we* handle the *were* and the mage," Cade said, his stern glance brooking no argument. "You did well against Billy Bob when he cornered you, but I think you'll agree he was more than you can really handle. You caught him unprepared to deal with a human with teeth, but he'd be a fool to make the mistake of underestimating you again."

Elaine had to admit Cade had a point but it stung to realize he thought she was too weak to fight her own battles.

"He was bigger and stronger, but I was faster." It was a matter of pride that she'd managed to outmaneuver a shifter who had fast, instinctive, animal reflexes.

"That may be, but I doubt he'll be as easy to defeat a second time. And you have no defense against a fire mage."

Knowing he was right didn't make it any easier to accept.

Chapter Ten

Cade hated hurting her. He could tell his words were landing like slaps in the face, but there was no way he'd let her come into contact with Billy Bob again. Not if he could possibly prevent it.

Billy Bob had been a friend of sorts. It had been a shock when he'd turned traitor on them. Cade cursed himself for not looking closer at the lone wolf who'd come to them with good credentials and a black heart.

Elaine's silence bothered him. He had to find a way to soften the harsh reality of their situation while still impressing upon her the seriousness of it. Even Molly was frowning at his blunt words.

"Look, Ellie, there are a lot of things you don't know about this situation. Shifters have some natural immunity to magic. Not a lot, but enough to give us some protection against Fidelio. Humans rarely have anything like it."

"They say some psychic humans have natural shielding," Ria added helpfully, frowning even more than Molly had at him.

"But that doesn't help me," Elaine admitted. "My grandfather was the strongest psychic in my family but I've never been clairvoyant."

It didn't help matters that Cade didn't know much more about Elaine than he'd been able to observe in the few days since they'd first met. He'd never even seen her fight. He'd never watched her practicing blocks and kicks with Harris down at the *dojo*. Cade regretted not attending more of those classes while he'd had the chance. He also regretted not investigating Elaine's background more.

He'd been in denial, plain and simple. Leaving her that first time had nearly broken him. He'd longed to give in and call her or go see her, but he'd fought against the attraction. He'd fought so hard in fact, that he couldn't even bring himself to do the routine background check he would have normally performed after their encounter. He'd wanted to put her from his mind completely but even going to such lengths as to ignore his duty, he'd been woefully unsuccessful.

She'd been in his mind constantly, in his dreams—waking and sleeping. He couldn't run fast enough to outrun the memories of their short time together.

And then she'd called. Her quaking voice over the phone as she had run for her life would be forever embedded in his memory. She'd very nearly died that night and he would have never seen her again. Never been able to hold her. Never been able to kiss her. Never been able to claim her as his mate.

That the last thought gave him pause. He still couldn't reconcile the instincts driving him to claim her with the harsh truth that humans and shifters rarely succeeded as mated pairs. Cade didn't feel particularly lucky enough to believe that he and Ellie could be the exception to the rule. That kind of thing would be too good to be true.

"Please, Ellie, for my sake." He squeezed her hand, imploring her. "I need to know that you'll be safe if we end up in another confrontation with our enemies."

"You can't keep her under lock and key, Cade," Ria broke in.

He grimaced at his cousin. "I can try."

Ria only shook her head.

"And there's the matter of how we're going to draw out Billy Bob and Fidelio," Charlie added calmly from the other side of the table.

"Don't even think it." Cade saw red. He knew without being told what the Escort was getting at. No way would they use Ellie as bait. They'd have to kill him first. Cade couldn't control the growl that sounded deep in his throat.

"This is getting us nowhere." Ria verbally stepped between the two men. "I suggest we adjourn and take this up in the morning. Cade, don't forget you have to explain a few things to Elaine." Ria's pointed look at Ellie's neck only caused his annoyance level to rise.

First Ellie wanted to step in where angels fear to tread, then Charlie had the nerve to suggest putting her in the line of fire and now this. He was being told how to run his love life by his younger cousin. Cade felt like he couldn't catch a break and everything was designed to annoy him. Not a good frame of mind for discussing life and death matters with the woman, who against all odds, might somehow end up being his mate. If the gods weren't finished playing games with his life yet.

"I'm sure I can dig up more information overnight." Charlie directed his words toward Ria, but Steve and Molly nodded in agreement. Cade knew they'd have their network of street informants activated within the hour.

The Underground boasted a worldwide network of shifters and sympathetic folks who had contacts that were far reaching and well informed. If any of them had heard anything useful about Fidelio or Billy Bob, Steve and Molly would soon know.

Cade waved to the others as they exited the room. Ria looked like she wanted to stay and talk but Charlie, thankfully, persuaded her out.

Cade could feel Ellie's displeasure with him and the way the meeting had ended. She sat silent at his side, steaming. He could almost feel the heat of her annoyance as a tangible thing.

"Would you mind telling me what that was all about?" Elaine's tone was as stiff as her backbone.

Cade breathed deep, searching for calm. "I'm sorry for embarrassing you in front of the others, but don't ask me to apologize for trying to keep you alive."

"I'm all for staying alive, Cade. I just don't understand why I can't take a more active role in keeping me that way." She held up one hand to forestall his reply. "I freely admit that you shifters have one up on us poor little humans strength-wise, but please remember I held my own against your werewolf friend. It wasn't easy, and I did have luck on my side, but I prevailed in the end and lived to tell the tale."

"Granted, but try to look at this from my point of view. I know how everyone else on the team handles themselves in a fight. Ellie, I've never even seen you practicing in a *dojo* under controlled circumstances, much less in a real world situation. From a tactical standpoint you're an unknown quantity. You can't blame me for wanting to limit the potential variables if we have to fight our way out."

Elaine was silent for a minute, and Cade hoped she was giving his words due consideration.

"I see your point. I don't like it, but I see it." Her posture loosened a tad as she turned to face him. "I want you to promise me one thing, and then I won't bother you about this again."

"What is it?"

"I want a chance to spar with you—or anyone you name. I want a chance to show you what I can do, so if it ever comes down to it, you won't make the mistake of underestimating me again."

Cade respected the firm belief she had in her own abilities. A good fighter needed to believe in themselves above all. That didn't mean she'd be a match for a shifter, but he had to give her points for bravery. Come to think of it, it would be good to let her go up against someone like Molly or even Steve, to let her learn how shifters really fought and how outclassed she probably was.

"Fair enough," Cade agreed without hesitation. "As soon as we have a spare moment—maybe tomorrow afternoon, depending on what the morning brings—we'll arrange a little sparring match. It'll be good practice for everyone involved, and I'll get to see your knockout leg sweep." He smiled, remembering the way she'd recounted taking Billy Bob down in that alley. Thank goodness she'd had the skill and luck to be able to escape. He'd never willingly put her in that kind of danger again.

"Sometimes I forget we've only known each other a few days. With all that's happened, it feels like I've known you forever."

Cade raised her hand to his lips for a gentle salute. "I feel that way too, Ellie, but I'm a Guard. I've trained most of my life for situations like this so I can't easily overlook the reality that us, together, is something new and magical, but fragile too." He hoped she could see the conflict in his soul. "You're the first human female I've ever let myself get attached to, El. You're the first female of any kind that I've considered asking to be my permanent mate. My panther knew you on sight. He's been roaring for you since the moment he first scented you, but the man has to be more cautious."

"When Bonnie took me upstairs to look through her closet for something to wear, she gave me an earful about how you and I could never work as a couple on a long-term basis. She was pretty nasty about how humans and shifters rarely ever make a go of marriage."

Cade made a mental note to have a few words with Bonnie when the danger was passed. The *tigre d'or* female had no right to interfere with Cade's personal affairs. She'd overstepped her bounds and elder or no, Cade would have something to say about it.

But he had to admit that some of what she'd told Elaine was no doubt true. Shifter-human matings seldom worked in this day and age. Legends abounded of the distant past when his people had mixed more freely and successfully with humans. But since the creation of the Underground and the need to hide so completely in the modern world, such pairings

171

happened less and less frequently and usually didn't end well.

"Bonnie has a big mouth, but it's essentially true. Shifters and humans don't have a good track record in the modern era though our history says intermarriage used to be commonplace. I haven't figured out where we're going, Ellie. To be honest, since the moment I met you I've felt like I've been in a whirlwind. I don't know which way is up anymore and, if going back to my old life means I can't have you in it, I'm not sure I want to go there. I don't know what the future will hold for us. Hell, I'm not even sure what the next few hours will bring. All I'm asking is that you trust me to make the best decisions I can, knowing all the variables and talents of the people on our team."

Elaine sat quietly for a long time, and he hoped she was seriously contemplating everything he'd said. He'd laid it all on the line. He didn't want to hurt her feelings, but he'd do it in a heartbeat if he thought it would keep her safe. The predator inside him demanded her compliance but the man knew it would be better to have her willing cooperation.

"Thank you for being honest with me." She took his hand, and he felt his heart rise with hope. "I think I understand better now and I'll do my best to follow orders like a good little soldier, but I have to warn you I've always been a free spirit and a bit of a troublemaker."

Her beautiful dark eyes lit with laughter, and Cade breathed a huge sigh of relief. She'd forgiven him for being such an unbending Alpha. Now maybe he could convince her to stay with him for a while after this was over. He hadn't yet had enough of her and thought perhaps he never would. He was beginning to hope they'd have a chance to discover if they could be the exception to the rule—or not.

"You're a beautiful woman, Elaine Spencer, and I'm not worthy of you, but I hope you'll keep slumming with me for a long time to come."

"That sounds serious," she quipped, but her eyes held

questions. "I hate to be pain, but what about the biting? Ria seemed to think I shouldn't let you off the hook until you've told me what it all means."

Cade gave her a dramatic sigh. "Oh, all right. Let's go upstairs, and I'll fill you in on all the sordid details."

Hand in hand they left the conference room and headed upstairs together. They passed Ray in the hall but didn't see anyone else as they made their way to the suite that had become their private retreat.

"When a shifter marks his lover it implies a mutual bond. In our case, it also states unequivocally that you're under my protection. Any other shifter seeing my mark would know immediately that to insult you is to insult me. Considering I'm an Alpha, the threat of my displeasure should carry a lot of weight."

They sat near the table where they'd eaten breakfast by mutual unspoken agreement. Cade knew it would be too tempting to sit on the bed with her. If she really wanted to talk, the table was much safer.

"Being an Alpha is that big a deal?"

Cade had to suppress a grin. She knew so little about his people even though she'd been friends with a tiger her entire life. In a way it was sad the *tigre blanche* had never been able to be completely honest with her best friend. Elaine was the rare human who would have accepted and even celebrated their differences while still being Gina's best friend.

"Being an Alpha isn't some kind of title we're awarded. It's innate. It's how I was born. Some might say it was my destiny. The majority of shifters follow an Alpha Pride or Pack leader. In the normal course of things, I would establish my own Pride once I found a mate. Other *pantera noir* could petition to join my Pride, or once my mate and I had adult cubs, they could join by marriage. There are other ways, but those are the main ones. Everyone in my Pride would be subject to my rule, and I would be responsible for them. As Alpha it's up to me to protect them and their cubs, to make decisions that allow them to flourish as families and individuals. It's also the Alpha's duty to settle disputes and dispense justice within the Pride."

"So it's sort of like being king of all you survey." Amusement danced in her eyes as she teased him.

"Watch it, you." Cade tugged on her hair playfully. "That's the normal course of events for an Alpha, but I'm relatively young and unmated. On top of that I'm a Royal Guard and close relation of the Nyx. With that combination, my life is a little different than the norm. Royal Guards are almost always Alphas and usually unmated. Bonnie and Ray retired recently because they want to start a family. Most consider being a Guard too dangerous when you also have cubs to protect, so a lot of Guards retire when they start their families."

"So Bonnie and Ray are both Alphas too?"

"You're catching on. Yes, they are and once they get pregnant, they'll probably get out of this game altogether. Right now they're helping out because of the fiasco with Billy Bob and Ria's presence in their chosen hometown."

"I saw the marks on Bonnie's neck when we were looking through her closet," Elaine said quietly. "It looked different than the bites you gave me."

"That's because what you saw was a mating mark."

"What's the difference?"

Cade shifted in his seat. "I was very careful not to break your skin when I bit you. Each time we make love and you agree to the bite, the drive will grow stronger in me to want to bite harder and deeper."

"That sounds painful," she said, but Cade heard the catch in her voice. He felt the same little gasp in his gut that made him want to find out exactly what it would be like.

"Pain mixed with pleasure so intense you barely notice anything other than the ecstasy. At least that's what my father told me when he explained the facts of life." Cade grinned, showing his teeth to her in a calculated display meant to flirt. Among shifters a showing of teeth often prefaced a steamy interlude. But Ellie was human. He had to keep reminding himself of that incontrovertible fact. That he had to remind himself at all was worrisome and divine all at the same time.

"I bet he said something like 'don't bite a girl unless you mean it', eh?"

Cade should have known she'd see the humor in things. She was a positive kind of person he was coming to discover. She tended toward optimism, while he too often took the other extreme. She was good for him, in that way—and in so many others.

"Something like that," he agreed, but he had more to explain. He'd promised he would give her the details before they went any further, even if what he told her made her turn away. He had to be honest with her. He had to take the chance.

"I've bitten you more than once. The first time I lost my head. I admit it. It wasn't my proudest moment." He tried to look regretful, but he really didn't regret a single minute of making love to Elaine. "The second time, I asked—and although you probably didn't know what you were agreeing to, which was a somewhat dirty trick on my part—you agreed. The first bite started something, the second made it stronger. Though I didn't break the skin, the panther wants it. Hell, he demands it. If we continue down this path, it could lead to lifelong bonding. Mating."

"But we can't. Humans and shifters don't mix if Bonnie is to be believed."

Cade rubbed his forehead with one hand. "I don't honestly know what to do about this, El. All I think we can do is take one day at a time. Maybe this will sort itself out somehow. Or maybe we can coast along for a while as we are, putting off any major decisions for later. I'm just not sure about that. But I am sure I want to be with you. I want you in my bed, and I want to make love to you as often as you'll let me."

Cade was gratified when he looked up and saw the fire in her eyes. His passion wasn't misplaced. She had just as much desire for him as he did for her. But of the two of them, she was probably the more cautious. She visibly tamped down her response, opting to continue talking.

Cade could have groaned, but he'd promised. He'd explain anything and everything she wanted to know. He owed it to her after the way he'd taken advantage of her ignorance the first few times they'd made love.

"And the mating mark?" she asked, getting him back on track.

"Results from a special bite given only when both parties intend to join for life. Breaking your skin with my teeth would let me taste drops of your blood and the enzymes in my saliva would enter your body, never to be removed. The level of certain enzymes in our systems increases exponentially when a shifter wants to mate. Nobody knows exactly how, but even a full-fledged break-the-skin bite at other times won't form the unique mate bond—only when the shifter wants it, body and soul."

"So you bite me full out and drink my blood. I thought that was a vampire thing."

"Only a small amount of blood is actually spilled, and we don't crave blood or need it like bloodletters do. It's a totally different thing. But we are hunters, top-of-the-food-chain carnivores. We don't shy away from blood. We like the taste of it. If you were a shifter, you'd bite me and if we'd agreed to mate, you'd want that reciprocal bond of my blood and your enzymes in me. Because of the enzymes, that kind of bite leaves a different kind of mark when it heals. Those are mating marks."

"So Ray has the same marks Bonnie has?"

Cade nodded. "If you saw his neck, you'd see Bonnie's marks on him, yes. They're joined for life. There's no such thing as divorce among shifters."

"So there's no going back?"

"No. No going back once the marks are made. Although with us I'm not sure how deep a mating bond would really go. My parents always taught me that mates needed to be near each other. The enzymes create a physical bridge between them. When mates are apart, they begin to crave one another, sometimes to a very serious extent. They can get irrational if kept apart too long and will attack anyone who stands between them and their mate. With a human in the mix, I'm not sure if the bond would be as strong, though there are some schools of thought that say it would produce an even stronger than usual bond because of the intricacies of human body chemistry. Some of our shifter doctors have studied this stuff, but I'm not an expert."

"Sounds like you've given it some thought."

She smiled at him, and he felt his heart lurch. If truth be known, he'd spent a lot of his free time looking into the matter since meeting her. He'd read through the findings of shifter doctors who'd put forward various theories on the subject and learned the intricacies of inter-species mating was an up-and-coming field of study. Apparently population specialists had figured that if shifters didn't start to mate with humans again, eventually many of their clans would die out for lack of members.

Weres had been known to mate humans more often than big cat shifters and seemed to have suffered no ill effects on their bloodlines from it. Cade took that evidence as hope for his relationship with Elaine—if it went that far. It was early days yet but if his panther had any say in the matter, Elaine Spencer would one day bear his cubs.

The thought gave him pause.

"I've looked into it." He reached over to tuck her hair back away from her face. "Strangely enough, I've developed a fascination with the topic of human-shifter mating of late."

She gave him a sultry smile. "Well then, why don't we give you a chance to do some hands-on research?"

Cade loved her playful side and loved even more her willingness to accept him—and all his many faults. He stood and swept her into his arms, startling a yelp from her as she scrambled to steady herself by wrapping her arms around his neck.

He strode over to the bed and lay her down upon it. She pulled the pretty caftan up over her hips and he did the rest, flinging it across the room before attacking his own buttons. Elaine worked on his zipper while he ripped the last few buttons clean off his shirt. Her touch made him impatient and unable to wait.

With a growl, he took over, slinging off the pants and throwing them after his ruined shirt. Elaine grinned at his lack of control, spurring him to even greater action.

He ran his hands down the sides of her body from shoulders to knees, loving the soft feel of her skin against his palms. She had the most luscious skin. He could stroke her for hours, but there were more important things to do. Namely, her.

Cade licked his lips as he crouched over her. She made room for him, eagerly spreading her legs so he could kneel between.

"I've thought about almost nothing else but this since this morning. If I haven't managed to say it well enough before, I'm crazy about you, Ellie." He looked deep into her eyes. "I've never felt this way before about anyone."

"Oh, Cade." She reached up and stroked his cheek. Her eyes held mysteries and so much caring, it made something inside him turn over and resettle in newer, more powerful lines. "I'm crazy about you too." She lifted to give him a quick, tender kiss, then whispered, "Let's go crazy together." A saucy wink fired his blood, revving his engines for more.

"How do you want it, Ellie?"

She wasted no time, pushing at his shoulder until he gave way. They rolled until she was astride him, over him, tantalizing him with her beautiful body and killer smile.

"I want to do you this time, Cade." Her sultry whisper nearly made him tremble as she leaned in to nibble her way down his neck to his chest. When she hesitated over the place where his neck joined his shoulder, rubbing lightly with her comparatively blunt teeth in the place where a shifter mate would leave her mark, Cade stiffened with fierce arousal.

"Ellie..." His voice was a low growl of warning as she tested his limits of control.

"Mmm." Her breath sent soft puffs of air against his skin, making him shiver. "I love it when you growl at me." She punctuated her words with gentle, biting kisses down his pectoral muscle. "And I've been wondering for a while what it would take to make you roar."

"Keep doing that, and you'll find out."

When she licked over his nipple it was all he could do not to grab her head and hold her still. She was temptation made flesh—a beautiful creature sent from the heavens to entice him with her alluring ways. He wanted to roll her over and plunge into her, but he'd agreed to let her have her way this time. The need to hold back might kill him, but he'd die with a smile on his face.

"Oh, I intend to do a lot more, Cade."

She moved lower, tickling his rippling abdomen with her teeth and tongue. He wasn't sure he could hold it together if she went any lower.

But his sweet temptation didn't let up, she moved steadily downward, pausing to tease his navel with her tongue, causing a loud rumble of satisfaction to echo through his chest. She was killing him...with pleasure.

And she didn't stop there. His little kitten went for it, circling him first with her delicate hands, then sheathing him in her mouth. Once again, her luscious mouth on his cock was the most delicious sensation he'd ever experienced. If he could freeze time, he'd stop right there to savor every lick, every nibble, every sucking squeeze.

Ecstasy snuck up on him when she did something with her fingers that made him convulse in pleasure. He was too preoccupied to realize she was still licking him when he came, but he had enough presence of mind to roll away from her.

"Don't swallow, Ellie." His voice was harsh, his breathing erratic. Yet he had to make her understand. This was important. "The enzyme," he gasped as his climax began to ease.

She sat up, stroking his shoulder and back with her soft hands, offering comfort when it should be the other way around. He should be the one comforting her. This woman never ceased to amaze him.

He rolled to his back, seeking her gaze. The gentle smile on her face humbled him and he couldn't resist pulling her in for a quick kiss. He held her, one of his arms around her neck and shoulders as she settled against his chest.

"I'm sorry, baby. I should have told you before. That enzyme I was telling you about? Its effects are pretty strong if you take it that way. Hey, I promised you full disclosure right?" He teased, grateful when she chuckled.

"What about when you come inside me?" she asked in a small voice.

He was glad to hear a revival of her curiosity. She was still with him. He hadn't managed to screw this up completely—yet.

"The oral transfer of enzymes is the key to creating and sealing the mate bond."

"That's probably a good thing," she tickled his chest with mischievous, roaming fingers. "Otherwise you tomcats would have a string of brokenhearted females following you around wherever you go."

He had to laugh at the image.

Chapter Eleven

Elaine didn't know what to make of Cade and the information he'd given her. To be honest, she was feeling overwhelmed with everything she'd learned in such a short time. All she could really do now was hang on and hope everything worked out for the best. She'd thrown in her lot with the shapeshifters, for good or for ill, and had to live with whatever consequences came.

It was worth it, she thought, for the chance to be with Cade. Nothing in her life to this point could compare with the way she felt with him. He was magic, in more than the obvious way. Sure, seeing him as a panther was something she would never forget, but the man himself was a study in contradictions. She thought she could spend the rest of her life trying to figure him out and never be bored. Frustrated at times, maybe, but always fascinated by the big Alpha male who could be so intimidating, yet so tender, so strong, so compassionate.

"Don't worry about me," she assured him. "I didn't uh...swallow anything." It was hard to talk about such intimate details without blushing.

Oddly enough, she'd wanted to taste him. She craved Cade. She craved anything and everything he could give her. She wanted to do it all for him, and she suspected the feeling was mutual judging by their previous encounters.

"Good." He sighed and relaxed fractionally, his arm holding her a little more comfortably as his heart rate slowed. She could feel it pounding against her, and the steady thrumming comforted her in a strange way. "Now how about we take care of you? Since you so graciously took care of me."

She felt the surprising rise of his ardor against her thigh and looked downward with one raised eyebrow.

"Isn't it...um...a little too soon for that?"

"You obviously aren't used to shifters, my dear." Cade gave her a challenging grin. "One of the many benefits of our constitution is that we recover faster—in all ways—than humans."

She eyed him suspiciously.

"What? You still don't believe me? After all we've done together?" He growled and tackled her gently, taking her to the bed beneath him. "I guess I'm just going to have to prove it to you. Believe me, it'll be a pleasure."

His mouth touched the place where he'd bitten her before, and the tenderness in her skin spiked a roar of desire through her body. He was potent, she'd give him that. His merest touch lit her on fire.

His big body covered hers, boxing her in with his arms and legs while he feasted on her skin. He kissed his way to her breasts, pausing there to bring her excitement level to a fever pitch. But as tempting as it was to just give in and follow his lead, this wasn't the way she'd had it planned.

"Cade," she nipped his shoulder to get his attention and felt him stiffen above her. Good, two can play the biting game after all, she thought.

"Don't bite me unless you mean it, baby." His growling words almost sent her into orbit.

"What if I do mean it? Will you let me bite you, Cade?" She was proud of the sultry purr in her voice.

He stilled completely, his rock hard body poised against her.

"Do you really want to?"

Cade pulled back to look deep into her eyes.

"I do."

Whoa, she thought, that sounded a lot like wedding vows. She wondered if her subconscious was moving things along despite what her rational mind had to say on the matter. But it would be okay as long as she didn't bite him hard enough to break the skin, right? She could do this. She could give this to him.

"I do too," he answered in a solemn voice that made her wonder if he also recognized the potential significance of their words.

Had they just made a vow to each other? It sure felt like it. But whether it was for a few days or a lifetime remained to be seen. For now, she'd take the moment and everything they could wring from it.

"Roll over," she ordered him gently. In what felt like slow motion, he complied, until she was over him, gazing into his quicksilver eyes.

This time, they needed no preliminaries. She sank onto him, both ready, both panting for more as she began to ride him with slow, even strokes.

The loving was languid, slow to rise to a boil and all that much hotter for it. Elaine held his gaze as she moved over him, responding to the need she read in his eyes. She began to move more quickly as their fever rose.

When his fingers squeezed her breasts, she gave a keening cry and began to lose control. Her hips moved erratically, a tempestuous force riding her, driving her onward. Cade's hands moved to her hips, guiding her and helping her shaking muscles last through the final few minutes of yearning toward a bliss they would share equally.

But she'd promised him one more thing. She couldn't let go until she gave him that final push.

Leaning forward, crushing her breasts on the solid wall of his muscular chest, she reached for his neck with her mouth.

She lingered at the last, while he controlled her hips with his strong grip, pulsing up into her now that she'd changed positions. She licked the strong pulse under his jaw, mouthing the cords of his neck until she found the sweet spot she wanted.

It was time.

She bit down hard, being careful not to break skin, but hard enough to show him how much she wanted this. How much she wanted to please him.

Elaine heard a big cat roar as she came, holding tight to his body everywhere they joined. She didn't let up the pressure on her mouth. If truth be told, she couldn't. Her system had gone into a rigor of pleasure that seized every muscle, every joint, while she experienced the most brilliant climax yet.

Every time with Cade only got better.

She remembered sighing with the satisfaction of that thought just before losing consciousness.

"Ellie, wake up." Cade's voice was low and urgent, and Elaine sensed immediately that something was wrong. His body vibrated with alarm as he slid from the bed toward the door.

"What is it?"

"Someone's in the house. Shit!" He threw her T-shirt and pants at her, followed by her sneakers. "There's a small door inside the bathroom closet," he whispered. "I want you to go through it and lock it behind you. It leads to the basement. Ria is down there."

Elaine understood what he didn't have time to say. He wanted her out of the fighting, away from the danger. His duty as a Royal Guard was to protect the Nyx. If Elaine was with Ria, then Cade could concentrate on his duty and protect them both at the same time.

"Okay." She reassured him as best she could, taking only a moment to place a hard, fast kiss on his lips. "Stay safe, Cade."

"You too, baby." He patted her butt as she scurried away, toward the hidden doorway she hadn't known about. She paused a moment to get Chuck out of the nest of toweling he'd claimed as his bed in the bathroom and opened the door to the big linen closet, looking for the hidden panel.

It was ingeniously disguised and popped open at her touch. She saw a steel bar and brackets across the back she could use to seal it shut behind her. With one last look into the bedroom, she turned to go.

Her breath caught when she met the glittering silver eyes of the panther. Cade had already shifted and bared his claws in preparation for battle. She closed the door and barred it, realizing idly why all the doorknobs in the big house were of the lever variety. Big cats could open those, no problem, with their giant paws where old-fashioned knobs might present some difficulties.

There was a steep set of narrow steps leading down, down, down as far as she could see. Light filtered in from somewhere above, but not enough to illuminate the hidden passageway completely. It was just enough for her to see where she was going, but no more.

Elaine let Chuck go so he could navigate his own way. He was more surefooted than she, and she didn't want to fall with him in her arms and hurt them both. She would need her arms for balance, and she knew Chuck would stay with her. He was loyal like that. Cobwebs brushed her face, but Elaine refused to think about the spiders that had spun them and were probably still in residence somewhere in the long passage.

The stairs looped around in places, and Elaine could just barely make out other doors connecting onto the passageway as she passed them. She realized that everything she'd seen of the house indicated the inside had been recently renovated. If they'd had to secure all new safe houses after Billy Bob's betrayal, they'd also had to have constructed all of this recently.

She'd just bet they'd bought an old house and in the guise

of renovations had completely redesigned the inside with these neat hidden passageways and expanded the basement beyond all proportion. Idly, she wondered what the neighbors would think if they knew just who—and what—was living next door as she flew down the stairs. She was out of breath when she neared the bottom, but otherwise okay. Chuck waited for her at the bottom, his kitty face looking up at her in concern.

Fright had kicked her into high gear, but she realized she had no idea what might be lurking on the other side of that final door. It would behoove her to be cautious. Moving as quietly as possible, Elaine crept toward the door that would likely lead her into the basement.

What she heard on the other side of the door when she pressed her ear to it didn't sound promising. Animal growls came to her through the door, and she couldn't tell whether they were friend or foe.

She debated what to do. Should she storm in and try for surprise? That might be a good strategy if there were bad guys on the other side, but it could get her torn up unnecessarily if they were friends and she didn't identify herself.

Then again, they probably wouldn't be making so much noise if something wasn't seriously wrong. So jumping into the fray could go either way.

Regardless, Elaine knew despite her promise to Cade, that she couldn't run away and leave Ria and the others to fend for themselves. If she could help them in any way, she'd do it. Dealing with Cade's anger was something she would worry about later.

She crouched to give Chuck a quick scratch and cuddle. "Stay here," she breathed, hoping the cat could somehow understand. He had the heart of a lion, and he might leap into the fight if given half a chance. She'd try to leave him in the passageway if she could, but he was quick and a good escape artist when he wanted to go with her.

Taking a deep breath for courage, and to center herself,

Elaine pushed open the hidden door, leaving quickly and letting it shut behind her. Chuck, thankfully, stayed behind. She needn't have worried about being jumped the moment she emerged. The fight was clear across the room. But it was definitely a fight.

Molly was on the floor, bleeding and unconscious by the door. That left a small black panther that Elaine assumed was Ria, facing a giant grey wolf in the middle of the garden room Elaine had seen for the first time only the day before. The fountain still gurgled, the plants looked only a little worse for wear, but the peaceful atmosphere had been forever sullied by fighting and bloodshed.

Billy Bob, if that's who he was under the shaggy grey wolf coat, had the panther at a disadvantage. Even Elaine could see the giant wolf would rip the little cat apart.

"You leave her alone!" Elaine shouted to be heard above the growls emanating from both panther and wolf.

Both creatures looked at her, and Elaine knew a split second of panic. What had she done? Did she really *want* to be mauled by a wolf?

"Shift back you scrawny bastard. I want another piece of you," she taunted him, hoping it would draw him away from Ria.

Elaine didn't think she stood much of a chance against a two-hundred-pound wolf, but she might be able to use her martial arts skills to fight a man long enough for help to get to them. There was no doubt in her mind that the rest of the team was working their way here. They would come for the Nyx if nothing else. She was precious to them, and they'd sworn to protect her.

Elaine hadn't made any oaths, but she felt protective of the young woman who'd been so kind to her. Ria was a special person who was both humble and sweet despite her position of power. She didn't deserve some cur like Billy Bob tearing her to shreds. Nobody deserved that. As a matter of fact, Elaine would do her best to avoid it herself.

The wolf prowled closer, and Elaine tried not to flinch when he barked menacingly at her. She refused to show fear, but she had to get him out of wolf form. She was dead—or at the very least, seriously injured—if he came at her with those huge, sharp teeth.

"Aren't you the wimpy fireman who was waiting for me in the dark?" she asked the wolf. If he wanted to answer her taunts, he'd have to change back so he could speak. She prayed he had the kind of foolish pride that would make him take her bait. "I whooped your ass then, you bastard and I'll do it again. How did it feel to be knocked on your ass by a girl? A human at that? I bet that stung, didn't it?"

The wolf faced her, pacing around as she countered his moves. She had to get him to shift. But how? An idea formed.

"I guess we'll be smelling smoke any time now, huh?" She tried for nonchalance but knew her eyes glittered with excitement as the confrontation unfolded. Her heart was racing double time, and her reflexes sharpened with adrenaline. "Or is Figueroa not with you today? He's the firebug, isn't he? You're just his minion. The one he sends out to attack people he's already got running from fires he sets. Is Figueroa—or should I say Fidelio—here, pulling your strings again? Seems like he's the brains in your operation. You're just the stooge. Aren't you, Billy Bob?"

That did it. The *were* couldn't take her trash talk. He shimmered and changed right in front of her while Elaine tried hard to hide her relief and satisfaction.

"You have no idea what you're talking about, human." He sneered the last word as if being human were something disgusting.

"Maybe I do, and maybe I don't," she admitted. "But I bet you're wondering how they found out so much about you and your keeper so quickly."

"You'll tell me before you die," he muttered, stalking

forward. He was naked and absolutely huge. And hairy. And clawed!

Billy Bob had done something when he shifted. It was like he hadn't shifted back all the way to his man form. He was sort of stuck...between. He stood upright like a man and could talk, though his voice was a low growl. But his hands were tipped with wicked claws, and his frame was way bigger than she remembered.

He'd been tall as a man, but now he towered over her and Elaine suddenly had a revelation. This was where the legends of werewolves came from. This in-between form was scary as all hell, and she'd be lucky if she could dodge him long enough to get in a few licks of her own before he brought her down.

It wouldn't be pretty either. Those claws would rip her apart.

She had to stay clear of them at all costs.

Elaine started dancing—jogging around like a boxer to stay focused and on the move. She had to stay alert and try to keep him off balance, but it looked more and more like a losing battle. What could she really hope to do against those freaking, huge claws? She breathed deep, trying to still the threatening panic.

Fear would take her down faster than anything. She had to master the fear and use the adrenaline rush to her advantage.

Billy Bob followed her every move, stalking her, playing with her. Elaine didn't like the feeling. He struck out fast as lighting when she danced a tiny bit too close, and she had to duck to avoid his flashing claws. She felt them graze by her cheek a hairsbreadth away. Too close for comfort.

"Why'd you do it, Billy Bob?" She tried to stall him as she backed away. "Why betray the friends you'd made here among the cats? Why betray your lover? You killed her, didn't you?"

Billy Bob actually winced. Maybe he wasn't completely evil if he regretted what had happened to Matilda.

"She knew too much," he rasped. "The organization

sanctioned her. It wasn't any of my doing. If it'd been up to me, the silly bitch would have lived."

"Pardon me if I think you don't seem too broken up about it. You let those Altor Custody people kill your girlfriend." Elaine scoffed at him, trying to throw him off stride as he advanced. He kept advancing, and she kept retreating. Eventually, she'd run out of room.

"*Altor Custodis*," he corrected her with a growling laugh. "And you're a fool if you think I work for them. They're small potatoes compared to the *Venificus*."

Elaine had no idea what he was talking about, but one look over his shoulder at the small black panther told her that Ria knew. She'd gone stiff with shock, and her animal eyes held a fear that Elaine would never have expected.

Elaine prepared as best she could when she saw Ria slink into motion out of the corner of her eye. Elaine danced closer to distract the werewolf hoping to give Ria some advantage as she pounced from behind.

Billy Bob was quicker that they'd given him credit for. He spun on his heel and knocked the young panther clear across the room. Elaine grimaced when she heard something snap as Ria's body crumpled against the wall. She'd hit so hard, she'd undoubtedly broken some bones.

It was up to Elaine now. If help was coming, it was too damned slow. Molly and Ria were already suffering. Elaine didn't want to be the next one lying on the floor bleeding and broken. She had to do something!

Elaine didn't wait. She didn't give Billy Bob time to recover, spinning around as she entered his range and delivering a highflying roundhouse kick to his head. It was a bruising blow, but the damned werewolf shook it off as if she'd only tapped him. A normal man would be on the floor, but the *were* only gave her a toothy grin.

"Is that all you've got?" It was his turn to taunt her, and Elaine didn't like it.

He swiped at her repeatedly, pushing her back as she scrambled to avoid those flashing claws. She was fully in defensive mode, and knew she couldn't continue to play this game by his rules for long. Eventually, he'd tire her out, then move in for the kill. She couldn't afford to let it go that far.

One thing was clear. His reach was too long. She'd have to jam him up by getting in close. It was a huge risk, but she didn't see any other alternative.

She'd do it smart though, using a spinning move that would present her back to him at the critical moment when she got in range of those wicked claws. Her safety depended on whether she could move fast enough and take him by surprise. If she didn't have either of those two elements, she was a goner.

And she couldn't use any of the standard targets. She'd already kicked the bastard as hard as she could in the temple, and it hadn't even fazed him. She'd have to go for the soft spots, much as it disgusted her. She'd never fought dirty before, but this werewolf left her no alternative.

Cade arrived just in time to see Elaine go on the offensive. She spun much too close to the werewolf, but she moved like lightning, faster than Cade would have believed if he hadn't seen it with his own eyes. She jammed up Billy Bob's long reach and delivered a shot to the groin that made every man in the vicinity wince in sympathy.

Billy Bob dropped to the floor like a stone, clutching his genitals. Cade didn't wait to see any more. He bounded inside, shifting on the run, to go to his mate.

Vaguely he was aware of Charlie, Ray and Steve ripping into the werewolf. He'd be dead within moments if the roars and snarls coming from that direction were any indication.

Cade wrapped Elaine in his arms and held her close.

"God, baby. Are you all right?"

Nothing had ever felt so sweet as having her in his arms, safe and sound.

"I'm okay, Cade, but Ria and Molly are hurt. We have to help them."

Cade gave her a smacking kiss as he pulled back. She was right. They had to tend their wounded and regroup while they had the chance. They'd prevailed above ground, but the safe house's location was no longer a secret. They'd have to flee as quickly as possible.

Elaine's nursing skills came in handy once again as she went first to Ria, who was already sitting up, holding her side as she grimaced in pain. It looked like the Nyx had broken ribs and a possible broken wrist, but otherwise she seemed okay.

"Don't worry, shifters heal fast as long as we don't lose too much blood. That's what weakened Molly. Go to her, Elaine." Ria touched Elaine's wrist as she turned toward the door. "And thanks for everything you've done here. Everyone, including me, underestimated you."

Cade was behind Elaine, blocking her view of the carnage in the center of the room where the growling was beginning to die down. He caught his breath at Ria's words. His cousin was right. Elaine moved like the wind, and she fought well under pressure—better than he ever would have given her credit for. She had the grace and style that could—and had—outmaneuvered a shapeshifter. Even Harris couldn't do that, though the old man had come damned close.

But for all Harris's skill, he couldn't move as sinuously as Elaine. That slinky way she had of executing lightning fast strikes was more than a match for the average shapeshifter—even one half-shifted, which was their most deadly form.

Cade kept himself between Elaine and the center of the room as she scurried quickly to Molly's side. Already injured in the attack on the *dojo*, Molly had been recovering slowly from blood loss. As Ria had said, blood loss was one of the few things that could really slow them down.

"She's unconscious," Elaine reported as she inspected Molly's still form for broken bones and other injuries. Elaine paused at her head, treading lightly around a head wound that seeped blood. "I think she cracked her skull."

"Thank goodness," Cade said in a low voice, drawing a disapproving glance from Elaine.

"That's nothing to be happy about, Cade. She's in very serious condition."

"No, baby, you don't understand. Shifters can heal from broken bones in a matter of a day or two—sometimes even in a few hours. Any swelling or injury will go away as easily. My fear was that she was bleeding out. That's one thing we can't mend so simply. A concussion? No problem. Broken bones? Piece of cake. But blood loss is serious."

Elaine shook her head as she ripped a piece of Molly's ruined jacket into strips and used them to cover and wrap the wound on her head. By the time she was finished, Molly started coming around.

"See? What'd I tell you?" Cade whispered in Elaine's ear as he bent over her shoulder to look into Molly's confused eyes.

"What happened?" Molly's voice was groggy and her pupils didn't match, but Cade wasn't too worried. "Billy Bob!" She stiffened as memory returned. Cade put a firm hand on her shoulder to keep her from rising.

"He's dead." Cade heard Elaine's gasp of surprise, but he couldn't hide the facts from her. "Ria's all right. A few broken ribs and maybe her wrist. Ellie downed Billy Bob, and the guys took care of the rest."

Cade darted a quick look over his shoulder to see that the cleanup had already begun. It wouldn't do to leave a shifter body around for anyone to discover. They always cleaned up their messes. It was the only way to keep their secret.

"You fought Billy Bob?" Molly asked Elaine as they helped her sit up to lean against the wall.

"In half-shift, no less," Cade said when Elaine only nodded.

He was proud of her, yet pissed off at the same time that she'd had to fight a creature twice her size. He hadn't been there to protect her, but she'd managed well on her own. Still, he hated that she'd been put in such a position in the first place. He could only thank the powers that be that she'd had the skill and courage to take care of not only herself, but Ria and Molly as well. He knew Billy Bob wouldn't have left anyone alive.

Molly's gaze tracked to him, and Cade saw her doubt and surprise. Grimly, he nodded to her silent question, and Molly tried to refocus on Elaine.

"Thank the goddess you were here, Elaine." Molly's words echoed Cade's own complicated sentiments. "I'm sorry I doubted you. You're the bravest human I've ever known."

"Thanks," Elaine answered, clearly uneasy with praise.

Steve ambled over in human form. His skin was streaked with blood, but Cade had the satisfaction of knowing it wasn't Steve's. His arm had healed sufficiently by this morning to allow him a comfortable shift to panther form, and he'd fought well against the small contingent of *weres* that had infiltrated the house.

"We need to move," Steve said in a low, urgent voice.

Cade nodded. "Bonnie was closing up when I left her upstairs. She should be down any time now with our packs, clothes and the essentials." As Cade spoke, Ray and Charlie left the room with their grisly burden. Billy Bob's body would never be found.

Ray returned with Bonnie a few moments later. She had packs for everyone that she passed around in a hurry.

Steve had crouched down next to Molly and was talking to her while Elaine had gone back to help Ria to her feet. Cade just watched, standing guard over them as best he could. He was proud of his woman and glad they'd all come out of this fiasco alive, but things had to change soon. They couldn't continue living like this, always on the defensive. They had to root out their enemies at their core. Soon.

Molly was able to stand with Steve's help a few minutes

later, and everyone convened around the pool in the center of the garden room. Cade took advantage of the fountain to clean some of the sweat and blood off his skin. He noticed Elaine averted her eyes since everyone except she and Molly were naked from shifting. His human lover had a lot to learn if she was going to hang out with shifters.

He saw her checking out her knapsack that was stuffed with clothing, courtesy of Bonnie, no doubt. He pulled jeans and a dark shirt out of his pack and dressed quickly as everyone else did the same. When he looked back, Elaine was rolling up cuffs on some dark stretchy pants and a shapeless dark T-shirt, Chuck the cat beside her.

Cade looked over at Bonnie and mouthed the word "thanks". Bonnie had unbent a little toward Elaine but Cade knew as soon as the former Royal Guard heard how a human had saved the Nyx's life, she'd give Elaine the respect she deserved. It ruffled his fur to have his woman thought less of only because she was human.

Bonnie was a hard case when it came to humans. Disappointed by her youthful experiences in a human high school, Bonnie had learned to hate the human bullies who had ganged up on her. Always being the new kid because her parents had been on the run much of her youth, Bonnie had never found a way to fit in. That she'd never turned on some group of nasty kids and shown some teeth or flashed a claw was to her credit, but the lasting bias was a real problem.

It was just as well they'd be going their own ways after this. They needed to disperse to reduce the threat and to figure out which target was the real one—Elaine or the Nyx.

"We'll need to split up," Steve said, echoing Cade's own thoughts.

"I agree." Cade went to stand by Elaine who was looking up now that everyone was mostly covered. Chuck was in her arms, purring as he snuggled into her. "At this point we don't know if they were after Ria or simply got lucky because they followed

Elaine's trail here. Either way, we should split them up."

"You're going with Elaine, of course," Bonnie said in an accusing voice as she rolled her eyes.

"Yes, he is." Ria surprised them all by stepping forward, anger blazing in her gaze. "She saved my life, and for that she deserves to be protected by our best. My *cousin*—" she emphasized their relation in a way she seldom did, "—will see to her safety as I'm sure, she will see to his."

Unspoken was the implied insult that without Cade, Ria would be stuck with the rest of these clowns. Cade had to suppress his amusement. His little cousin was becoming a master of veiled putdowns.

"I've done what I came here to do," Ria continued, stepping in front of Elaine. Ria limped a little and held one wrist close to her aching ribs, but she looked as royal in that moment as Cade had ever seen her. "I wanted a chance to meet you, Elaine, and I'm glad to see my instincts weren't wrong. You're a friend to the Clan, and a friend to me."

Bonnie gasped as Ria leaned forward to kiss Elaine's cheek. Ellie didn't know it, but she'd just been given entrée into the Clan, if she chose to accept it. It seemed Cade had more explaining to do once things quieted down a bit.

"Now..." Ria turned back to the stunned group around her. "I assume the rest of you are coming with me, no?"

Chapter Twelve

The plan was to leave *en masse* from the compromised safe house, then split up once they'd reached a certain point. Only Cade and Charlie Gantry knew their intended final destinations.

Bonnie had unbent enough to give Elaine a modicum of respect. Ria had seen to that, and Elaine was grateful. She didn't like Bonnie's attitude, but even more, she could see it hurt Cade when Bonnie treated her badly.

They left the basement as a group, exiting to the topside garage where Cade's motorcycle waited. The garage was bigger than Elaine remembered. She'd been in such a state when they'd arrived she hadn't even seen the two vehicles besides the bike. Then again, maybe there had only been one when they got there. More than likely the second vehicle had brought Ria, so it wouldn't have been there the day before.

Charlie got into a dark sedan with Steve and Molly while Bonnie and Ray took Ria in their SUV. Elaine and Cade were on the motorcycle, so Chuck the cat went with Ria.

Elaine didn't like to be parted from Chuck, but it wasn't safe to have him on the motorcycle the way they'd done it the night before. Besides, it was daytime and someone was bound to notice an orange tabby cat riding on a motorcycle. Elaine knew it was better not to draw attention.

So she said goodbye to Chuck and gave him to Ria. The traitor seemed to like Ria even more than Gina and paid little attention to Elaine after he found a comfortable spot on the bench seat next to the Nyx.

"I can see why you like this cat. He's a charmer," Ria said with a grin, one hand on Chuck's orange fur.

"He is that," Elaine agreed. "Thanks for keeping an eye on him."

"My pleasure. Elaine," Ria's tone turned solemn. "Good luck on your path. I'll pray to our Lady that She keep you and my cousin safe."

"Blessed Be." Elaine knew the proper response from having hung out with Gina her whole life, and it popped out of her mouth without thought. Ria tilted her head, eyeing Elaine with surprise, but said nothing more as Ray took his place behind the wheel. Elaine backed away and let Bonnie shut the door to the SUV.

Elaine and Cade mounted the bike only after the men had checked it and the vehicles for any trace of tampering. They'd been looking for homing devices, Cade told her and she'd been jolted to remember she was in the middle of a real life cloak and dagger thriller.

One she was more than willing to end. Any time now. She'd had enough of fighting for her life and running like a bat out of hell every other night.

The small convoy exited the row of garages with little fanfare, and Elaine was surprised to see it was still early morning. They joined the flow of traffic from the suburbs along with regular people on their way to work. Elaine felt a pang of regret that her life would never be so uncomplicated again, but by the same token, she wouldn't give up having met Cade for anything.

Having him in her life made all the rest seem almost worthwhile. Though she figured she could do without the constant threat of danger.

The sedan was in the lead, the SUV following close behind and Cade and Elaine brought up the rear of the parade on the motorcycle.

A van came out of nowhere and clipped the back wheel of the bike, sending it spinning into an alleyway. The sedan and the SUV sped out of sight as Elaine and Cade took a wild ride that ended when they smashed into a brick wall. Elaine heard a sickening crunch and when everything stopped spinning, Cade was unconscious with blood gushing down the side of his face.

Elaine tried to crawl over to him, but her world was spinning and strong hands held her back. She had just enough presence of mind to realize she was being manhandled into the back of the van, but she was too out of it to offer any real resistance. She cried out for Cade, but he couldn't respond.

"What about the guy?" Elaine heard one of the men ask the other.

"Leave him, dude. We're supposed to get the girl. He didn't say anything about killing the dude." The casualness of the man's remark cut through her disorientation. "He's dead anyway. Nobody takes a hit like that with no helmet and lives."

Anguish clouded her brain until she realized one of the men was fastening her hands behind her with a cable tie. It hurt like hell and would be impossible to escape. She started to struggle in earnest, but it was already too late.

The blond guy who seemed to like the word "dude" climbed into the driver's seat and put the idling van in gear. The dark haired one bundled her ankles together in one thick hand and used another cable tie to completely immobilize her, then climbed up front to sit in the passenger seat as the van shot forward into traffic.

They'd gone less than a mile when Elaine became aware of an annoying popping sound. The dark haired one was cracking his knuckles repetitively in a way that set her teeth on edge. She decided to give them names since it was unlikely they'd ever introduce themselves.

The blond "dude" with the killer tan became Beach Boy and the dark-haired one immediately became Knuckles in her mind. Elaine had to stifle a laugh, which she realized bordered on the verge of a hysterical. She was losing her mind. She knew it. Naming her captors like it was some sort of game. Something had to be very wrong with her responses if she couldn't even work up the energy to fight back against these two losers.

Elaine looked down at herself and took stock. She was scraped up and bruised, but nothing felt broken or too badly damaged from the wreck. She'd bet anything Cade had controlled the crash in such a way so that he took the brunt of the impact.

She prayed to any deity that would listen for him to be all right. Beach Boy and Knuckles hadn't seemed to realize Cade was a shifter, or they probably would have checked him out better. Elaine hoped Cade hadn't been exaggerating when he'd said shifters could heal fast, but then, he'd been bleeding a lot when she saw him and she remembered him saying blood loss was the one thing that really messed them up.

Thoughts circled around and around in her head, which hadn't really stopped spinning since the crash. Idly she wondered if she hadn't hit her head too, but there was no way to feel for bumps on her skull with her hands tied behind her back.

Elaine settled in to wait. They'd have to stop driving at some point and maybe she'd get some answers then—or, even better, a chance to escape. She'd have to stay sharp and do her best to take advantage of any opportunity.

That was the last thought she remembered before falling unconscious in the back of the van.

Elaine woke when someone splashed cold water in her face. She sputtered and coughed, coming awake with a jolt. She was indoors, propped up on a chair in the center of what looked like a giant, empty warehouse. Her hands were still bound behind her, but it looked like the cable tie on her feet had broken when they moved her and nobody had replaced it. So that was something at least.

Dark windows made black outlines on the far walls, giving her the impression it was night. They'd left the safe house early in the morning and crashed soon after. So where had the day gone?

She realized with a sickening lurch of her stomach that she'd been unconscious through it all. That was the only explanation that made any sense. Her head hurt, and her vision was a little fuzzy. She probably had a concussion.

"Glad you could join us, Ms. Spencer. Sorry for the headache, but you did that yourself when you fell off the motorcycle."

Elaine looked up to find the man who'd first introduced himself as Detective Figueroa standing in front of her. The warehouse was dim with weak pools of light descending from light bulbs in the rafters high above, but she could see enough to make out the walls in the distance. The place was huge.

"I didn't fall off the motorcycle." She was mad as hell at the man who'd hunted her and burned her home. She let the anger carry her through. It was either that or whimper in fear, and she wasn't going to give this bastard the satisfaction. "I was pushed."

"Semantics," he said offhandedly as if it didn't matter in the least that he'd ordered Beach Boy and Knuckles to cause a potentially fatal accident. "All that matters is that you're here, ready for the next part of my plan."

"Your plan? And can I ask what that is? I'm nobody, buddy. I have no idea why you've been hounding me."

"Hounding?" He guffawed. "I like your choice of words, but I'm not the hound in this operation." He opened his hand and a flame sprang to life within it. If she hadn't been sitting down already, Elaine's knees would have given out. She'd seen a lot of weird stuff lately, but this had to take the cake.

"You don't look surprised, my dear."

"Believe me, I'm stunned." The irony was completely lost on him, and Elaine began to suspect the man wasn't necessarily playing with a full deck.

He started juggling with fireballs, moving closer to her seat. When she started to feel the heat of the flames, she steeled herself not to cringe backward. That was what he wanted she knew. He was testing her.

But he went beyond the testing stage right into swimming down the river, crazy as a loon when she smelled the distinct stench of burning hair. That got her to jerk backward, and he finally stopped. The fireballs winked out of existence, and he patted her head like a poodle.

It took her a moment to realize he was patting out the embers of her hair that were still smoldering. A few little wisps had turned crunchy, but vanity was the last thing on her mind. This was life or death.

"You must learn to respect the flame, Elaine. Do that and I'll go easy on you until your rescue arrives."

"Rescue?" What in the world was he talking about?

"Oh, they'll think they're the cavalry riding to your rescue, but in reality it will put them exactly where I want them. One of them in particular, anyway. I've sent a messenger to the cats. I need royal blood for my spell, and they're going to deliver it. For a while I thought it was you, but you didn't smell right."

"I didn't *smell* right?" That explained the sniffing thing back at her apartment.

"Not royal. Not magical enough," he said dismissively. "I was most put out until I realized the cats had grown fond of you. They'll send what I need, or you'll pay the price."

Elaine saw no advantage in trying to deny her knowledge of the shifters. This guy didn't seem to care what she said. He was just using her as a means to an end.

"Not magical *enough*? I'm not magical at all."

Fidelio gave her a strange look, tilting his head to the side as he studied her. "That's not entirely true. You have something... I can't put my finger on what it is, but there is the scent of magic about you. At first I was hopeful it was shifter magic, but alas it is human in nature. Strong, but human, and of a variety I have never before encountered. Odd really, considering how long I've been around, but it's of no importance. Whatever your power, it's not offensive in nature so it's of no concern to me. All I care about is that you are the tool to bring me what I need. I divined it in the flame, and the flame never lies to me."

Elaine tried to figure out what in the world he was talking about. Unless...could it be that psychic phenomena somehow equated to magic in this guy's mind? It was the only thing she could think of. While she wasn't clairvoyant, her grandfather had been incredibly powerful in that regard, as were others in her family. Maybe somehow this nut could pick up on a faint echo of that ability. It was in her genes, even if she didn't have the gift.

More worrisome at the moment was the idea that he was using her as bait.

"They'll never trade their leader for me. I only just met them after you torched my apartment."

"Ah, that was a thing of beauty, was it not? Too bad I was so preoccupied with the flame that I had to send that incompetent dog to catch you. When he let you get away I almost killed him myself, but he had his uses."

"He's dead, you know." She felt some satisfaction in telling Fidelio he'd lost one of his faithful minions, but the mage didn't seem fazed by the news.

"As I expected. He'd ended his usefulness to me anyway. I can't figure why he thought you were one of the royal cats. Do you know why he thought that?"

Elaine shook her head even as she thought of Gina. Maybe the wolf had somehow discovered his target worked at the hospital or lived in the building. Maybe he'd simply picked the wrong woman.

"From all accounts, Billy Bob wasn't very bright."

"Yes, that's true, but like I said, it was an asset at times.

He was easily led into the games that I wanted him to play."

"What for? I still don't understand what you get out of this."

"The magical work of a lifetime, my dear." He moved out of the light, but she could still see him. "With such royal blood supplementing my own magic, there's nothing I can't accomplish."

"Why? What are you trying to do?"

"My flame will pierce the veil and return the founder of my order to this mortal realm. When Elspeth returns, I will rule at her side."

Yep. Nuttier than a fruitcake with delusions of grandeur to boot. But he was in a position of power over her, and Elaine couldn't give in to fear. Fear was one of the few things that could make her say or do something that would drive him to action. And action was to be avoided at all costs while she was trussed up like a Christmas turkey.

"And what happens to me and the shifter afterward? If we agree to help you, will you let us go?"

A flame appeared in the murky darkness. Fidelio was playing with his fireballs again. They bounced from hand to hand and back again.

"Unfortunately not, Ms. Spencer. The royal will die in the course of powering the spell, and you'll make a suitable sacrifice when Elspeth arrives."

Sacrifice? Elaine hoped the shifters had some idea of what they'd be dealing with because this was looking grim. Elaine doubted the cats would actually let Ria come, but Cade was another matter entirely. She knew in her heart that if he survived the wreck, he'd find her. Even if he had to do it by himself, he'd at least try to rescue her.

She only hoped he didn't lose his life in a vain attempt to get her out of this. As it had been the last two times she'd been in danger recently, it was up to her. She had to act. She couldn't wait around depending on a rescue that might never come.

"So you expect me to just sit here quietly and wait for you to kill me?"

Fidelio laughed long and loud, echoing through the empty warehouse. The reverberations of sound gave her chills, but she refused to let him see her fear.

"You can scream, if you like. We're on a deserted dock in the middle of the night. Nobody will hear you except me and my men and we'll find it very amusing, I assure you."

Elaine cursed him as he walked away, but he didn't look back. She followed his movements hoping to learn more about her surroundings. Fidelio met up with Beach Boy and Knuckles near a side door, talked to them a few minutes and sent them on their way—each going in opposite directions.

She heard distant clicking sounds and felt her heart lurch when metal gleamed darkly in their hands. They were armed this time and she feared for anyone that might approach. Beach Boy and Knuckles weren't too bright and she had a feeling they were the type to shoot first and ask questions later.

Elaine began to wiggle her toes and rotate her ankles as discreetly as she could. She'd been stationary so long her muscles were cold and cramping. That wouldn't do if she needed to move quickly.

She didn't know what kind of chance she might have, but she wanted to be ready for anything. At the very least she could run for it if she had to. Elaine didn't think her chances were very good with that kind of lame plan, but it was all she had at the moment with her arms tied behind her back.

Her legs were coming along, and Fidelio had disappeared out the side door so she took the opportunity to raise and lower her legs a few times while still seated. Her thigh muscles protested the movement, but she knew she had to work through the pain if she wanted to be ready to move. If her captors realized she was unfettered and able to walk, none of them seemed to care. At least, nobody came running over to tie her feet again, for which she was grateful.

She made it to the far wall and leaned back against it to get her bearings and take stock of the room behind her. Just the simple act of having her back against a wall gave her comfort. She could see the empty warehouse spread out before her, but nothing else of interest. Beach Boy and Knuckles were out of sight, as was crazy Fidelio.

There was an opening to her left. It was dark and it looked like a short hall that might lead to the outside. Elaine inched toward it certain that at any moment someone would tell her to stop, but nothing happened as she neared the dark rectangle.

She looked toward it, trying to peer into the darkness and that's when she saw it—or rather—*him.* Gleaming silver panther eyes shown in the darkness. They were only open a fraction, giving off the faintest glow. She was pretty sure nobody else could see him, but Cade had to know she was there.

Doing her best not to give him away, she turned slightly, keeping her back to the darkness. The panther's claws could take care of the binding on her wrists with a single swipe.

Cade took her hint, and she felt her arms come loose, but she did her best not to give away the fact that she was now free. She moved her fingers and wrists behind her back, trying to ease the muscles. It was going to hurt like hell when she finally moved her arms in front of her, but she'd save that for when she could no longer hide the fact that she was free from her captors.

Someone had to be watching her, but they thought she couldn't get anywhere. That meant the door had to have been locked. They'd probably expect her to try it, then come back out when she realized she'd been unsuccessful.

Ducking into the hallway, she leaned against the wall and gave a deep sigh before moving her arms forward. She did her best to hide the gasp of pain torn from her throat as she absorbed the agony.

Strong arms came around her. Cade had shifted shape and

reached for her in the darkness. He bent to whisper in her ear, while rubbing her arms, helping relieve the pain.

"Are you all right?"

"Fine. You?"

"I'm good."

"Can he hear us?" she began to panic.

"It's okay. They can't see you in this hallway, and I don't hear the electrical hum of cameras or mics. If we're quiet, they shouldn't be able to hear us."

"It's Figueroa. He's the fire starter. He had two goons snatch me from the crash. He sent them around opposite sides of the building and they were armed, Cade. They had guns."

His strong hands continued to rub her shoulders in soothing circles. "It's okay. Charlie's out there hunting with Steve. They'll take care of anyone they find then work their way to us."

As Cade found his way to his mate, Charlie Gantry called in a favor he'd been keeping in reserve. He had a lot of contacts from his time working among humans, and he used one of them now. It was time for his people to become aware of something Charlie had only just verified for himself earlier that day.

The *Altor Custodis* had gone rotten from the inside, but there were people in the organization Charlie trusted. People he'd worked with and called brother in earlier times who he knew would watch his back if asked. The time had come to ask.

And so, Charlie Gantry, former special operative, called a number he hadn't dialed in years.

When he ended the call, Charlie went hunting. He found the blond man who'd been driving the van easily enough. Charlie took him down soundlessly. An arm around the neck, a quick jerk and the hit and run driver would never speed away again.

Charlie had seen just enough in his rear view mirror to

know who'd been responsible for Cade's take down. Powerless to do anything at the time, Charlie felt satisfaction at being able to at least do this much now. He stalked the perimeter in human form, a bag slung over his shoulder, but he found no others.

This operation had the earmarks of being hastily assembled. That could work in their favor, but Charlie wasn't taking anything for granted.

He found Steve, in panther form, near the body of the second assailant from the van. Charlie threw the bag at the panther's feet.

"Shift and get dressed. We need to move."

Steve didn't argue, shifting form in the blink of an eye and reaching for the clothes in the bag. Charlie had planned ahead, knowing he'd more than likely get a positive response from his call. Now he just had to tie up one last loose end...Steve.

"What's up?" Steve asked as he pulled on his shirt and slipped into lightweight shoes.

"We need to leave."

"Leave? What the hell are you talking about?"

Charlie knew Steve would argue. He only hoped he could talk him around. Otherwise, he'd have to resort to more drastic measures.

"Do you trust me?"

Steve eyed him for a moment before answering. "I trust you."

"Then trust me on this. We need to clear the area. I called in a favor, but they won't show if we're here."

"You'd gamble with Cade's life? Are you sure, man?"

Charlie swallowed hard. He was about ninety percent sure his contact would show, but he wasn't sure about the timing. This could get too close for comfort considering they'd had little lead time.

"I'm sure that if they come in time, Cade will have the

firepower he'll need against a fire mage. I'm also sure that the longer we stand in the way, the more likely it is they won't get to him in time. Make a decision. Trust me or don't. It's your call."

"This is one hell of a time to pull your spy shit on me, Charlie." Steve grumbled as he picked up the bag that had held his clothes and scrunched it up into a ball. He stuffed it in his pocket with angry motions.

"So are you coming quietly?" Charlie thought he knew the answer, but he'd take Steve down if he had to and carry him out of here unconscious.

Steve grit his teeth, but Charlie could tell he'd made the right decision. "Let's go. But know this, if Cade buys it because of you, you're next."

"Heard and understood, Steve. When this is over I'll be sure to inform Cade of your loyalty."

"You'd better pray you have the opportunity to do so."

With that last quip, they both ran for the perimeter and didn't look back.

"Cade, he wants a royal shifter. Something about needing to kill a royal to fuel a crazy spell he wants to perform."

He placed a finger gently over her lips, following it up with a hard kiss. "I heard him. You did a good job of getting him to talk."

"It wasn't hard. The guy is looney tunes. But did you see the fireballs? It's like Ria's vision. A man who can throw fire. He's dangerous, Cade." She pressed her head to his bare chest, reassured momentarily by the steady thrum of his heartbeat.

"That's why I want you to stay here until we clear a path, and then we're going to run like hell."

"I can help, Cade. Don't make me sit on the sidelines and watch you take all the risks. I can't do it. And with my luck, I'll get drawn into the thick of things somehow. That's what always happens since I got mixed up with your people." She had to laugh or she just might cry, and they couldn't afford her having an emotional meltdown at the moment.

Cade held her for a long moment while the silence stretched.

"I hate seeing you in danger," he finally admitted.

"Then you know how I feel when you do it."

"Ellie..." He hesitated. "I love you. I don't care what my people say. I can't deny it anymore."

"Cade, I—"

"When this is over," he cut into her reply. "I want you to be my mate. My wife. The mother of my children. My partner for the rest of our lives. Don't answer now. I want you to think about it." He kissed her hard and fast, sealing his incredible words with a kiss that sent her senses reeling. All too soon, he pulled away.

"Cade—" A sharp noise in the warehouse cut her off.

"I let you have a little leash, but it's time you come out of there, Ms. Spencer," Fidelio shouted harshly from a few yards away. He'd come out of a closer door than the one he'd used to leave.

Cade moved silently to the outside door, returning just as quickly after pulling it shut.

"There's a group of men out there," he reported. "They're armed, and they're not ours. We can't get out that way."

"Then we have to go out and face this guy. All he has to do is send one fireball into this enclosed space, and we're both toast."

Cade nodded in grim agreement. "I'll go first. When I engage him, make a break for the closest door and see if you can get out."

"No way. I'm going out. He doesn't know you're here. I can buy you some time and give you the element of surprise. It's the best chance we've got."

"I'm getting impatient, Elaine," Fidelio called. "Don't make me come after you." Orange light flared from the direction of the warehouse, and Elaine knew Fidelio was playing with his fireballs again, trying to intimidate her. It was working too.

"I'm going first," she insisted as she steeled herself.

After a timeless moment, Cade nodded, agreeing silently to her plan. He was taking a chance, showing his faith in her and it meant more than she could say.

The orange light died down, and she peeked out to see Fidelio reaching for a black box on his belt. It was a walkie-talkie that she'd missed noting before.

"Jorge, Samuel," Fidelio called over the small radio. "Get back in here."

"They won't be coming." Elaine took a deep breath and strode out of the darkened alcove.

"What do you mean? And how did you get free?" Fidelio looked at her in surprise, walking closer, just as she wanted. Just a little closer...

"Oh, come on, Figgy, you said yourself you didn't know what my magic was. Maybe I'm an escape artist." She made an elaborate movement with her hands, trying to distract him while she moved into perfect position. If he reacted the way she figured he'd react, she had to be ready.

Sure enough, the fire started growing to an enormous size in his palm. He was going to throw that sucker, and she wasn't going to be anywhere in the vicinity when he let loose. Not if she could help it.

She timed her move and sent a quick prayer toward heaven that Cade would know what to do with the opening she was about to give him. She waited for the exact millisecond, then tucked her head and dove for all she was worth. She rolled, keeping low as Fidelio let loose with a fireball that hit the spot on the concrete floor where she'd been standing only a second before.

She rolled to her feet in one smooth move and aimed a

knife-handed jab at Fidelio's throat. She wasn't going easy on him. She had to make every move count because this guy could kill her in horrible, painful ways.

A furry black blur raced out of the darkness, tackling Fidelio just as her jab connected, ruining the full effect of her strike, but Cade's claws were much more effective. He had the magic user in his grip as Elaine backed away from the action. She couldn't do anything now. It was up to Cade.

She watched as they tussled, claws and teeth flashing while Cade tried to get a grip on the slippery bastard. But then the worst happened. Fidelio got a hand free and summoned his fire. Cade roared as the magician pressed a hand to his side. Where Fidelio touched, hair singed and skin burned. Cade writhed in agony and in that moment of inattention, Fidelio slipped out from under the big cat.

"Cade! Get out of there!" Elaine shouted, already on the move. She didn't even have to think about her response. Cade was hurt. He mattered more than anything in her life. He mattered more than her life.

In that split second she knew she loved him and would do anything to stay with him. Up to and including bearing the brunt of his people's disdain or living in hiding for the rest of her days. She'd do whatever it took to have him in her life.

But first they had to get out of this alive. Frankly, she didn't think their chances were that great.

Cade limped away, but Fidelio was gathering his flame for the biggest fireball he'd summoned yet. Elaine didn't think. She just reacted, putting her body between Fidelio and Cade. She saw the fireball too late. All she could do was duck with Cade behind her and pray it didn't hurt too bad to be burned alive.

She felt the impact of the flames, the force of the blow making her sway, but oddly she didn't feel any pain. Elaine wondered if that's what it was like to die. Maybe there was a point when something was so painful, you didn't feel anything anymore, but then she realized she wasn't on fire.

Her head came up, and she saw flame all around her. She felt heat on her skin, but it was manageable. It felt like the sun on a hot summer day, but it didn't burn. The flames licked around her, dissipating behind her—well off to her sides. She looked back at Cade and realized whatever she was doing shielded him as well. The fire mage's flames had no effect on her. She had no idea how or why, but she was going to take advantage of this lucky break.

Elaine stood and faced Fidelio. He met her eyes and cursed.

"You're a Shield? A gods damned Protector? That's your power? Of all the—"

Fidelio began to rant, so Elaine tuned him out and went to Cade. She had no idea what Fidelio was talking about, but it sounded like she had a tiny bit of grandpa's magic. The flame bounced away from her, which was a very handy trick just at the moment.

Cade, still in panther form, was already on his feet but Elaine could see he was in pain. There was a handprint singed into his coat on one side of his torso and angry red marks in his hide. He rubbed against her leg as she stood at his side and roared his displeasure with the mage.

Fidelio's rant wound down, and he was watching them with calculating eyes.

"It seems we're at an impasse," Elaine said in her best calm voice though she felt anything but calm at the moment. "Your fire can't hurt me, and there's no way I'll let you kill this panther so you're going to call off your dogs and let us walk out of here. Understand?"

"I think not." Fidelio spit a little when he talked, and she knew he was riding a knife's edge toward insanity. "You're going to leave and forfeit the royal panther in exchange for your life."

"He's not royal." She laughed, trying desperately to forget the fact that he was so closely related to the Nyx. That didn't make him royal, did it? "He's my boyfriend. He came to get me. Do you honestly think they'd send their monarch out to save one measly human life? You've overestimated my importance to them from the beginning."

Fidelio inhaled loudly and for a moment she thought he'd gone completely around the bend. Then she remembered the sniff test. *Please don't let Cade smell royal,* she prayed silently.

"Your boyfriend's been holding out on you, my dear. He's as royal as they come. I have a nose for these things." Fidelio tapped the side of his prodigious proboscis. "He'll do very well for my spell, in fact. Male, in his prime, full of his power and royal. He'll make my job easy. Much better than the scrawny female I was anticipating." Fidelio practically licked his chops in anticipation, but Elaine wasn't about to make his day easy.

"Aren't you forgetting something? You'll have to get through me—and him. Neither of us will go along quietly with your plans. You lose, Figgy. Give up, while you're still alive."

The grind of metal as the giant warehouse door opened made all three of them turn. Elaine could see the shapes of men—a lot of men—filing into the warehouse and her heart sank. She doubted they were shifters. She didn't recognize any of their faces as they walked in and took up positions.

Within moments they were ringed by men, some of whom carried weapons of various kinds. All wore stern expressions on their faces and Elaine feared the balance of power had just shifted in Fidelio's favor.

One of the men stepped forward. He wore some kind of semi-automatic rifle slung casually around his shoulder and looked like he knew damn good and well how to use it. He looked at Fidelio, then over at Elaine and Cade. His expression gave nothing away of his thoughts.

"Step away from the shifter, ma'am."

Chapter Thirteen

"Sorry," Elaine said in a tight voice. "That's the one thing I can't do."

"And why is that, ma'am?" The stranger tilted his head as if considering her words.

"Because if I do..." She hated the sob that welled up and would not be denied. Tears tracked down her face as she knelt at Cade's side. This was it. It was over for them both. She could protect them against Fidelio's fire, but bullets were another matter. All they had to do was shoot her, and Fidelio would have a clear field for whatever sadistic games he wanted to play. "If I do..." She tried again but couldn't speak for the emotion clogging her throat.

"Who the hell are you people?" Fidelio asked, making Elaine and Cade both start in surprise. If they weren't the mage's people, then who were they and what stake did they have in this mess?

"You'll get your turn to speak," the stranger addressed Fidelio with clear annoyance in his tone. "Call me old-fashioned, but I'd like to see to the lady's safety first."

Hope rose so fast, she nearly choked on it. "I am safe. I'm the only thing protecting this shifter from that jerk's fireballs. Speaking of which—" Elaine moved in front of Cade as Fidelio lost patience and started gathering flame again. The men, surprisingly, started chanting in some strange tongue, and Elaine's skin prickled as an unseen force rose in the midst of their circle. More of that velvet-wrapped electricity she'd felt before. Only much stronger this time. "Are you people magicians?"

"No, ma'am, not in the strictest sense, but we do have a few tricks up our sleeves." The stranger's voice rose to be heard over the chanting.

Fidelio let loose with his fireball, but it couldn't penetrate the circle of chanting men. It stopped about three feet in front of them as if it had hit an invisible brick wall. The deflection pattern was different than the way it had parted around Elaine, but the effect was the same. Fidelio's fireballs were harmless against it.

Fidelio aimed another one at Elaine in pure annoyance. It parted over and around her while she shielded Cade from it. The fire starter screamed in rage.

"Now, would someone care to explain this little drama?" the stranger asked, casually leaning one arm on his weapon.

"I don't have to explain anything to you. You're trespassing in a private matter, and I demand you leave now before you stir up forces you'll regret to have awakened!" Fidelio screeched but the stranger looked unimpressed.

"Is that a fact? What kind of forces?" It sounded almost like an idle question, but Elaine saw the flashing intelligence in the stranger's eyes.

"Ancient power the likes of which you cannot even imagine." Fidelio was nearly foaming at the mouth as Cade tugged Elaine's hand with gentle but insistent teeth backward, toward the stranger.

She was inclined to agree with the move. Fidelio was insane, and she knew his plans for them ended in certain death. She had no idea what this circle of men wanted, but so far their leader had seemed both polite and reasonable. She began to hope they might come out of this mess alive.

"Oh, I don't know," the stranger replied casually, "I can imagine quite a bit. Why don't you tell me? Are we talking fourth realm power? Fifth realm? Or maybe one of the forgotten realms?"

Fidelio's eyes sparked red with flames. "You know nothing of what you speak. When I bring Elspeth forth with the royal shifter's blood she will destroy you for daring to interfere in her return."

"Elspeth, eh?" The stranger signaled with one hand to his men and the circle started getting smaller as they moved closer and the chant changed. "Then you're the one we want."

The man raised his weapon and with a giant boom that reverberated through the empty warehouse, he blew a big hole in the center of Fidelio's head.

Just like that, the threat of burning to death in agony was removed. Relief washed over her, but it was tempered by fear. The stranger had killed another being in cold blood. He was so casual about it she feared Fidelio wouldn't be the only one who died that night. Elaine looked away from the gruesome body, burying her face against Cade's soft fur, praying they wouldn't be next.

"It's okay. You can get up, ma'am."

"You're not going to shoot us too, are you?"

The stranger actually cracked a smile when she looked over at him. He shook his head, resting his hand once more on the weapon now slung downward at his side.

"No, ma'am. I reckon you two are the ones we came here to rescue, but our contact didn't have a lot of time to pass on particulars."

"Who are you people?" Elaine asked as she got to her feet. Cade was a warm presence at her side.

The stranger shook his head. "Not here. The guys will handle clean up, but I think maybe you, your furry friend and I should have a little talk somewhere more private."

Elaine was curious, but after the past few days she'd had, she didn't trust anyone anymore except Cade. He was the only one who had been honest with her. He and his people were her friends now. She wouldn't do anything to endanger them and wouldn't trust anybody she didn't know.

"First things first. We had two friends outside. What happened to them?"

The stranger stepped closer, speaking in a low voice. "I sent the other panther home with Charlie. He's my contact. Code Leviathan."

Cade nudged her hand, and she looked down to see him nodding vigorously. He knew the code. She had to trust he knew what they'd be getting into if they went anywhere with this man.

Elaine looked over to where Fidelio had gone down, but the body was gone and so were most of the men who had formed the circle. They moved silently and fast with almost military precision. The chanting had given her pause, but otherwise these folks seemed like some kind of army.

She wished that Cade could shift and tell her she was doing the right thing but she knew the fewer people who saw his face, the better. She was getting pretty good at reading his body language, and he seemed all right with the idea of talking more with the guy who'd just blown Fidelio away, calm as you please.

"All right," she said. "Where do you want us to go?"

The stranger tipped a nonexistent hat to her. "Follow me, ma'am. I have a vehicle waiting."

Cade hopped into the dark SUV and claimed the back seat. His black coat blended in against the dark upholstery so that he seemed like a ghost. Elaine climbed more slowly into the passenger seat, her muscles complaining with every movement. It had been a very long day.

Their rescuer got behind the wheel and started driving. They were clear of the dock area within minutes. Elaine felt better the more distance they put between themselves and that horror show of a warehouse.

"There are some gym clothes in the back if you want to shift," the stranger said to Cade. "My name is Theodore. You can call me Ted."

"I'm Elaine." She left it to Cade to decide whether or not to give Ted his name. "Thanks for helping us back there. It was a Mexican standoff until you showed up."

"I feel like getting a hamburger. How about a diner?" Ted asked, seemingly out of the blue.

"The one on the corner of Main and Mayflower has good steaks," Cade put in as he pulled on some dark grey sweatpants. Elaine was so glad to see him in one piece she reached out through the gap between the front bucket seats and took his hand.

Her heart was in her eyes, but they weren't alone. Cade took her hand and raised it to his lips, letting her know without words he felt the same. He squeezed her fingers once before letting her go and grabbing a sweatshirt that had been behind the driver's seat. It had a U.S. Navy emblem on it and Elaine could only suppose it belonged to Ted. She wasn't surprised. He had a very military bearing.

"You're in the Navy?"

Ted glanced into the rear view mirror at Cade before answering. "Yes, ma'am. Actually, scratch that. I'm not in anymore. I recently retired."

Elaine smiled at him. "Must've been very recent if you're still thinking like you're in."

Ted lifted one corner of his mouth in an answering smile. "Yes, ma'am. It still needs some getting used to, but it was a good decision. I can use my skills in the civilian world now and still work for the good guys."

"You're not *Altor Custodis*, are you? I thought they had a policy of non-interference."

"They do. But lately some of us have broken with that tradition and struck out on our own. We believe the *AC* has been compromised at the highest levels, and we're not willing to sit around and let the bad guys take over. The firebug tonight was just one of many I've had reports of over the past months. They seriously want to bring back Elspeth, an immortal creature known as The Destroyer of Worlds."

"Oh, Lord, I hope you're kidding," Elaine had heard and seen a lot of weird stuff recently but this was by far the weirdest.

"Afraid not, ma'am."

"Please, call me Elaine. When a guy saves your life, I think he's entitled to use your first name."

"All right. Elaine." Ted shot her a small grin that said he would have to practice to remember not to be so formal. "The long and short of it is—the *Venifucus* are back."

"The who?" Elaine asked over Cade's swearing.

"*Venifucus.* An ancient order that according to legend once tried to rule the world. Their figurehead leader was a sorceress named Elspeth who was banished to another realm centuries ago. A new movement has recently come to light that wants to restore her to our world. I'm not really sure if that's even possible but these people are doing everything they can to try, and wreaking havoc in every corner of the globe in their various attempts. Your guy was actually one of the tamer ones, if you can believe it. All hell has been breaking loose in other parts of the country for a while now."

"I've heard rumors," Cade said. His tone was as solemn as she'd ever heard it. "I didn't believe it could be possible but it makes sense with some of the things Fidelio and Billy Bob said."

"Billy Bob?" Ted asked curiously.

"A werewolf who worked for the mage. We took care of him yesterday but our monarch told me he also mentioned bringing Elspeth back."

"Yeah, I heard him say something like that," Elaine recalled. "I thought he was just ranting."

"Ranting, it may well have been," Ted agreed. "But the

intent is real if everything we've observed is taken together and looked at as a whole. They've got multiple groups with multiple talents out there working toward the same goal. My fear—my nightmare—is that one of them will succeed. That's why a number of us have broken away from the *AC.* They don't know it yet, and we don't want to show our hand too early, so I'm trusting you with this information. I need to ask you not to tell anyone how many of us you saw, what we did, or—if you can manage it—that we were there."

"I understand your need for secrecy," Cade admitted. "But I will tell one other. The Nyx needs to know."

"Then you're really not the monarch?" Ted asked, clearly surprised.

"Just a royal cousin," Cade said with a shake of his head.

"And a Royal Guard, I bet."

"You'd win that bet." Cade held Ted's gaze in the rearview mirror. "I tell you this in the spirit of cooperation. Few outside the Guard and my Clan know exactly who or what I am."

"A secret for a secret." Ted nodded. "I can get behind that."

Ted checked his mirrors and pulled into the well-lit parking lot near the diner Cade had selected. For the first time in hours Elaine became aware of her stomach. She hadn't eaten all day and was still woozy from the accident, but she was starving. A burger with all the fixings was in her immediate future.

But she stopped short when Cade opened the car door for her as a startling thought occurred to her. "Cade, we don't have any money!"

Ted strolled around the front of the SUV, no doubt catching the tail end of her words. She was embarrassed as she took Cade's hand and hopped down to the pavement.

"Don't worry," Ted said in his casual way. "I won't let them make you wash dishes. This one's on me."

Elaine looked up at him with a chagrinned smile. "Thanks, Ted. We've...um...sort of had a rough day."

He looked her over and nodded. "You might want to hit the ladies room first and clean up a bit. You have some dried blood on your temple from a cut that clotted just above the hairline."

She tried to touch the area, but it hurt so she left it alone. Cade bent over her inspecting the area, and she was touched by his concern.

"It must have happened when they made us wreck the bike this morning," she mused. "I was unconscious most of the day and I've been feeling a little woozy since I woke up, but I think at this point it's mostly from hunger."

Cade's eyes narrowed as he held her gaze. He was probably checking her pupils, she realized. "All right. Food first, then we'll see how you're feeling. If we have to, I know a doctor we can wake up to check your head. Are you hurt anywhere else, baby?"

"No. You saw the rest. My arms and legs are sore from being tied, but I'll be okay. How about your burn?"

In answer Cade lifted the side of the sweatshirt. The burn mark was already fading. She traced it with a finger.

"That's amazing," she breathed. "I was so upset when I thought it would leave a permanent mark."

"I told you we heal fast. By tomorrow you'll never even know it was there. Good as new."

"That's one ability I wish I had," Ted piped in, reminding them of his presence.

"With the way my life has been going recently," Elaine agreed, "I could use it too."

"It comes in handy every once in a while. That's for sure." Cade tucked Elaine under his arm as they walked together toward the entrance of the diner.

They went in, and Cade escorted her to the rear of the building where the restrooms were located. Ted grabbed a booth facing the door and started looking over the menu.

"Go on in and freshen up. I'll be right here standing guard.

Call out if you need me."

Elaine reached up and gave him a quick kiss, a promise of more once they were alone and had time to sort out their personal matters. She knew things had changed—for her at least—when they'd faced the danger of Fidelio together. He'd said some things too, that gave her hope, but they needed time alone to talk it out and just hold each other.

She drew away and went into the ladies room. They'd have time to discuss their future as soon as they got this other business out of the way. She looked forward to it.

Chapter Fourteen

Cade signaled one of the waiters and a minute later saw the man on the phone. He was calling the owner of the diner, a lion shifter named Rich. If Cade needed backup, the lion and his Pride would provide it. Most of the big cat shifters tended to stick together when necessary, and Rich owed Cade a favor or two.

Elaine came out of the bathroom looking much neater. He gave her a peck on the cheek, unobtrusively checking the extent of the gash on her head. It wasn't as bad as he feared, but he'd keep a close eye on her tonight and he'd damned well wake the doctor if she showed any signs of more serious injury.

They walked together to the booth Ted had chosen. Cade was pleased by its location out of sight of most of the windows and facing the door. Easily defensible, should it become necessary.

Cade let Elaine slide into the booth first, closest to the wall. He wasn't letting her get too far away from him ever again. They'd have to sort some things out once they were alone, but he had high hopes after the things they'd both said that night. She'd learn soon what it meant to be a shifter's mate. It'd be his pleasure to teach her about it, for the rest of their lives.

"So, you're a Shield," Ted led off the conversation by asking Elaine. She looked blankly at him, bless her heart.

"That's what Fidelio said, but I have no idea what it really means except for the fire not hitting me."

"You didn't know?" Ted seemed surprised.

Elaine shook her head. "I thought I was toast when he hit me with that fireball. You could've knocked me over with a feather when it went around me and Cade, thank goodness."

Ted sat back and looked at her. "I didn't realize you were new to this. Charlie didn't have time to tell me much about what was going on. He only said the *Venifucus* were probably involved and some innocents would be paying the ultimate price if I didn't get my ass down to the dock in time. I didn't realize just *how* innocent."

"I didn't even know about shifters until about a week ago," she admitted, and Cade noticed she carefully didn't mention her best friend. He liked her loyalty and her ability to keep a secret. That would come in handy in their future together.

Ted whistled between his teeth, the noise grating on Cade's sensitive ears but he didn't flinch. He'd trained himself against reacting to things humans would take for granted. He'd had to in order to pass in human society. It was something they taught youngsters and something he'd pass on to his own cubs—once he and Ellie started having them.

But he had to stop daydreaming. They'd get to it soon enough. Business first. That had always been his mantra, but he was having a hell of a hard time sticking to business with Elaine's soft body and alluring scent right beside him.

"Shields—sometimes called Protectors, among other things—have the innate ability to hide the magic of anyone they're near. For example, if a Sensitive—someone who can sense magic—came over here, they'd think Cade was completely non-magical because your presence masks his inner magic." Cade finally understood why the *tigre blanche* had been able to hide in plain sight for so long. Her best friend was shielding her, whether either of them realized it or not. "You can also deflect magic away from you, like you did with the fireball," Ted went on. "Though I've never seen such a powerful Shield as the one you possess. You're damned lucky you were that strong, Elaine.

Otherwise, you really would have been toast. That guy was the strongest fire mage I've ever seen."

"Seen many, have you?" Cade challenged.

"A dozen or so, actually." Ted surprised him by answering. "They seem to be more common in military circles because they're naturally drawn to explosives."

The waiter came over and took their orders, leaving behind tall glasses of ice water. Cade received a subtle signal that the Pride leader was on alert. Cade looked around and saw Rich, the owner, emerge from the kitchen as casual as could be. Only Cade realized the lion Alpha was watching everything that transpired with discerning eyes.

"I'm grateful for your intervention, Ted, if I haven't said it before." Cade raised his glass to the man. "Thanks."

"Glad we could help. As a matter of fact…" Ted tapped his glass, seeming unsure how to proceed. "That's the main reason I wanted to talk to you privately. For a while now I've believed that if we're going to succeed in keeping our world safe, we're going to have to start working together. Humans, magic users, shifters, hell, even bloodletters if we can find any reasonable ones." Ted ran one hand through his spiky blond hair. "What I'm proposing is an alliance."

"I can't speak for the Nyx," Cade said after considering the idea. "But I'll talk to her. If she agrees, I'll talk to some of the others, if possible. The Nyx only speaks for *pantera noir*. You realize that, right?"

"I'll admit I'm not completely up on how your Clans and Packs are organized, but I get the general idea."

"My cousin leads the Clan as Nyx, but my father is Alpha of our familial Pride. Lots of Prides make up a Clan and some Clans have more Prides than others." Cade decided this was safe enough information to pass along as a show of good faith. If this guy really was former *Altor Custodis*, he probably knew or suspected a lot of this already. "The Nyx can interface with the other Clan monarchs, but it'll be up to each of them whether or not they want to form an alliance. It could take some time to organize. We're not used to the idea of working with humans. Hell, we're not even used to the idea of mating with humans, but times are a-changin' and they're going to have to get over it."

"So you're mated?" Ted looked from Cade to Elaine and back.

"Not officially, but after tonight that's one of the things we'll be sorting out." Cade put his arm around Elaine, gratified when she moved into him, not denying his words or his possessive touch. She looked worn out and wasn't talking much, which he took as a sign of her bone-deep fatigue.

"Congratulations," Ted said, and Cade felt the genuine good wishes behind the man's words. "I'm doubly glad I got there in time tonight. Everyone deserves a shot at happiness."

"Why, Ted," Elaine said with a sleepy grin as the food arrived. "I didn't know you were a romantic."

The ex-Navy man actually blushed and ducked his head as he pretended undue interest in his burger. Cade winked at Elaine, glad to see the spark of amusement in her eyes. He took an extra moment to check her pupils, relieved to see they looked normal. She'd be all right. She just needed a few solid hours of sleep to get her strength back. Food first, then sleep, as soon as he could get her someplace safe to do it.

Cade dug in to his steak and eggs, needing the protein to aid his body in recovering from the abuse it had been dealt that day. Being knocked unconscious by his abrupt contact with a brick wall had been the worst of his injuries but by no means the only one he'd suffered. His body's repair systems had been working overtime, and he needed to refuel.

"I've seen a lot of the bad side of the world," Ted said to Elaine after the silence had stretched. "It's good to see a happy ending once in a while to sort of balance things out. For what it's worth, I hope things work out for you two."

Elaine reached across the table to put her hand on Ted's

wrist, so he'd meet her eyes. Cade suppressed the instinctive growl that rose in his throat at seeing his woman touch another male. The panther wanted to rip and tear and claim its mate but the man knew better in this instance. Of course, the man was as eager for the claiming part as the panther, so on that they both agreed. Soon, he promised his cat. Very soon.

"You're a good man, Ted, and I can't thank you enough for the second chance you've given me. Despite the ugliness that came before, the end result is a good thing." Elaine pulled her hand back, and Cade relaxed, a fraction off high alert. "If I have anything to say about it, this will only be the beginning of humans and shifters working together. What do you think, Cade?" She turned to him, her eyes flashing, daring him to join her in the bold pronouncement.

"I think..." He chose his words carefully. He had to secure one last promise from Ted before they adjourned this meeting. "As far as the world is concerned, you, my dear, are strictly human. Your ability is something we can use to our advantage." He shot Ted a questioning glance and was gratified to see understanding in the man's expression. "As far as human-shifter cooperation, I can't speak for all of my kind, but I'll do my part to make it happen."

"That's good enough for me," Ted said, finishing up his burger and wiping his chin with a napkin. "As far as Elaine's talent goes, I agree. I'll keep it under wraps as much as possible. My team saw what happened, but they don't know who you are and we'll keep it that way for now. They all know enough not to talk about anything that we do when we get together, but I'll give them a gentle reminder."

"We'd appreciate it." Cade reached over and shook the man's hand as he rose and threw two twenties on the table.

"I'm outta here. I suspect you'll be able to make it back to your people from here, right?"

Ted shot a knowing glance to the counter where Rich, the owner, sat nursing a cup of coffee while he talked with a few of the wait staff. All were members of his Pride and on alert though it was hard to tell if you weren't a shifter. Apparently Ted recognized the signs, which told Cade the man had either spent a lot of time around shifters or been well trained by someone who had.

"Yeah, we'll get a ride," Cade acknowledged, standing also. It was time to take his mate home. "Thanks for everything, Ted. We owe you."

"Don't worry. Some day I plan to collect." Ted shook Elaine's hand while Cade watched. This time he wasn't as successful repressing the growl while another man touched his woman, but he respected Ted for not backing down. He lifted Elaine's hand for a gentlemanly kiss and let her go with a wink in Cade's direction. The man really did like tempting fate, it seemed.

Cade pulled Elaine to him for a hug as they watched Ted leave. One of the waiters went out to smoke a cigarette, and Cade knew Ted would be watched at least until he cleared the immediate area. Cade tugged Elaine along with him toward where Rich held court at the counter. It was time to introduce his woman and make their way home.

Rich gave him the once over as Cade stood before the Pride Alpha. They were friends from way back, and Cade respected the older man who had been a Royal Guard in his day. He'd been one of those who'd trained Cade as a matter of fact, and they were good friends.

"Would you mind telling me why I had to get up in the middle of the night and come down here to babysit you sharing a meal with this beautiful girl and an ex-Navy SEAL?"

"Navy SEAL? How do you know?" Cade wasn't surprised to hear the news. Ted had skills above and beyond those of a regular seaman, and he took killing way too casually.

Rich pointed to a big kid standing by the kitchen door. "My son's buddy is home on leave from Coronado. He's a tiger," Rich shrugged. "You know how they love the water." A signal from the Pride Alpha brought the younger man forward.

"This is Lenny, my oldest son's best friend. Lenny, tell them what you told me." Rich instructed.

"Is she cool?" The young man looked quickly at Elaine and back to the Pride Alpha.

Rich looked at Cade, waiting for an answer.

"Cooler than you can even imagine." Cade pulled her close to his side and placed a kiss on top of her head. He saw Rich's eyes flare.

"Is it serious?" Rich eyed Elaine in a whole new way.

Cade nodded. "We're working on it. She's met my family and she knows about us, so you can speak freely. She's proven herself trustworthy many times over. Elaine..." Cade could feel the tension in her shoulders as he made the introductions. "This is Rich. He used to have my job."

"It's a pleasure to meet you, Alpha." Cade was proud she'd remembered that little detail, which no doubt impressed the lion. "I'd wondered why Cade chose this diner. It all makes sense now. Thanks for watching our backs."

"She's quick," Rich complimented her as he smiled. He still looked a little puzzled, but was clearly warming to Elaine. Cade took it as a good sign. Rich turned back to Lenny, prodding him to continue.

"I've seen your friend around the base at Coronado, but we've never been introduced. In fact, the instructors discourage us from asking questions or seeking out any of the Ghost Team members that occasionally make an appearance on base."

"Ghost Team?" Elaine asked.

"Yes, ma'am. It's not official and it'll never be acknowledged, but we've all heard rumors of a top secret spec ops Team. Your friend is definitely a SEAL and more than likely a Ghost. Rumor has it one of the Ghosts just retired for medical reasons—a bum knee was the most popular rumor. A few of my buddies are trying unofficially for the vacancy."

Cade was interested in hearing more, but one look at Elaine told him she was fading fast. She'd put in one hell of a day and didn't have a shifter's recuperative powers.

"How long will you be home, Lenny?" Cade asked the young tiger.

"Another week, sir."

"Good. I'll look you up in a day or two if that's all right. I need to know everything you can dig up—if you can dig up any more. Our new friend told us his name was Theodore, if that helps. He goes by Ted."

"Yes it does help, sir. I'll make a few calls and see if anybody has heard anything."

"Good man. I'll be in touch."

Lenny left with a nod to the lion Alpha.

"Do you have a secure phone for me?" Cade knew he didn't have to go into specifics of what he needed. Rich had been one of the men who had written the modern handbook for Royal Guards. He'd know, and better yet, he'd be prepared.

Rich didn't let him down, handing him a brand new prepaid cell phone. "I activated it before I came down here. It's clean and untraceable back to any of us."

"Excellent." Cade took the phone and checked it over as he knew Rich would expect. Royal Guards were taught to never take anything for granted.

"You can use my office in back if you want some privacy."

Cade declined the generous offer. Few people were ever invited to make use of a lion's private den.

"If you'll just entertain Elaine for a while, I'll make my calls from here. She's got a slight concussion, I think."

Rich's concern at that news would have been laughable if it wasn't so touching. Rich was a gentle giant with a soft spot for women of all ages and descriptions. He charmed grandmas and toddlers alike with his easy manner. Cade knew she'd be safe with him. The panther inside didn't see Rich as a threat because Rich was a happily mated man.

Cade walked just out of listening range even for sharp shifter ears. He kept Elaine in his sight, glad to see her perking up a bit under Rich's supervision. The big lion had even talked her into letting him take a look at her head wound. He had a clean, wet dishcloth and some of his staff was already making ice packs out of plastic bags for her sore arms. She had him eating out of her hand, but Cade figured she deserved to be spoiled. He would do the same thing, once he got her home.

Cade called Charlie first, knowing the Escort would have the ability to check their phone connection from his end, just to be sure. Even retired Royal Guards could slip up from time to time, but Cade needn't have worried. Charlie cleared the line and proceeded to fill him in on his part in tonight's adventure.

"Everyone's safe. I take it my friend made an appearance."

"He just left. Interesting man, your friend." Cade watched Elaine being fussed over by the lion. She looked happy, but the poor thing was almost dead on her feet. "He was very helpful."

"I'm glad. I got Steve out of there. It was a condition of my friend's arrival. He wanted as few witnesses as possible."

"I can understand that. He took care of Fidelio. We won't have to worry about him ever again, but there are some things we ought to talk about just the same."

"I agree. Hang on a sec, your cousin wants to say hello."

Cade was relieved to hear Ria's voice come on the line. She was well, as were the rest of the people who'd been in the compromised safe house.

"How's Elaine?" she asked immediately.

"What? No concern for my health?" Cade couldn't resist teasing her. "She's okay. Just banged up and maybe a slight concussion from this morning's wreck, but I think she's through the worst of it. We've eaten, and now I'm taking her home for a good long sleep. I just wanted to check in and make sure everyone was all right before we take some downtime."

"You've earned it. Take all the time you need. If Charlie's

right, the danger is past."

"I wouldn't ease up on the precautions just yet. We got the firebug, but there might have been others pulling his strings. I got the distinct impression he was flying solo today. His target was definitely Ellie. That doesn't jive with the attack on the *dojo*. She was just an innocent bystander at that first attack."

Ria was silent a moment as she absorbed the news. "I hate to say it, but you're right. When they hit the *dojo*, it was because they knew I'd be there. They only started tracking Elaine after she walked in on us."

"I'm glad you see the distinction. Elaine's probably in the clear now, but you aren't, so you need to take precautions."

"I hear and obey, Alpha." Ria tried to joke but Cade knew living on the run, constantly in hiding, was starting to take a toll on her.

"Elaine needs sleep in a bad way. So do I. We'll be off the radar for at least eighteen hours. You have my new number. Call if you need me. Otherwise, expect to see us tomorrow night. We have some interesting things to discuss about Charlie's friend. Get Charlie to fill you in on the basics if you can. I'll give you the details when I see you. This is important stuff, cousin. We may be facing things we never could have expected, and we may need to ally ourselves with people we never could have imagined."

"You've got me curious."

"No surprise there, you were born curious, kitten." Cade signed off soon thereafter and went to collect his mate.

Rich tossed him the keys to one of the Pride's vehicles and handed him a wad of cash.

"I'll return the car in a day or two and reimburse you for this," Cade indicated the pocket on his borrowed sweat pants into which he'd stuffed the money. "I owe you big time for your assistance here tonight. The situation is graver than you know. If all proceeds as I think it will, that man you saw here tonight may become one of our strongest allies."

"A human? I know he's a SEAL, but he's still human. What can he possibly help us with?"

"There's more going on here than I can tell you now." Cade took a pointed look around the room. There were too many curious ears present to discuss such a sensitive subject. "We took care of one threat tonight, but an even bigger one looms on the horizon. An ancient one that we thought long vanquished. She has allies of her own here that will do anything to bring her back."

"You can't mean—" Rich was alarmed, as he should be.

"Elspeth."

The single word was all Cade needed to impress upon the Alpha the seriousness of their predicament. All shifters knew the legends from ancient times when the supernatural races had banded together to fight a great war against Elspeth's forces.

Rich's mouth firmed into a thin, grim line. "I'll look forward to talking with you more about this after you've recovered."

"Look for me the day after tomorrow."

"Come to the house." Rich issued the rare invitation to his lair, and Cade was grateful the Alpha was taking this so seriously. In all likelihood, Rich's Pride would be one of the first to sign on as an ally with the *pantera noir* Clan and the Ghost, Ted.

Elaine was so tired when Cade led her in to an uptown apartment that she barely looked around before heading to the bathroom for a quick shower. After that, it was straight to bed. She couldn't keep her eyes open any longer. She was only vaguely aware of Cade climbing into bed beside her before she was unconscious.

Golden light streamed in through the cracks in the Venetian blinds hours later. Elaine stretched, glad to find the pounding in her head had subsided. She felt much better, though her arms still ached from being tied behind her back so long the day before.

Cade slid onto the bed next to her, rubbing his hands over her bare shoulders as she blinked up at him. He wore a black silk robe that made him look very Lord-of-the-Manor. She liked the look on him. He was sexier than all get out.

"Still sore?" His low voice rumbled through her, waking her fully.

"How'd you know?" She smiled at his concern.

"You're moving stiffly, and you winced when you raised you arms." He moved off the bed just when she'd been about to drag him down and pounce on him. "I ran you a bath. The water's hot, and it'll feel good on your muscles. Come on."

Now that sounded like heaven. Pouncing on Cade could wait until after the bath, she decided.

The tub wasn't as big as the Jacuzzi in the safe house so Elaine had to bathe alone. Cade brought her hot tea as she soaked, and he fed her tidbits of fruit with his fingers. She felt like a spoiled Roman empress at his tender treatment. There was only one thing missing from this picture.

"Did Ria mention how my cat is doing?"

"Chuck didn't come up in conversation, but I'm sure he's being spoiled rotten. I think you might have noticed house cats generally like us. And I know my cousin likes Chuck. She's probably feeding him tuna at every meal. He'll be fat by the time you get him back."

Elaine laughed at Cade's exaggeration and realized there were probably no better people to take care of Chuck than a group of cat shifters.

"So what did I miss while I was dead to the world?"

"Not much. I had some groceries delivered so we could eat, and clothes for you. Steve called to check in, but it was nothing important. He just wanted to touch base. He felt bad about leaving us last night but Charlie insisted. Nobody says no to Charlie when he insists." Cade rolled his eyes. "Everybody's safe and tucked away for now. I realized last night that while we neutralized the threat to you, the attack on the *dojo* had nothing to do with you, really. Ria's still in danger, so we're all on alert."

"But Fidelio started the fires, so at least that threat is gone."

"True, but there are more people involved. There've got to be. Fidelio was more or less on his own in going after you. Otherwise he would have had a lot more backup. I think he saw you as a target of opportunity to advance his own private agenda. The threat to Ria exists. They may have been set back by the loss of their fire mage, but they're still out there."

"Damn." Elaine contemplated the situation while her muscles soaked up the warmth of the water. She was beginning to feel like her old self again. Cade's nearness warmed her from the inside while the hot water took care of the outside.

She was submerged to her neck in the hot water so her shoulders could soak. Cade picked up a bath sponge and trailed it down her neck. It felt so good she tilted to give him better access.

"Did you mean what you said before? In that hallway?" The words popped out before she could sensor herself. She'd been in a whirlwind of confusion since the accident but his hastily spoken words stood out in her mind.

Cade stilled, dropping the bath sponge. When she opened her eyes, she was almost afraid what she might see.

He trailed his fingers over her neck this time, pausing at the place where he'd left his mark before. It was fading, she knew from seeing herself in the mirror before. Did he really want to renew them—permanently this time?

Lord, she hoped so. She was crazy about this man, and she didn't want to live without him.

"Every word." He leaned down to kiss her as his fingers tightened over the fading marks. "I love you, Ellie. I want you for my mate. The question is—" he drew back to study her, "—do you want me?"

Elaine launched herself out of the water and into his arms. She was getting him wet but she couldn't bring herself to care at the moment.

"Yes, Cade. Of course I want you. I love you too!"

Cade lifted her clear of the water and snagged a towel from a shelf above the toilet. He swiped at her wet skin, getting rid of the worst of the damp, but it was by no means a thorough job.

He didn't seem to care as he lifted her in his arms and carried her into the bedroom. He lowered her to the bed and lay next to her, side by side, staring deep into her eyes.

"This time it's forever, El. I'll never let you go again. Be sure."

"I've never been surer of anything in my life, Cade. You're it for me. Forever."

He growled as he moved closer. "Goddess knows I love you, Ellie. I can't wait to make you mine."

"Then don't wait. I want my mating mark." Her demand startled a laugh out of him as she'd intended. His hand cupped her cheek, and his eyes glowed briefly with power.

"My greedy kitten wants it all, doesn't she?" She loved the growl in his voice as he teased her.

"And you're just the man to give it to me." She pulled him in for a tempestuous kiss that got them both breathing hard.

She pushed at the robe he wore, loving the feel of warm silk against her palms, but it had to go. She untied the belt and the silk parted, much to her satisfaction as she touched him all over. She lifted one knee up over his hip. She wanted him, and she didn't want to wait. With Cade, it felt like she was always at the boiling point within moments of his first touch.

"Easy, baby," he whispered. "I've got you." His big hand wrapped around her thigh, raising it higher on his body so he could fit himself to her, rubbing against her, driving her wild.

"Cade!" He sucked one nipple into his talented mouth, making her writhe.

She cried out again when he lowered one hand over the curve of her bottom, his long fingers teasing her lower, lower, to finally touch the moist center of her. It took little more than that to send her into a lovely climax, keening his name as he rocked her against him and she knew they were just getting started.

"Baby, you're hot." Cade smiled at her as she gasped for air. He took her by surprise, rolling them over until she was on her stomach. She whimpered when he lifted her hips until she was resting on her knees. He stuffed a couple of pillows under her stomach to help support her, and she knew he was just getting warmed up.

"Are you okay, kitten? Comfortable?"

"You take such good care of me, Cade." Her thoughts drifted in a sea of excited bliss that turned her bones to jello.

His low chuckle warmed her. "Hold that thought, my love. It's time we ratcheted this up a notch."

Higher? She didn't know if she could take it, but that last exquisite completion had left her hungry for more. She perked up as he moved behind her.

His fingers roamed over her body and soothed her into a deep languor. When he smacked her bottom with a loving spank, she yelped.

"You sleeping on me, baby? Wake up."

"I'm awake, you fiend. Did you just *spank* me?"

A husky chuckle filled the air, rolling over her body like a caress.

"You liked it?"

She wasn't completely sure, so she thought about it for a minute. "I'll get back to you on that."

"Be sure you do." His voice was nearer now as a wet tongue rasped its way up her spine, making her wriggle in delight. He knew how to touch her to bring her pleasure. "I don't think I can wait much longer, El. I wanted this to be perfect for you."

"It is perfect. Being with you is always the best there ever was or ever will be. Take me, Cade. Make me your mate."

He needed no further urging. Seating himself behind her, he joined with her in the most basic way, filling her body as he nearly draped himself over her back. He held most of his weight off her with strong arms that bracketed her shoulders, but she loved the feel of him against her in this new and exciting way.

She'd never been so completely overwhelmed by a man in her life and knew she never would. Cade was it. Forever.

He rocked them toward ecstasy, increasing his pace with each leap of her pulse. He wasn't rough but this kind of claiming was complete and utterly decadent. He moved faster as the promise of pleasure loomed. She was almost there.

And then he struck.

The pain in her shoulder was both terrible and tantalizing. Normally not a fan of pain in any format, Elaine knew there was something utterly different about this kind of pain. It was tempered somehow by Cade's magnificent presence. For just a moment, she felt possessed by both the man and the beast, working in tandem through Cade's gorgeous body. She heard the cat roar in her mind and felt his teeth break her skin, his tongue lap at her blood, bringing peace and renewed sexual hunger every time he touched her.

Elaine was almost too far gone to realize Cade was right there with her, holding her, grounding her one every level throughout the orgasmic ordeal. He was hers as she was his. Forever.

He took exquisite care of her after they'd both managed to catch their breath. Cade wrapped her in his arms and held her while they both shuddered. It was, without a doubt, the most intense moment of her life to date. She loved him so much. It was hard to believe he was finally hers. She loved his sense of humor and his protective side. She loved everything about him.

She wanted to feel his laughter once more before they succumbed to the bliss.

"I don't know why they call it doggy style." She yawned as satisfaction made her drowsy. "Cats seem pretty good at it too."

As she wanted, Cade's laughter followed her into sleep.

Chapter Fifteen

"Where are we anyway?" Elaine looked around at the apartment. Cade had made breakfast in the kitchenette, and they ate at the large dining table that could double as a decent sized work space.

"It's a place we keep for clients or visitors from out of town."

"Clients? Of what?"

"The business. What? You thought being a panther paid really well all on its own?" Cade chuckled, and she joined in. "How could my mate not know I'm the CEO of one of the most successful publishing companies in this burg?"

"You have an actual job?" She was dumbfounded. Since she'd known him, they'd been in crisis mode and she'd never thought about how he usually spent his days.

"Well, I don't go in to the office as much as I used to. Things pretty much run themselves at this point, which is good because it's the only reason I can spend so much time with Ria. But I planned it that way—at least hoped it would work out that way—or I wouldn't have suggested to my father that they send her here. She wanted to go to school downtown, but I'm not sure it'll even be possible for her to stay here. Not unless we can make it safe for her."

"So you live here, then."

"Outside of town in the burbs. I have a large estate with room to roam the grounds when I feel like it. I wanted Ria to live there with me, but she wanted an apartment downtown near the university. That's what we were talking to Harris about when you arrived at the *dojo*. But there's no way I'm letting her live on her own now. Not until I'm absolutely certain she'll be safe. For now, everyone's holed up at my place. It was too far for us to drive after everything we'd been through, and I knew the guest suite was free this week, so I brought us here instead. Plus, I wanted some time alone with you, El." He leaned in to kiss her cheek.

"So," Elaine smiled at him when he pulled back. "Panther Publishing. That's you?"

His grin was downright sinful. "What gave me away?"

"Is everyone who works for you a shifter?"

"Not everyone, but a large percentage are. As a race, we tend to have a creative streak and a lot of us find enjoyment in literature or the arts. Panther Publishing is a subsidiary of Wild Cat Investments. The parent company is a conglomerate that has its paws in all kinds of enterprises. One of their main missions is to provide startup capital and expertise for the rest of us. It's something the elders put in place about fifty years ago, and it's been a boon to us. I bet we could even find you a job as a nurse for one of our shifter medical practices, if you wanted to work. Skilled medical help is sometimes hard for us to find since we have to be careful who we let treat us."

"You've got this all figured out, haven't you?" She climbed over his lap and wrapped her arms around his neck.

"Just trying to keep my mate happy. By the way…" He moved the collar of the robe aside to touch the incredibly tender spot on her neck. "My mark looks absolutely stunning on you, baby."

She shivered as his fingers danced over her skin. Just like that, she was ready for him again. Elaine was coming to find that when it came to Cade, she was downright easy.

"I was thinking." She tugged at the black silk tie holding his sexy robe closed. He caught on to her game and untied the smaller red robe he'd had delivered for her.

"What were you thinking about, baby?"

"I was wondering." She pushed the robe off his shoulders as he did the same for her. His hands went to her breasts, touching her in a way guaranteed to send her into orbit. She fought the response, needing to say what was on her mind, but it was hard. And so was he. She stroked him, gaining his attention once more. "I was wondering if I could return the favor of biting you." He jumped in her hand, and his eyes glowed. She forged ahead, uncertain. "I mean, it probably wouldn't make the lasting mark since I don't have those shifter enzymes in me, but I could try. If you want."

"I want what you want, El. Always." He leaned forward to place a gentle kiss on her lips, then drew back. "But if you want to try, I'm all for it. You can bite me anytime you like. It makes me want to roar, as you probably have already realized."

She was relieved by his words and the devilish expression on his handsome face. He was more man that she'd ever expected and everything she'd ever wanted. Although he could get bossy and Alpha on her, he was also considerate, kind and protective. As she was of him. This would work. They'd make it work.

She ran her fingers over him again, lingering longer this time, ready to put her plan into action. She'd thought about nothing else since waking in his arms. She wanted to return the claim that would mean the most to him—the claim his people would recognize. It might not be exactly what a shifter mate would have given him, but she'd try to make it close. She wanted to do this for him—and for herself as well.

Something inside her craved it, though she'd never felt this kind of animalistic urge before. She began to suspect mating with a shifter had changed her on some basic level and so far, she liked the changes.

Cade caressed her, claiming her mouth for a lingering kiss as she touched him, arousing them both. She was so ready for this, so eager to please him. Elaine lifted up and positioned him under her, lowering herself onto him so she could control where they went from here. She'd give him the ride of his life.

She started slow and the pace built rapidly. Cade helped, his strong arms supporting her as she moved on him. He licked at her skin, each touch of his tongue sending her closer to bliss. But this wasn't about her. She had to focus.

Elaine moved into position, the mere act of kissing his neck driving her higher. When he started to purr, his chest vibrating against hers, she knew this was going to be one of the most amazing experiences of her life. She licked along the tense cords of his neck and searched for just the right spot. It had to be perfect if he was going to wear her mark even for a day or two.

She was desperately in need when she finally bit him, her orgasm crashing through her at the exact moment she tasted the faintest hint of blood. She hadn't thought she could actually do it, but with the added push of climax, she'd managed to break his skin the tiniest bit.

Cade roared, nearly deafening her with the panther's voice in his human form, climaxing with her in a maelstrom of pleasure that left them both wrung out and gasping for air.

Elaine relaxed her jaw but kept her mouth over the small wound, licking his salty skin as the vibrations in her body went on and on. At length, she slumped against him and he cradled her against his chest. They didn't move for a long time, and she could tell he'd been as profoundly affected as she by the fine tremor of his arms around her.

"I love you, Cade," she whispered, kissing his chest.

"You are my perfect mate, Ellie."

The touching compliment followed her into sleep as she dozed against him.

Elaine woke a few hours later in the bed. Cade had taken care of her while she slept, cleaning her up and tucking her in and she hadn't even been aware of it. He really was the most amazing man.

Her mate.

She repeated it a few times, loving the sound of those words.

They'd mated in the eyes of his people, but her family was going to want an old fashioned wedding. She chewed her bottom lip, wondering how to go about this. The direct approach had always been her strong suit, so she got up, threw on the red silk robe and went to find Cade.

"Cade?" she called.

"In here."

He was at the computer in one corner of the living room, answering what looked like business email. He coaxed her into sitting across his lap as he laid a hot kiss on her in greeting.

When he let her up for air, she pushed against his chest to get his attention.

"Cade, there's something I need to ask you."

"Ask me anything. If it's in my power, it's yours."

Elaine took a deep breath. "Cade, will you marry me?"

His eyes widened in surprise. "We're already mated." Understanding dawned. "Oh, I see. You want a human wedding for your family and friends, right?"

"Well, we could just go on living in sin, but I think it would be best for the future if we tied the knot officially. Don't you?"

"Absolutely. And it's not unprecedented. Some shifter couples have ceremonies. We can do the same."

"What do shifter couples do otherwise—to make it all legal, I mean, so their children are...um...legitimate, in the eyes of the law?"

"We have officials who can fill out marriage certificates. It's usually done after a mating to keep us in line with the human legal system. If the shifters are prominent in their communities or have appearances to keep up for human friends or employees, sometimes they'll do a ceremony with a shaman or priestess presiding."

"So we could do something like that, right? I don't have a big family, but I do have some and I'd like them and my friends, to see me get married. We don't have to do it right away, but maybe in a few months, when things have settled down..."

"I think it'd be perfect."

"You're the one who's perfect." She kissed him, and it was some time before Cade got to finish his email.

Much later that day, Cade and Elaine drove out of town to the suburbs where he had an estate set back in some woods and walled off to provide both security and privacy for when he wanted to prowl in his fur.

He was somewhat concerned by the attitude Elaine may face from the hardheads like Bonnie and Ray once they got a look at her new mating mark—and his own for that matter. The bite she'd given him so generously that morning was starting to look more and more like the real thing.

He didn't know how it all worked, but maybe a little of Elaine's hidden magic had helped her replicate the mark on her own neck. The bite she'd given him was smaller, of course, and the teeth patterns different because she was human, but from all he could see at this early stage, the mark itself was forming just like the one on her neck. He'd have to talk to the doctors who studied this sort of thing to find out why, but he was thrilled beyond belief to have the visible evidence of their bond.

But Cade worried about how news of their mating would be received by certain shifters. There was a lot of snobbery in certain Clans in regard to humans.

"You should be prepared." He chose his words carefully. "Some of the others may give you a hard time about our mating. If they do, I want you to tell me. I don't expect you to face a den of obnoxious cats on your own, Ellie."

"Is that buyer's remorse I hear in your voice?" She turned to him in the small cabin of the sedan, and he could feel her gaze on him as he drove. He thought he recognized humor in her tone, but it was mixed with a tiny bit of worry as well that made him wince.

He reached for her hand, holding it warm against his thigh. "Never." He dared a glance at her. "I just don't want you to be uncomfortable, and I want to nip any bigotry right in the bud. I won't tolerate anyone in my home who disrespects you or our relationship."

"You say the sweetest things, sometimes." She squeezed his hand and smiled as he returned his attention to the road. "So just out of curiosity, what would you do if someone did insult me?"

"I'd throw their sorry asses out of our house!"

Elaine laughed, and he knew things would be all right. She was a strong woman—the strongest he'd ever known—and she'd already done well in feline company. He did worry about how his people would take the news of their mating but ultimately he and Elaine were a team. They would face whatever came their way together.

"I've been thinking about retiring from Guard work."

Her hand tensed under his. "Because of me? Because of us?"

"I always knew I'd have to retire when I settled down."

"But what about Ria? She needs you, Cade. Until the threat to her is taken care of, she needs everyone to stick by her—especially you."

He raised her hand to his lips for a quick kiss.

"You're one hell of a woman, Ellie, and I'm glad you care for Ria and her security. The truth is, I want to make sure she's safe, but I'm torn. I don't ever want to put you in danger because of my work as a Royal Guard and if I'm guarding Ria, her watchers may somehow trace me back to you."

"What if I helped?"

"What? Protect Ria?"

"Sure, why not? I've done okay against everything that's been thrown at me so far and if I can really Shield people from magic, that might be an asset if they send another mage after her."

Cade had to admit she had a good point.

"I'm sorry, baby. There's never been a human Royal Guard that I know of."

"Not even unofficially?"

That gave him pause. Indeed, Elaine had probably been an unofficial Guard her entire life, merely by her association and protective instincts toward her best friend.

"If anyone could fill the bill, it's you, Ellie. Did it cross your mind that your presence has probably been hiding Gina's magic all along?"

"Yeah. Actually, I got an inkling about that when Ted explained what a Shield was. Do you think it's true?"

He squeezed her hand this time. "I think there's little doubt about it. Your presence probably masked hers this whole time."

"But then how did you know she was a shifter the moment you met her?"

"The scent I picked up isn't magical in nature. When she came close enough, I could smell the slight variations in her body that told me she wasn't human."

"But then other shifters could smell her too, right? Why hasn't she ever been discovered that way before?"

"Who's to say she hasn't? Maybe she played lone cat on the prowl if anyone was curious enough to ask. It used to be common for cats to want to roam alone before they settled down. She'd fit that stereotype, living alone and exploring the single life. And she works in a human hospital. She's not likely to run into shifters there. We stay away from human doctors as a general rule."

"But she treated shifter patients privately. *Shihan's* wife was one of her patients."

"A few here and there who wouldn't be trained well enough to recognize a royal *tigre blanche* when they sniffed her, she could get away with. Under normal circumstances, most shifters never get close enough to a royal to learn the subtle differences in their scent. Even I didn't recognize the *blanche* distinction right off. It took Mitch to recognize that, if you recall."

Elaine sighed and sat back, leaning her head against the seat. She moved toward the center on the wide bench seat so she was closer to him. He liked that instinctive move on her part. He needed to be near her, now that they were mated.

He couldn't believe he really had a mate. He'd never been so happy or felt such satisfaction in his life. Having Elaine in his life had changed him for all time, and he never wanted to return to a time when she wasn't with him.

"I'm glad Gina was able to go her own way for so long. Now that I'm learning more about your world, I see she could have led a very different life. Knowing her as well as I do, I don't think she would have been happy growing up with the restrictions your people would have placed on her. She's a free spirit, Cade. She needs her space. Just like her dad."

Cade had almost forgotten that Elaine had grown up knowing the former *Tig'Ra*, the Sun King of the tigers who'd abdicated his throne in a rage years before. Elaine had known him only as her best friend's father, but in reality he was so much more. There were loads of stories about his exploits as a young man. He'd been a powerful ruler in his time, but personal tragedy had changed him from a daring young man to one that wanted nothing to do with ruling his people. Cade had always thought it a shame.

"What's he like?"

"Gina's dad? He's great. Warm, caring and protective of us when we were little. He was like a second father to me. I spent so much time at Gina's when we were little, I always felt like part of their family. That's why it hurt so much when I realized they'd all been keeping such a huge secret from me for so long."

Cade patted her hand, his fingers stroking along hers in comfort. "They didn't mean to hurt you."

"I know. I still have a lot to learn about your people and the rules of shifter life, but I do understand they were living Underground. They were only protecting themselves. I hope that someday I'll get to see them again. With all that's been going on, I'm really worried I've lost my best friend."

Cade hated the tremor in her voice. If he hadn't been speeding down the highway, he'd have pulled her into his arms to comfort her.

"Have faith, Ellie. She'll take care of Mitch and if I know that tiger, he'll take care of her too. It might take some time, but I believe Gina will come back into the fold. Mitch can be very persuasive when he sets his mind to something. I should know. We grew up together much like you and Gina. I'd trust him with my life, and have on several memorable occasions."

"But if Gina goes back to her Clan they'll want to make her queen, right? I know Gina. She won't like that. Not at all."

"They'll sort it out. I think your friend Gina is a stronger woman than even she realizes. To have lived in hiding her entire life could not have been easy."

Elaine sighed and closed her eyes. "I suppose you're right. I can't help but worry about her though. It's a habit of long standing." A gentle smile graced her luscious lips when Cade glanced over at her. "We used to get into such trouble together as kids and her father would get so mad sometimes, he'd growl." Elaine's eyes popped open, and she started to chuckle. "I just realized he really was *growling*! All this time I never realized the tiger was growling at us when he found us doing something he didn't like. I guess I just thought it was his way of not yelling. Sometimes my dad would count when we were bad so he wouldn't yell. All the while Gina's dad was growling so he wouldn't *roar*."

"I bet he roared plenty when you weren't around to hear it.

I remember my own father's roars when I got into mischief." Cade had to smile at the childhood memories.

"I'm glad Gina's going home. She needs her parents, even if they are hiding out. They've always been a very close-knit family. Now I understand a little better why."

Cade took the exit that would ultimately lead to his estate. He navigated through the town and into the residential area, coming eventually to the gate and perimeter wall that surrounded his place. He'd called ahead when they left the city to let the others know they were on their way. He was glad to see they were vigilant when he pulled up to the gate. Ray met them there and paused to say hello before they passed through the gate onto the grounds.

The house came into view around a short curve, and Cade felt satisfaction run through him when Elaine gasped and her eyes widened. She liked the place, of that he was almost certain.

"You live here?"

"Most of the time. Do you like it? If you want to change anything, let me know. This is your home now too. Unless you'd rather live somewhere else." He parked the car in the front drive and got out.

"I couldn't imagine a lovelier place to live, Cade." Her eyes were swimming with emotion when he came around to her side of the car. He hugged her, proud that she liked his lair. That she would share it with him.

"Wait 'til you see inside." He lifted her into his arms, taking her by surprise as he bounded up the steps and through the open door. Bonnie had come to greet them and was completely nonplussed when she saw Cade carrying Elaine over the threshold.

But Cade didn't give a damn. It was his house. If Bonnie was going to be obnoxious about their mating, she could damned well leave. He'd tell her and her mate that at the earliest opportunity, should it become necessary. For now, he wanted to show Elaine around their home and seek out his cousin. As Nyx, she had the power to make or break their future as a mated pair within the Clan.

One thing he knew for certain, if Ria somehow surprised him and objected, he'd wash his hands of the Clan, his familial Pride and go out on his own with Elaine. No way would he give her up. Not for the Clan. Not for the Pride. Not for anyone or anything. Never again.

Cade turned in to the living room, hoping to corner Ria there since it was early evening. Most likely they'd all already eaten dinner and were relaxing together before bed.

Cade had just lowered Elaine to her feet when an orange furball hurled itself at her. Cade realized at once they'd found Chuck the cat, but Elaine screeched as Chuck's claws latched on to her new blue jeans. She laughed at her own reaction a second later, bending down to pick up her furry friend and smother him with hugs and kisses.

Cade never thought he'd see the day he'd be jealous of a house cat, but there it was. Just when he was about to start growling, Chuck decided he'd had enough of Elaine's antics and wriggled out of her arms. He flounced to the floor, stuck his tail up in the air and walked away without a second glance.

"Aw, Chuck, don't be that way," Elaine called after him. Cade couldn't help himself. He burst out laughing, earning a glare from Elaine. "What?"

"Nothing." He held up his hands, palms outward, all innocence.

"You did something. I know it."

"I didn't do a thing. I swear. It seems Chuck is mad at you for abandoning him, and he's decided to ignore you. Don't worry, he'll come around eventually. When he feels you've suffered enough."

"Chuck Norris, you little stinker." She shook her fist at his retreating tail in outrage that was only partially feigned. Cade hugged her to his side as they shared a laugh at the house cat's expense.

"Did anyone see Chuck?" Ria's voice came from the hallway, growing closer. "Elaine will kill me if I lose her cat." Ria came into the room, surprise on her face when she saw them. "Cade! Elaine!" She rushed over to hug them both. "I'm glad you're here. Oh, and, um... I didn't really mean that about Chuck being lost. He's around here...somewhere. He took off a few minutes ago and raced around the house like a crazy kitten. He must've sensed you were back."

"Yeah, we saw him already," Cade reassured her. "The little brat snubbed us."

"He wouldn't dare." Ria's eyes narrowed.

"It's all right," Elaine piped in. "He has a right to be upset. I did abandon him with relative strangers."

Ria looked pointedly at Elaine's neck. "Relative being the operative word." Cade held his breath to see what Ria would do. Her acceptance mattered a lot to him both on a personal level and in her role as Nyx. He shouldn't have worried. Ria grinned and gave Elaine another, even bigger hug. "Welcome to the family. This is gonna be great."

Cade loved to see her youthful enthusiasm back in full force. Ria hadn't been herself since the attack at the *dojo*.

"It's true then," Bonnie said from the doorway. Cade wasn't surprised to see a disgusted expression on her face.

"Might as well gather everyone together. There are a few ground rules I need to establish if you're all going to stay here." Cade walked over to a small console that blended in mostly with the décor. He hit the intercom button and spoke briefly to summon everyone to the living room.

When they were gathered—Charlie, Ray, Steve, Molly, Bonnie and Ria—Cade put one arm around Elaine's shoulders. They'd face this together, as they would face every challenge in the future. Greetings were exchanged, and he noted the way they reacted to the mark on Elaine's neck.

"As you can see, Elaine and I are mated." Cade unbuttoned

his collar and the first few buttons on his shirt to display his own mark, much to everyone's surprise. Ria, bless her heart, bounded over to make an inspection, and he allowed it only because she was Nyx, and family.

"That's amazing," she said after a thorough study. "I didn't know humans could leave a mark like that. It's a little different than the norm, but it's definitely a mating mark. You should let Doctor Brundy look at that. I bet she'd be fascinated."

"In due time," Cade agreed. "But for now, I just wanted you all to know that Elaine and I are a couple and if any of you have a problem with it, you're welcome to leave our home at your earliest convenience."

Bonnie shifted on her feet but seemed to simmer down at that pronouncement. Nobody wanted to be left out in the cold to fend for themselves with the current threat hanging over them.

One by one, they came forward to offer their congratulations and Cade was pleased to note that every one of his friends—with the exception of Bonnie, perhaps—accepted Elaine with open arms. She'd proven herself to this inner circle, at least. Molly, much recovered from her injuries, even thanked Elaine for what she'd done at the safe house.

"I don't know how you handled Billy Bob, but I'm grateful. He took me by surprise, and I was down before I knew anything, I'm ashamed to admit." Molly flushed with embarrassment, and Cade knew it was tough for the female Alpha to admit her own weakness. "I hate to think what could have happened if you hadn't been there."

Molly took them all by surprise when she leaned forward and placed a kiss on Elaine's cheek. Elaine still didn't understand the significance of that expression among their people, but Ria saved Cade the effort of explaining.

"A kiss of friendship in our Clan is a special honor, Elaine," Ria told her. "Molly just offered her friendship and respect in a very public way. Do you accept her friendship and ally your Pride with hers?"

"That sounds complicated." Elaine made a stab at humor that luckily was well received.

"It can be," Molly said. "In this case, however, it's not that difficult. My Pride, such as it is, consists of me alone. All my family members were killed several years ago." Sadness passed over her features, and Cade recalled that terrible day that had seen a young girl blossom into an Alpha warrior before her time. If she hadn't she would have been dead now as well. "So allying with me doesn't carry any real strings. You're correct to be wary, however. Until you know all the ins and outs of who's related to whom, be careful. An overture from you commits not only you, but your mate now as well and any cubs and others you may add to your Pride later."

"Well then..." Elaine gave Molly a hug and a kiss on the cheek. "I'd be honored to have your friendship and alliance."

One hurdle crossed, Cade felt relief well up inside him. Slowly, Elaine would win them all over—not just this close circle of friends—but the entire Clan. She was too special for them not to see it, given half a chance.

The others were less demonstrative but for the most part just as friendly. One by one they paid their respects then filed out until only Ria, Cade and Elaine were left in the room—with Chuck pouting and pointedly ignoring Elaine as he sat by the window.

Charlie was the last one out the door. He shot Cade a quick signal to indicate he'd stand watch outside the door. It shouldn't be necessary in his own home among friends, but the things they had to discuss were of such a sensitive nature, it was worth the extra precaution to keep a lid on this. The time would come when the rest of them would have to be told, but when and how was really up to Ria. The Nyx would have to decide the Clan's course of action, as was her right.

"Charlie told me a little about his friend, but he was characteristically tight-lipped on what happened with Fidelio." Ria sat on the couch facing them while Cade and Elaine cuddled on the love seat. Aptly named piece of furniture, that. He'd never thought about it before, but it was just the right size for them to share. He liked it.

"Charlie's friend is a recently retired Navy SEAL. He told us his name was Ted, and he's claiming *Altor Custodis* ties. He says his group broke with the non-interference rules because they believe the *AC* has become corrupt at the highest levels."

"And what do you think of him?" Ria asked.

"I'm inclined to believe him. We had breakfast at Rich's diner." Cade knew Ria was aware of Rich's position in the city's shifter community because he'd introduced them when she first arrived in town. "One of Rich's sons has a tiger friend who's become a Navy SEAL. The kid is home on leave, and he recognized Ted right off. Said he was rumored to be part of an elite Ghost Team that specialized in black ops."

"You seem to agree. Why?"

"Well, he shot Fidelio in the head, casual and neat, and never batted an eye. He's a tough man, and the group he had with him all seemed cut from the same cloth. If they turn out to be on the level and we could recruit some of them to help with the Underground, I think we'd all be better off for it."

"They were that good?" Ria seemed impressed.

"Better. And they have at least some basic knowledge of defensive magic. They formed a circle around us and Fidelio, and used some kind of chant to keep all magic within it. When Fidelio launched his fire at us it didn't touch the men in the circle and didn't leave their ring. It was constricted and died within the circle."

"But you were in the line of fire? Like in my vision? How did you escape?"

"That's the other thing you need to know. It seems—" Cade put his arm around Elaine's shoulders, "—my new mate is a Shield. The flame parted in front of her and never touched either one of us." He dropped a kiss on her hair.

"A Shield." Ria looked at her, a grin creeping over her face.

"That explains a lot. I've been seeing strange things since I met you, Elaine. You and...a white tiger."

Elaine kept her poker face, which Cade had to admire. He couldn't lie to Ria. He could, however, let her know certain things were not to be discussed at the moment, but Elaine beat him to the punch.

"I understand what that means, but I can't tell you anything more right now, Ria. I'm sorry."

Ria's eyebrows rose in surprise. "Really?"

Cade nodded with finality, backing up his mate. "Really, cousin. The time may come soon when we can clarify things for you, but that story is not ours to tell."

"Hmm. Well, you certainly have piqued my curiosity, but I respect your judgment. I'm just happy you're both safe. And mated." She clapped her hands together in joy. "I can't tell you how happy I am for you. I truly believe your union is the start of something."

"Which brings me to another thing. Ria, I'll probably have to retire from the Guard. I won't leave Ellie behind. She and I go together, wherever our path leads us."

Ria held up one hand to forestall his words. He'd had a speech prepared, but she wasn't letting him deliver it. The gentle expression on her face made him curious.

"You don't have to retire. At least not until you settle down and start a family and maybe not even then. It's completely your choice, because if you're willing, I'd like to ask Elaine if she'll accept the commission as my newest Royal Guard."

"You mean it?" Elaine's voice was full of wonder and excitement. Cade wasn't sure he liked this idea, but in all good conscience, he couldn't stand in the way of Elaine fulfilling her potential. She'd been given her gifts for a reason, and he was a great believer in fate. Elaine had been brought into their lives for a reason. He wouldn't be a good Alpha, mate or Royal Guard if he stood in the way.

"I was willing to offer you the position based solely on what you did back at the safe house, but now that we know you're a Shield, I'd be a fool not to recruit you. Especially because if I don't, we'll lose Cade. He's our leader, Elaine, though you may not realize it. He leads the Guard contingent of the *pantera noir*, and it was only because he was here, in this city, that my parents allowed me to study here. They knew Cade could keep me safe, and he has."

"Since when did you become such a good strategist, cousin?" Cade was proud of the way she'd matured over the past few weeks. Adversity had brought out the best in her, and he was glad he hadn't called out the cavalry to come get her and whisk her away. She'd been in more danger than he liked, but she'd come out a stronger woman for it.

"Since I've been hanging around with you, cousin." She winked at him, and they all laughed. "Seriously, Elaine, I'd like you to consider it."

"And I'd like you to consider living with us, Ria," Cade said, hitting on another important matter they had to settle. "Once we make this city safe again, I don't see any reason why you can't go to school here, but I want you to live with us where we can watch over you and Elaine's Shield can protect you. What do you say? I know you wanted an apartment by yourself but recent events have convinced me that there are just too many possibilities for discovery in a city this size. You never know who might sniff you out or sense your magic. At least this way, they won't be able to find where you live easily because once you get near Elaine, your magical trail will go cold."

Ria was silent a long time but finally nodded. "Okay. I see the wisdom of what you're saying, and I'll do it. Besides, I like cubs, and I think you'll be starting a family sooner or later. Won't you?" She blinked at them in comical innocence, and Cade threw a pillow at her in retaliation. Chuck came over and pounced on it, claiming it as his own while they laughed.

When Elaine finally got around to checking her messages,

she burst out laughing. Cade came over and rubbed her back.

"What's so funny?"

She pressed pause on the keypad.

"My brother left the most amazing message. You've got to hear this." She busied herself pressing buttons while he took a seat next to her.

"You've never really told me about your brother."

It hit her again how much this wonderful man had changed her life in so short a time. They'd have years together now, to explore each other and learn all that had come before to bring them both to this point.

"I don't see him much. He spends a lot of time out of the country or in inaccessible places. The last I knew, he was in a Tibetan monastery."

"Sounds like an interesting character, your brother."

"Oh, you have no idea." She held the phone out to him. "Here, listen to this."

Cade took the handset and raised it to his ear. After a short pause, a man's voice came over the line.

"Hey sis, it's me, Jake. Congratulations on your marriage. I would have called to warn you, but there weren't any phones where I was and I knew despite it all, you'd come out on top. Tell your new husband I think he's not a bad guy, even if he isn't human, and he better take good care of you. For what it's worth, I think you're both in the clear but watch your backs anyway, okay? Love you, El. I'll be in touch when I get back to the States."

Cade eyed her warily. "When did he leave this message?"

Elaine grinned like the cat who swallowed the canary. "Oh, didn't I mention that my grandfather's gift passed down to my generation? Jacob is clairvoyant. He left that message the night my apartment burned."

Cade stared. He looked like he was in shock, but then he had it coming. Elaine liked the idea that he wasn't the only one with supernatural surprises in his background. They'd have years together to explore them, and Elaine was eagerly looking forward to each and every one.

About the Author

To learn more about *Bianca D'Arc*, please visit *www.biancadarc.com*. Send an email to *Bianca* at *biancadarc@gmail.com* or join her Yahoo! group to join in the fun with other readers as well as *Bianca!* http://groups.yahoo.com/group/*biancadarc*.

A forbidden union forged in love—and tempered in hellfire.

Inferno
© 2009 Bianca D'Arc
A Tales of the Were Story.

One last task and Megan will be free of the debt of honor owed by her family. Spying on Dante, a powerful vampire with questionable friends, sounds simple enough. But her mission is complicated by the fact she's got something every vampire wants—tangy, powerful, werewolf blood.

It's easy to capture his attention. The hard part will be getting out with her heart—and soul—intact. Not to mention her life, thanks to a crazed bomber.

Dante isn't the kind to forgive or forget easily, especially the grudge he holds against werewolves. Still, he is instantly drawn to the injured lone wolf in his care. When he and his friend Duncan treat her wounds, they discover something that marks her as much more than she seems.

That mark is a neon sign warning to be careful, but Dante can't help himself. He wants her and nothing will stand in his way. Not her species. Not his. Not the strange woman who keeps trying to kill him.

Not even the magical poison in Megan's blood…

Warning: This book contains sexual healing, ménage a trois and quatre, hot sexy vampires, an irresistible fey warrior and a lone wolf bitch on the prowl.

Available now in ebook and print from Samhain Publishing.

Love—it's the real thing. And complicated as hell...

The Egyptian Demon's Keeper
© 2009 Ciar Cullen

Archeologist Eliza Schneider assumes her meeting with an exotic stranger in the Egyptian desert was a heat-induced hallucination...until he materializes in New York. She has to give the tall, handsome Egyptian high marks for originality with his pick-up line: they're fated to save the world together. The master/servant thing goes a long way toward sweeping her off her feet, but it's easier to believe he's just another in her long line of poor romantic choices.

Kasdeya, the Fifth Satan, waited eons for his Keeper to find her way to his tomb amongst the ancient ruins. He only has a limited time to convince Eliza that her role is critical to help defeat the loathsome Deumos, a female demon who has laid her claim to bearing his child—a child that will bring down mortals.

Trouble is, Eliza doesn't even believe Kasdeya is real. If he can't convince her he isn't an illusion—and neither is their love—Deumos will win.

Warning: This book is not work safe! May cause hot fantasies about sexy immortals and lead to poor productivity.

Available now in ebook from Samhain Publishing.